ON GRANDMA'S PORCH

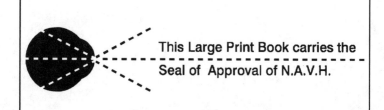

This Large Print Book carries the
Seal of Approval of N.A.V.H.

On Grandma's Porch

Sandra Chastain
Debra Leigh Smith
Martha Crockett

THORNDIKE PRESS
A part of Gale, Cengage Learning

GALE
CENGAGE Learning

Detroit • New York • San Francisco • New Haven, Conn • Waterville, Maine • London

GALE
CENGAGE Learning™

LIBRARY OF CONGRESS CATALOGING-IN-PUBLICATION DATA

On grandma's porch / by Sandra Chastain, Debra Leigh Smith and Martha Crockett.
    p. cm. — (Thorndike Press large print clean reads)
    ISBN-13: 978-1-4104-0756-6 (hardcover : alk. paper)
    ISBN-10: 1-4104-0756-X (hardcover : alk. paper)
    1. Short stories, American. 2. Southern States — Social life and customs — Fiction. 3. Southern States — Social life and customs — Miscellanea. 4. American fiction — 21st century. 5. Large type books. I. Chastain, Sandra. II. Smith, Deborah, 1955– III. Crockett, Martha.
PS648.S5O5 2008
813'.0108975—dc22   2008007935

TABLE OF CONTENTS

6

DEDICATION

When you read *On Grandma's Porch,* think of Virginia Ellis. Gin was a founding partner of BelleBooks, and her talent and commitment shine brightly in this collection. An award-winning writer (and a good ol' southern gal from Florida), she contributed a wonderful southern sensibility to selecting the stories for this book. She encouraged the writers, many of whom she sought out personally, giving them opportunities to publish their work. She found, purchased and edited most of the stories in our previous collection, *More Sweet Tea.* This book would not be what it is without Gin. We'll continue to celebrate her work and her life in every sip of sweet tea, every wonderful southern sunrise, and every heartfelt tradition she loved. *On Grandma's Porch* is dedicated for now and always to our friend, partner, and sister of the heart, Gin Ellis.

"I was blessed with humble beginnings."
— *Dolly Parton*

- Soft drink machines always had a metal rack next to them for the empty bottles. If you took your drink with you, you were supposed to leave a two-cent deposit for the bottle. You put the two cents in the machine's coin slot.
- Kids' toys included serious, sometimes dangerous, chemistry kits.
- Telephone numbers included words as well as numbers. For example: "Poplar 67056," which was written as PO67056, or "Plaza 39824" which was written as PL39824.
- Your parents took you to a nice dinner at the local cafeteria, where young men in waiters' coats carried your trays to the table for a small tip.
- A "bag boy" always took your groceries to the car for your mother, and she tipped him fifty cents.
- Gas stations had attendants who pumped your gas, cleaned your windshield, and checked your oil and tires.
- Men and women always wore hats in public. Women held their hats in place with long, thick hat pins. Women routinely wore white gloves in public. They didn't wear pants in public, and they always wore hose with their dresses or skirts.
- Blue jeans were called dungarees.

- Kids played with Erector Sets and hula hoops.
- Playground equipment was made of sharp steel.

THE GOOD SON

BY MAUREEN HARDEGREE

> "Anything to do with the South resonates with me, because I'm Southern."
> — Mary Steenburgen, actress

The dead, pretty much, have to take whatever we want to do to them "lying down," so to speak. But can you use the dead, I wondered, to make the living happy?

I hadn't ever contemplated that question until recently, and why would I? Why would anyone other than a physician, mortician, or anatomy instructor?

Guess I'd better begin at the beginning.

It was the first cold, crisp day of fall when I walked through the back door of my house and encountered my mother sitting at the kitchen table. She raised her gray head, dabbed her teary eyes with some tissue, and sighed.

I glanced out the window at the yellow leaves, which earlier in the week my wife had informed me were actually a burnished gold. The sky was a pretty blue. It was the kind of day that made most people happy — but not my mother.

"Hi, Mom," I said with forced joviality and tossed my keys onto the desk.

Rather than answer in kind, she blinked at me, then her small face crumpled like the tissue in her plump hand and she started boo-hooing in earnest.

From the hunger-inducing smell of mozzarella, beef and garlic, I suspected my wife Hannah was baking a lasagna, which didn't usually make my mother cry. It often did, however, prompt Mom to tell my wife how our family had never eaten Italian food for supper.

Maybe Hannah had borrowed one of Mom's dishes again. All hell broke loose several months ago when Hannah pulled out the electric frying pan with the intent of using it to make pork chops. You'd have thought my wife had committed murder the way my mother had carried on.

Food cooking in the oven was only adding to my confusion. School was in session. Why was my wife home before sundown and preparing a hot meal? Had someone died?

"What's wrong, Mom?"

"Why did you let me leave your father in

Augusta?"

Mom's genteel Piedmont accent often lulled people into thinking she hadn't truly meant whatever hurtful thing she'd said, but I wasn't most people. I heard the veiled accusation — his being in Augusta was somehow my fault.

"Maybe because he's been dead for six years," I said. "I don't think he minds."

"Well, I don't want him there anymore. I can't drive down to see him without taking the whole day. Besides, I don't want to be in Augusta when I die. I want to be in Rutledge."

"Your plot happens to be in Augusta, Mother. In fact, you've got seven of them."

"Can't we move him?"

Hannah, who was tearing the lettuce for a salad, drew her breath in sharply. Mom's question didn't shock me. She'd been talking about moving him ever since the questions began about when Davy, my father, was going to get his tombstone.

"Daddy," I started to say, and my wife snorted.

The way I say "daddy" amuses her to no end. My wife, a Yankee I married to help the height of my gene pool, claimed "daddy" sounded like "diddy" when I said it.

I tried to ignore the snort. "Daddy didn't

13

want to be buried in the first place, and now you want me to move him to the Rutledge Cemetery? He hated that town."

Mom stood. Her little body shook like her voice. "I don't care."

My father, a former Army officer, left the sleepy Georgia town where he'd grown to manhood as soon as he was able. He'd also provided clear instructions on what he wanted done at his death, which had come much sooner than any of us had imagined it would. A heart attack at fifty-three. He lingered in the hospital for a week.

Of course, the fact that Daddy was a drinker and smoker didn't help. Since his death, though, who he'd been and what he'd wanted and liked had morphed into a person I didn't recognize. His name changed from Davy to Ezekiel, his middle name, and he'd become a saint, a teetotaler, and a man who was kind to all animals including the deer viewing his garden as an all-you-can-eat buffet. Several family members had even attempted praying his atheistic soul into heaven.

Dad had wanted to be cremated and to have his ashes added to the soil in his garden, which had rivaled the one on the PBS show "The Victory Garden" in neatness and beauty.

He'd canned his own vegetables, and his days in the summer and spring were spent weeding and protecting his fenced domain from the bed of his white Chevy pick-up. Deer and other animals daring to trespass for a little nibble got a load of buckshot. His company during his garden-guarding vigil? A shotgun, a pack of menthol Benson & Hedges, and a tall glass of sweet tea. A screwdriver, the drink, not the tool, was actually his favorite beverage but wasn't appropriate during those after-hours guarding episodes.

Even if his remains wouldn't be in the ground, he'd wanted a monument in a cemetery, and he truly liked the plot in Augusta, which had belonged to my mother's great-grandmother and had passed down to Mom. A tall oak shaded the ground, the perfect spot, in his opinion, for a nice granite headstone that mentioned his service to his country.

When Dad died, my mother was a mess, so I couldn't count on her to follow through on his wishes. She'd always been what her family referred to as high-strung.

Since she couldn't, I voiced what he'd wanted to the family at large, and the mention of cremation made one of my elderly relative's pale skin go stark white. Her blue eyes widened like she'd seen a ghost. I was afraid she would have a heart attack, and we'd have two funerals to argue over.

My uncle quietly suggested a traditional burial, complete with displaying the dead body in the dining room of my parents' house and what we call "sitting up with the dead." I didn't sit up with Dad all night, and no one that I know did. I slept upstairs almost directly above the casket, which might be close enough. My Yankee wife was pretty shocked when I told her about that little tradition years later. I explained that I was only trying to be a good son, nephew, and grandson.

In the years since Dad's funeral, Mom had never pulled herself together (which is why she was living with me and my wife), nor could she bring herself to buy Dad's monument. I was still trying to be the good son — "trying" being the key word, because she was trying my patience to no end.

If I wasn't dreaming, Mom wanted me to move my father, a man who never wanted to be buried, to their homeplace, Rutledge, a town he hated. I had to take a stand for him. "You can't move him there."

Mom worked her lips in and out in a down-turned pout. "Why not? I don't care how much it costs."

16

"You know he didn't want to be buried at all, much less in Rutledge."

"That's not true." She worked her lips faster. Her eyes brimmed to full pool.

"Yes it is. Why don't we just pick out a monument? I'll come home early tomorrow afternoon and take you to the place on the highway."

She scraped her chair back from the table and fisted her small, puffy hands. "You've taken everything from me, and now you want to keep your father where I can't go see him."

My wife pulled the lasagna out of the oven and slammed it down on the stove. Her face was flushed, with anger I suspected. I knew what she was thinking. Right, being newly married we wanted nothing more than to take care of my crazy mother just so we could have all her things, such as the circa 1968 burnt-orange bedspread in the guest room and her deviled egg tray.

"Look, Mom, you can't exactly see someone who's buried, anyway."

"You're just being hateful," Mom said, now fully into the drama of her role. She'd be the first to tell you she liked to emote. With her lips pursed and the tears flowing, she stomped through the den to her bedroom and slammed the door behind her,

17

her trademark gesture.

She'd played her trump card to perfection, accusing me, her perfect only son, of being hateful.

Now I was angry, too.

"Fine," I yelled from the other side of the door separating us. "You want to move him, we'll move him."

My wife probably thought I was as touched as my mother.

I stormed into the living room and dug through the drawers in the secretary to locate all the funeral papers. I unzipped the pouch from the mortuary that overflowed with sympathy cards Mom couldn't bring herself to throw away, and I found the phone number.

"You aren't serious, are you?" Hannah asked. She must have finished with the salad.

"He was used to moving around with the army."

"You aren't kidding."

"Nope, I'm trying to be a good son. If moving him will make my mother happy, does it really matter where his body is?"

"Correct me if I'm wrong," she said. "But didn't he make her promise not to ever bury him there?"

"It's not like he's even going to know. And

if it'll get my mother to stop crying and obsessing, I win."

"I hate to tell you, Clay, but I don't think it's possible for her to stop crying and obsessing."

"Very funny," I said.

I dialed the number. What sort of message would I leave on the answering machine? You buried my father six years ago, and he's ready for a change of scenery. I had no doubt this would be expensive and involve more than one funeral home, two county governments, and a mountain of paper. But the move would be worth it if it helped Mom settle down. I listened to the recording providing the funeral home's viewing hours. The line must have been busy, so I'd been transferred to the automated service.

The beep sounded, and I said the first thing that came to mind. "I want to move my dad to a different cemetery. What do I need to do? Please call me at. . . ."

I walked back into the kitchen, where Hannah was setting the table with our stoneware rather than Mom's off-limits dishes, and I placed the phone in its cradle.

My wife shook her head. "If your father starts haunting you, don't say I didn't warn you."

■ ■ ■ ■

Several days later, as I remained on hold with the Rutledge Cemetery, I wasn't plagued by Daddy's ghost as much as by worries about the potential disasters that could occur while the Augusta funeral home moved him. Apparently, they would transport him vault-and-all via truck (for the vault) and hearse (for Daddy) up Interstate 20. That concrete-and-asphalt corridor from Augusta to metro Atlanta hadn't yet encroached on the small-town serenity of Rutledge, where my parents had been high school sweethearts, but one day soon it would.

The route along I-20 was appropriate, considering Eisenhower had started the interstate road system, and he'd been a soldier like my dad. I wondered what Eisenhower would think of interring a soldier twice — a soldier with a full beard, buried in his dress uniform without his medals. At my uncle's urging, I removed them before we closed the casket.

Our request to move his body wasn't as unusual as I'd thought before embarking on this strange quest. Mom's family agreed with me that it was well worth the money to try to make her happy. They knew as well as I did that if I didn't at least try, there would be no peace for the living.

A thought paralyzed me for a second or two. What if Dad wasn't where we thought we'd put him? Mom hadn't ever bought the marker.

Worse yet, what if they dug up the wrong body? They could get confused since my dad's body wasn't the only one in my great-great-grandmother's plot without a marker.

Visions of the truck losing the vault and hitting the hearse with my Dad's casket inside flashed through my mind as well. And the potential news bites — Dead Man Dies Again, Imperishables Wrecked on I-20. Considering all the formaldehyde in him, he probably didn't look too bad. Except for the Mohawk.

The mortician who worked on my dad did a great job except he parted Daddy's hair on the wrong side. It drove me crazy during the viewing, and I just couldn't have my father buried with his hair wrong. Failing to factor in the copious amount of hairspray, I tried to fix it. His comb-over stood straight up like a Mohawk.

I decided I wouldn't mention my worries to my mother. She didn't need to be any more upset than she already was, and I didn't need the stress of her emotional upheavals compounded with interest.

Finally, a man from the Rutledge Cemetery, who had an accent much like my mother's, returned my call. "Mr. Thackery," his gravelly voice drawled, "if you want him buried on Sunday, there'll be an extra charge."

"Why?" I asked.

"It's the Sabbath. We've got to pay overtime for the workers."

"Any other holy days cheaper?" I asked, hoping the man had a sense of humor. "How about Friday night?" Which might be the Jewish Sabbath, but Dad had always felt an affinity with the Jews. He'd never failed to praise them in his Sunday school days.

"I don't believe there are other holy days, Mr. Thackery." The man must be a Southern Baptist.

"Okay, fine. Sunday it is, then. I'll send the check." I put the phone up and found my mother watching Wheel of Fortune in the den.

"Mom, Dad's all set to go."

A smile lit her face. A sparkle returned to her pale-green eyes. I was the good son again.

"Where's our plot?" she asked. "Near Mother and Daddy?"

22

A few days earlier, I had purchased two plots yet had delayed in telling Mom where they were.

I'd have to spoil my moment of triumph. "I couldn't purchase plots for both of you in the old part of the cemetery."

Her upturned lips flattened into a tight, thin line. "But I want your father to have a monument, not one of those brass doormats they mow over."

"Some of those plaques are nice. They even come with urns for flowers. Besides, there aren't spaces in the old part available. It's not like I can move the bodies that are already there."

"It's not what I want, but at least he'll be . . . home." Mom started crying again, softly, which tore me up more than her usual loud bawling. My wife shook her head at me.

I knew what she was thinking. I couldn't win.

Now that moving day was imminent, I also had to argue with the cemetery director about which side of Dad and Mom's double plot Dad would get. Mom wanted him in the ground the way he and she had slept, which I came to find out was opposite most of the rest of the world. My dad preferred sleeping on the right, my mom the left.

Mom picked out a double brass plaque for them, which had a nice urn in the middle. My wife started on a beautiful silk arrangement for it, which pleased my mother to no end.

Another minor glitch arose when I discovered the one person Daddy disliked most in Rutledge was buried in the same row I picked. I guessed my father would have to roll over in his grave so his back would be to Cleetus. Cleetus, who'd never seen any action in Vietnam beyond a filing cabinet, whose only injury might have been a paper cut, had come back and claimed disability due to the war. Everyone in Rutledge had gone along with the lie, which had only added to Dad's contempt for the town.

Wait a minute. Daddy was dead. Why should he care that someone he'd hated was in his row? By next week, he'd be where Mom wanted him. Whether he would have liked it or not was beside the point. He was beyond aggravation.

Unfortunately, I wasn't.

"Clay," my wife whispered in my ear, about a week after the reburial, which went well, all things considered. No accidents on I-20, and Mom still liked the brass plaque she picked out at the monument store. I suspected the ease of the move was too good to be true, and I was right. Hannah nudged my shoulder, forcing me from a warm, sound sleep. "Clay!"

"I'm sorry," I said reluctantly, assuming I'd been snoring again. I rolled over.

"Clay, wake up."

"What?" I lifted one eyelid and peeked in her general direction. "What's wrong?"

"I smell cigarette smoke."

I squinted at the digital alarm clock, not that I could see it. I'm blind without my glasses. "What?"

"I smell cigarette smoke."

I sniffed, smelling nothing. "It's probably someone burning leaves, and the scent's drifting in from the window."

"The window's shut," she said.

Being the good husband that I am and wanting to prove my wife wrong so as to gloat, I moaned then dragged myself out from under the warm flannel sheets and heavy quilt and put on some pants and my glasses to search for the phantom smoker.

The carpet muffled my steps as I walked through the house. Mom was in bed. The front, back, and basement doors were locked. No cigarettes, no cigarette packs, no

25

cigarette butts, ashes, or smoke to be seen anywhere. I even checked the old ashtrays my mom kept.

My wife's active imagination was at work again.

I returned to bed and hoped I'd get a few hours of sleep before work. My wife, however, wasn't through with her torment.

"It's probably your Dad," she said. "I don't think he's happy."

"Let me get this. Dad, being an atheist, finds it too difficult to haunt me, also an atheist. So he chooses to haunt you, my Catholic wife, a woman he never met?"

"You're going to have to appease him in some way," she said.

"Yeah, right. And you think Mom is crazy."

When it came to pacifying my father, my wife had an idea, not that I would admit to her that I smelled the smoke, too, or what was worse, that I'd heard the second prong of attack that had started several days after the first. Someone or something was walking along the upstairs hall in the wee hours.

I told myself that was nuts. Houses creak at night. But what about the continuing scent of menthol cigarette smoke? Well, I couldn't explain that, nor did I want to. It might upset my atheistic equilibrium. If you don't believe in life after death, how can your father haunt you?

Whatever was causing that smell lingered in the house like burnt biscuits for weeks after his reburial. I kept telling Hannah it was her fertile imagination. She writes novels in her spare time, and I'm hoping I'll be a kept man some day — once she rakes in the royalties.

Mom didn't smell the cigarettes or hear the footsteps in the hall at night, which meant, in my wife's on-going opinion, that Daddy was still trying to haunt just me. He knew who'd done the dirty work. I couldn't help but feel that in making Mom happy, in being the good son to her, I'd somehow now failed in being a good son to my father.

I should have taken this opportunity to have him cremated and just have the casket buried without him in it. Who would ever have known? I should have ensured his wishes were respected, but it all gets so complicated when a person dies.

Thinking their wishes will be honored, people make elaborate plans, but what about those who are left to carry on? You've got to respect their wishes, too.

My father's mother, who never expected to outlive any of her children, was raised

Baptist. She was devastated when her first-born died, though she'd tell you she wasn't the type to go to pieces. The idea of cremation horrified her and the rest of the family. Should I have made my Dad, who was gone, happy at the expense of his own mother?

That's the problem with being the good son and the good grandson. I couldn't make everyone happy. I still can't.

It had been three weeks since my dad's big move, and my mom wasn't even happy. Now, she cried that he didn't have a monument. She obsessed about how she'd wanted him to be buried in the old part of the cemetery and that I had forced her into the brass plaque.

When I came home from work one day, I could tell she'd been crying again. Her eyes were red rimmed, and she was clutching the tissue box. I suspected it wasn't just because she'd burnt dinner. I wanted to believe Mom's bad cooking created the cigarette smell and that Mom had thrown the evidence of the ruined dinner in the trash.

"What's wrong now?" I asked.

"How do I know they dug up the right man? What if those people took the wrong vault? I could spend the rest of eternity buried next to Mr. Jurgen. And your father would be in Augusta." Her last word ended in a high-pitched whine.

It wasn't that Mom didn't like Mr. Jurgen. She did. He was a laborer who'd worked for her great-grandmother. They'd buried him in the family plot even though technically he wasn't family.

"Mother, you're just going to have to trust these people. I draw the line at exhuming Dad's body. I'm not opening that casket. Besides, Mr. Jurgen most likely didn't have a vault."

"I should have just left your father in Augusta." She dabbed her eyes with a tissue. "Why did you let me do this?"

Buyer's remorse of a magnitude I'd never expected.

"Well, I'm not moving him back," I said.

"Why not? It's my money." Mom marched back to her room and slammed the door, then opened it to give it a second slam for good measure.

When my wife arrived home and I told her the latest installment in the burial saga, she refrained from reminding me she'd told me so. I appreciated that.

She sniffed the air, too, saying nothing. I knew what she was thinking. The cigarette smell was back.

"Mom must have been cooking before I

got home," I said.

Hannah arched an eyebrow. "Really?"

"Rolls, I think."

"Your mother doesn't cook anymore except for Thanksgiving," Hannah said. "And when she does, it's Jell-O fruit mold, which doesn't smell like cigarette smoke at all."

"So maybe she burnt some toast." I wasn't going to admit to Hannah that the smoky scent was more tobacco-like than bread-like.

She smiled. "We can buy some vodka and sprinkle it on his grave this week. Maybe he'll stop."

"Any ideas on what we can sprinkle on Mom?" I asked.

I stubbornly refused to go along with the appeasement of my father's ghost, but I suspected my wife would pretty much do as she pleased. She can be stubborn, too.

When she told me she was going to be especially late getting home from work as opposed to her usual late, I knew something was in the works. She taught composition at the university in Athens, and sometimes she came home well past quitting time due to meetings or paperwork, but I'd seen the brown paper sack from the package store in her car when I'd scraped the frost from her windows that morning.

I figured clearing her windows was the least I could do since my dad was haunting her.

As I suspected, her late meeting was in the Rutledge Cemetery.

In the twilight, I pulled my sporty SUV behind her car and cut the engine. I got out and shut the door gently. Leaves crunched under my feet as I walked to where she stood, waiting for the last vestiges of sunlight to fade from the sky.

No need to let the people in the houses across the street in on what she was doing.

The monument's brass urn was empty. So much for the silk flower arrangement Hannah had made. She'd chosen a red, white and blue theme for my career-army dad. My great-aunt had contributed a small American flag, and damned if it wasn't gone, too.

"Just look," Hannah said, pointing to the empty floral foam cone riddled with holes. "Who would be so callous as to steal flowers from your father's grave?"

"I don't know. Maybe a person who had an empty spot on his mantel?" I looked around in the dwindling light to see if they were in someone else's urn nearby. When presented with a problem, I try to fix it. I'm trying to be a good husband, too. "All the other bouquets seem to be in place," I said. "I guess our thief was a patriot."

"Well, I'm putting barbed wire in the next one, that way it'll cut their fingers when they go to steal it."

I love how she gets so indignant.

"It's probably for the best that the bouquet is gone," I said. "My dad didn't like flowers much. They reminded him of funerals."

Hannah tried not to laugh at my feeble joke, but as usual she didn't succeed.

"What's in the sack?" I asked.

She smiled. "As if you didn't know."

The lights came on in a small house across the street. Unaware of the peace offering about to take place, the people who lived in that house were moving on with their evening, preparing dinner, watching TV.

Hannah pulled a half-gallon jug of Smirnoff vodka from the bag. When it came to quantity, she wasn't messing around with pleasing my father's ghost.

"Should I do the honors, or you?" she asked.

"I will," I said. "You do have the orange juice to go with it, don't you?"

"Nope, sorry."

Maybe he wouldn't mind.

As I unscrewed the cap, the barely there scent of this liquor reminded me of my dad and how vodka had eased him through his post-traumatic stress disorder and, later, retirement. We'd had good times and bad. "Good" being chats on the phone about my golf game (hole by hole), when I was in college, rough-housing when I was a kid, the years we'd spent in Germany. The bad times being the years he was in Vietnam, and I could only hear his voice on reel-to-reel tapes he'd send us — none of which I had kept, now that I couldn't remember what he sounded like.

I'd found his letters from Vietnam, both tours, in Mom's old suitcase in the basement, and I'd started cataloging them. His narrow scrawl proved how much he'd loved and believed in me, believed I'd do great things. He somehow thought I'd one day grow up to be President. I guess being a government bureaucrat wasn't too far from the mark.

Had I been a good enough son to him?

While I poured the elixir he'd needed onto the grave, I got my answer. An overwhelming sense of tranquility came over me.

Yes, I was a good son.

His spirit wouldn't be angry for long that

we'd brought his body back to Rutledge. He'd be glad I was trying to make my mother happy. That is, if I was the kind of person who believed in ghosts, and I'm not saying I do.

I was at peace, and if I was wrong about the ghost stuff, maybe he was at peace, too.

"This should do it," I said to Hannah as the last drops of vodka hit the sod. I guess he could take it straight, and so could I.

The question I began with was this: Can a person use the dead to make the living happy? The answer, I discovered, is no. But there is nobility in trying.

What Grandma Bought At That New Place Called A Shopping Mall
(1970s)

1 carat diamond ring $300
2-quart pressure cooker $8
Atari game cartridges $20
Eight track tapes $5
La-Z-Boy recliner $190
Bean Bag Chair $20.00
Play Doh Fun Factory $3.00
Sleeper sofa $300
CB Radio $150
Clothes Dryer $220
Polaroid Camera $18
RCA 23 Inch Color Television . . $370
Smith Corona Electric Typewriter . $200
Radio Shack TRS80 Computer . . $400

Getting to the Heart of the Watermelon

BY LYNDA HOLMES

"It was not a Southern watermelon that Eve took; we know it because she repented."

— Mark Twain

Being an only child growing up during the 1950s, I always looked forward to visiting my cousins in a big way. Mama's folks lived on a farm way out in the Georgia countryside, and a few of my cousins and I managed to convince our parents to let us spend some time there during the summers, "helping" our grandparents with the running of the farm. Besides milking the cows and feeding the hogs each day, we knew we would participate in two other rituals: going to Sunday church meeting and helping harvest (and eat) the farm produce, including Granddaddy's prime, home-grown watermelons.

Now, Granddaddy's melons were a delicacy, wetter than a swimming pool on a hot,

36

summer day and sweeter than a ripe peach, and he grew them with yellow meat as well as red meat. People from that community raved about Granddaddy's melons being some of the best they ever tasted. Our job was to retrieve the watermelons from the patch as needed. Granddaddy let us pick the ripe melons a couple of times each week and load them on his truck to take into town for selling, along with fresh eggs from the henhouse.

We got to choose whether we wanted to help gather the eggs or pick melons. I always chose picking the melons because I was scared the chickens would jump on me and peck me to death. Getting through the pasture to the melon patch was always less formidable to me than the possibility of confronting the chickens in the henhouse. On an earlier summer farm visit, one of my cousins decided I needed some egg education.

"Hold out your hand," she said to me. "Just hold it out, palm up."

As I held out my hand, I had a sinking feeling that I would regret that moment.

Before I realized it, she had placed a soft-shell egg in my palm, and I could feel the small body moving around inside. I suddenly felt nauseous, because of the mental picture I had created of chickens jumping around, so I dropped that egg and took off running. I ran all the way to the smokehouse as I heard my cousins' taunting laughter and chanting behind me. "Fraidy cat, fraidy cat." I was a coward, and I did not care one bit. I'll take watermelon picking over egg-gathering any day.

Getting to the watermelons was always a challenge. Two boondoggles stood between us and them: Cow manure and bees.

"Watch out or you'll cut your foot," Granddaddy would holler as we set out for the melon vines. Getting a "cut foot" was Granddaddy's reference for stepping in cow manure. "And don't be pointing (pronounced pintin') at those melons cause you'll make 'em fall off the vines too early." We could hear Granddaddy's snorting guffaw as we hightailed it over toward the watermelon patch. Sandy, Granddaddy's collie dog, romped along with us, barking excitedly all the way.

"Look out over there, and over here, too," I shouted, as I tried to offer guidance to us all.

"Oh, no, I think I already stepped in it. Ugh," one of us replied.

"Watch out. I think I did it, too."

We knew that the consequences of "cut

feet" included an hour or more of shoe cleaning and scolding if we tried to bring the shoes into the house before the odor was mostly gone. Once we got out to the vines, we momentarily forgot about the shoes as we tried to dodge the bees that were swarming nearby. The ultimate low point would be to let a bee sting get the best of you. Only a sissy would let a bee sting make you go back to the house for treatment of the pain and swelling (probably a little baking soda or tobacco juice rubbed on the sting) instead of eating and fetching the watermelons.

We decided that *pintin'* at the melons only counted when you did it with your index finger — not with your elbow — so we wiggled our elbows at every single melon we saw. "Looka here at me," we hooted to one another, as we elbow-pointed at all of those watermelons. Granddaddy taught us that the ripe melons were the ones that had come off the vines prior to the *pintin'* and had a yellowish spot on their bottoms where they showed evidence of being "ground-ripened."

We would take our first-picked ripe melons over to the fence posts and crack 'em in two, eating out the heart, which was the sweetest portion, and spitting the seeds out as we pleased. This behavior was acceptable because we were with family and not "mixed company."

Finally, we gathered up a ripe melon apiece and navigated our way back through the pasture to the truck, where we loaded our bounty onto the bed. Since it took several trips to the melon patch and back to accomplish this task, most all of us had "cut feet" by the time we finished it. Granny had us to leave one or two melons beside the door of the house to have with her special roasting ear (corn) soup for breakfast the next morning. We knew we would be out picking corn for the soup and other vegetables from Granny's garden later in the day when we got back from town.

When the truck was half-full with melons in the back and several baskets filled with fresh eggs in the cab, we loaded ourselves and Sandy into the remaining space in the back of the pickup and away we went into town. Holding on tightly to the sides of the truck as the wind whipped our hair awry, we screamed over Sandy's barking most of the way into town. As Granddaddy stopped at each "selling point," we took turns jumping down from the truck to haul the melons out for the buying public. Granddaddy called himself a "she-Grandpa" until years later when our two boy cousins were born into the family, and he introduced us girls to folks as "his boys."

When we stopped at the home of Mrs. Kate, the Sunday school teacher, she bought some eggs and asked Granddaddy if she would be seeing us at Sunday school. Granddaddy assured her that we would be there. "I will expect to see every one of you at Sunday church meeting, now," Mrs. Kate replied with her admonishing tone.

"Yes ma'am," we responded, much to Granddaddy's relief.

"And can you bring along your smallest ripe melon to Sunday school?" Mrs. Kate added. "I believe we can use it in our Bible lesson."

"Yes'm. See you Sunday," we called as Granddaddy drove off to the next stop.

I wondered how on earth a watermelon could be part of a Bible lesson, but I knew from other Sunday school visits at Granny and Granddaddy's church that Mrs. Kate was an inspirational teacher. Whatever she had planned would be worth knowing. She had us hooked from that instant, by appealing to our curiosity. Sunday was two days away, so we would have to wait to find out the mystery.

When we arrived back at the farm, Granny

41

had a snack lunch ready for us: Peanut butter and jelly sandwiches with some cookies and milk. She knew we wouldn't eat much because we were hankering to get outside and move on with our explorations around the farm. Granddaddy had some work to do at the farmhouse before getting back outdoors, so Granny gave us our directions:

"Children, now go out and pick two baskets of vegetables from the garden during the afternoon for the evening dinner and bring them back in time for cooking. Best not go over to the little pond alone, and best not get into the old barn. Now, scoot."

We told Granny we would pick some vegetables, and away we went. The plan always worked. We made sure we got most of two baskets full of ripe vegetables from the garden: Corn, squash, okra, tomatoes, cucumbers, and whatever else appeared ready for picking.

Next, we stashed the mostly full baskets in a cool hiding place (usually the porch swing), where we could grab them later on to prove we had, in fact, been picking. Then we headed off to the little pond, about a half-mile through the pasture behind the barn. If we stayed close to the beaten path we didn't have to worry as much about getting "cut feet" with this adventure. Sandy went along with us, but we petted him all the way so his barking would not betray us with our whereabouts.

We were careful to take off our shoes and roll up our britches legs before the wading so we could dry off pretty well afterward and evidence would not remain to reveal our disobedience. As we waded into the cool water of the little pond, we pondered Mrs. Kate's words.

"How can a watermelon be part of a Bible lesson?" I asked out loud.

"Well, I read my Bible regular, and I sure don't remember that part."

"Mrs. Kate can find a way to do it if anybody can."

"Sunday school will at least be interesting, so I don't fall asleep there."

After wading long enough to feel that we had showed our childlike selves in disobedience, we sat down on the bank to dry off a spell while Sandy shook his watery body all over us, making us scream in spite of ourselves. When we had dried out enough to put our shoes back on and roll down our britches, we proceeded to the next forbidden escapade: Going into the old barn.

We had to be quiet and stealthy about getting into the old barn because it was closer to the main farmhouse, and we didn't want to get called in for "wash up" before we completed our explorations. New kittens were in there, and we could hear them mewing, and we tried to get a distant look at them without disturbing their mother cat. My older cousin decided to be bold and climb up the ladder to the top floor. As she ventured out onto the creaky boards in the center of the room, I decided to follow her up the ladder and wisely stayed on the top rungs, peeking in so I could see her.

"Come on out here in the middle of the rafters," she beckoned.

"No, it's not safe," I said, as I shook my head and motioned for the two younger cousins to stay down below.

"You're just scared again, like with that egg thing."

"You better come on back," I yelled, but it was too late.

The rotten board she stood on began to crack in two pieces, and she barely made it back to the ladder before she slipped all the way through, too. We all screamed, and when we made it out of the barn, we ran back to the house as fast as we could, hollering all the way. Granddaddy came out and asked us what was going on, and we settled down and said that we were just playing chase. Our disobedience had nearly backfired on us.

We reclaimed our baskets of vegetables from the front porch swing and took them in to Granny, washing them for her, and realizing that we were getting mighty hungry for evening dinner. While Granny cooked dinner, we washed up and settled down in the front porch swing to rest from our afternoon adventures. We took turns swinging as high as we could go, and then seeing if any of us would be brave enough to try jumping out when the swing was at its highest point in the air. Pretty soon, we could smell dinner cooking, and we could hear Granny whistling as she worked in the kitchen.

Granny would cook every cousin's favorite dish, and mine was fried okra.

No one could make fried okra the same as Granny. Hers was light and sweet, due to the freshness of the just-picked okra and the slight amount of cornmeal she used to coat the okra before frying it in bacon drippings. I pulled up a stool and sat watching Granny's expert moves as she heated the cut up okra on high heat, lightly browning the okra pieces and turning them over and over in the cast iron skillet. Then she lowered the heat, simmering the okra until it was completely tender and ready for eating. I didn't much like sharing it with anyone else, and I did so grudgingly. I made sure I got the last serving, too.

I called the okra "my Annie Okra," after Annie Oakley, the legendary sure-shooter. I even had a cowgirl suit with a red vest, skirt, and hat, and two cap guns so I could pretend to "be" Annie Oakley when I wore that outfit. Although I brought the outfit with me to the farm, I figured that Granny probably wouldn't let me wear it to Sunday church meeting. I decided to ask Granny if she knew how a watermelon could be part of a Bible lesson.

"Granny, is there a Bible lesson with a watermelon as part of it?" I inquired, as we helped Granny clear the table after evening dinner.

"Child, I don't remember one, but Mrs. Kate may be planning to use the watermelon to help you children learn a Bible lesson."

We took our baths after dinner and piled into the big beds, ready for slumber after our busy day at the farm. We fell asleep after saying our prayers and wondering how our parents were getting along at our homes without us. We decided they could make do all right, and we knew they would be coming to visit us Sunday afternoon, anyway, to see how we were doing at the farm.

The next day was Saturday, and we went with Granddaddy to milk the cows early that morning before breakfast. When we returned to the house, Granny had her roasting ear (corn) soup ready for us with hearts of watermelon slices to go with it. After breakfast, Granddaddy gave out the fishing poles, accompanying us on a "sanctioned" visit to the little pond.

We followed him along the path, never breathing a word about how we'd already been over there the day before and waded around in the water for a spell on our own. Each cousin wanted to be the one who caught the most fish, of course. The problem was that I wouldn't touch the red wiggler worms. So somebody had to bait my hook for me.

"Granddaddy, will you fix my worm on the hook, please?" I begged.

"You can do it for yourself."

"No, I can't. They're wigglin' all around. I'll be sick if I do it."

"Scaredy cat, scaredy cat," my cousins chanted.

"The rest of us can put our own worms on the hooks. You just won't catch any fish."

When I was almost in tears, Granddaddy gave up and had mercy on me. We all caught some fish, but Granddaddy threw them back into the pond after taking them off the hook because they were so small. We were catching the same fishes over and over again, but we still counted up to find out how many we caught all together. Being there at the pond with Granddaddy and having him take up time with us was the main part of the fun.

Later that day, Granddaddy reminded us to go out to the watermelon patch again and find a small, round melon for Mrs. Kate's Bible lesson the next morning. Granddaddy's melons varied in shape and size, from large, oblong, and striped to small, round, and solid dark. We picked out a small, round, darkish melon with the telltale ripened yellowish spot on the "grounded" side for Mrs. Kate. That was one of the few trips to the melon patch when I think no one got any "cut feet."

Sunday morning dawned, and Granny was calling us early on to get dressed in our Sunday clothes to go to church. We wore our napkins around our necks at breakfast so as not to get our church clothes messed up. Granny fixed roasting ear soup again (at our request) and some freshly gathered scrambled eggs with bacon and grits, too.

I had brought my Bible with me from

home, along with my embroidered bookmark that Mama made and used to mark her favorite Bible stories when she was growing up. She gave it to me so I could use it as she did. It was delicate and lacy around the edges with irises embroidered in dark blue and yellow down the center part. I intended to use the bookmark to mark the mystery passage that related to a watermelon and then to impress all my friends back at home with this knowledge. I tried to wear part of the Annie Oakley cowgirl suit, too, over my good clothes, but Granny made me take the cowgirl suit off and leave it at the farmhouse.

When everyone was ready, Granddaddy pulled the blue pickup to the house, and Granny got into the cab with him. Granddaddy had put a quilt down over the bed part of the pickup, and we climbed in and sat down on it. Granddaddy handed us the chosen watermelon, and we wedged it in between us so it wouldn't roll all over the back of the truck and get split apart before we got to church. Sandy barked loudly, wanting to jump in and go with us, but Granddaddy told him he had to stay at home this time. We moved on down the long, gravelly driveway and into town.

The Baptist church building in town was

an architectural marvel, and it is still standing today. The story goes that William Tecumseh Sherman himself and his soldiers did not burn this church building during the Civil War when they marched from Atlanta to the sea in Savannah; instead, they occupied the building, keeping their horses in the rounded basement part overnight. That same basement portion of the church building is where Mrs. Kate and the Junior Children's Department held Sunday school meeting.

As Granny and Granddaddy took us into Mrs. Kate's Bible class, she asked each one of us our names. To Granny's horror, I replied that my name was "Annie Oakley." I decided that God would want Annie Oakley to go to church, too, and why not pretend to be her? Granny made me redeem myself by telling her my real name. Although Granny was embarrassed to death, I am sure that I heard Granddaddy chuckle before Granny stifled him with her stare. We handed Mrs. Kate the small, round melon, and she said that it would be just right for the Bible lesson.

Mrs. Kate introduced all of us girls to the other local children in the class, and I sat down by a pretty, blond girl who smiled at me and told me her name. The boy sitting across from me looked bored and about to fall asleep. Mrs. Kate played the piano and led us in a chorus of "Into my Heart" and "Standing on the Promises." Then Mrs. Kate told us to get our Bibles ready for a sword drill.

Now, sword drills are very important because they make you test your knowledge of the order and location of the books in the Bible, which is the "Sword of the spirit, the Word of God." Mrs. Kate would call out a book of the Bible, along with a chapter and verse number, and we all would try to find the verse first and read it aloud to prove we had found the proper verse.

Sword drill came before the Bible lesson. Right before we started the sword drill, I laid my precious bookmark down on the table where I had been sitting earlier during the singing time. We had to stand up for the sword drill, so I presently forgot about the bookmark as I got caught up in the excitement of the drill. My older cousin won the sword drill (just by one verse, though).

Next came the highly anticipated Bible lesson. Mrs. Kate informed us that the Bible text would be from the Old Testament: I Kings, Chapter 3. Now, this chapter is the story about King Solomon, who asked God for an understanding and wise heart during his kingship, rather than riches or material wealth. She told us to read along silently as she read aloud until we got to verse 24. At that point in the chapter, the boy who sat across from me would help act out the remainder of the chapter (using the watermelon as a prop) as he spoke the words of King Solomon in verses 24, 25, and 27.

I still wondered how a watermelon could possibly relate to the Bible lesson. Apparently, we were about to find out. Mrs. Kate read on about the two women, one whose baby died during the night, and the other whose baby was alive and well, and how both women claimed to be the living child's real mother. What would King Solomon do to solve the problem? Mrs. Kate got to verse 24, reading, and the boy across from me suddenly stood up (as Mrs. Kate had coached him to do in advance) and spoke King Solomon's words: "Bring me a sword."

The boy grasped an imaginary sword and held up our chosen small, round watermelon as a symbol of the living baby. We all sat up very straight in our chairs and began paying close attention. The boy continued speaking as King Solomon with the words from verse 25, "Divide the living child in two, and give half to the one, and half to the other." We all gasped as we wondered whether the boy would crack open the melon then and there.

Mrs. Kate read on with the words first of the mother who wished the living child divided and then with the words of the mother who begged King Solomon to give the child to the other mother rather than harm the baby. Once more the boy, speaking as King Solomon, read the King's words from verse 27 as he laid the intact watermelon on the table. "Give her the living child, and in no wise slay it: she is the mother thereof."

We all let out sighs of relief, as we realized that King Solomon had used God's gift of wisdom and understanding to reconcile the situation. Mrs. Kate then led us in prayer, thanking God for all blessings.

Mrs. Kate thanked the boy who played King Solomon's part, and then she got out some cookies and juice for a quick snack before we left to find Granny and Granddaddy and go into the big sanctuary for the worship service. She told us we could pick up the watermelon after church, but we agreed that Granddaddy would want her to keep it and enjoy it. From that day forward, eating watermelon took on a whole new meaning for me.

It was during the snack time that I realized

my embroidered bookmark was missing. I frantically looked around the room and scanned the tables, but no bookmark. I asked my cousins whether they had seen the bookmark, but no one seemed to know anything about it. I sat through the worship service thinking only of my loss, and how I would ever get the bookmark back again. Riding in the back of the truck back to the farm, I asked my older cousin if she had any suggestions.

"Oh, we'll be going back next Sunday cause we're staying one more week. At least you and I will stay another week. We're not homesick like the younger cousins. They'll probably go on home with their parents this afternoon."

"Do you think the bookmark will turn up next Sunday?"

"Well, it's a possibility. Ask Granny about it. She'll know what to do."

I took my cousin's suggestion and talked to Granny about the problem. She said she would call Mrs. Kate and ask her if she noticed the bookmark left in the room after Sunday school. After their phone conversation, Granny said that Mrs. Kate didn't know anything about the bookmark, but she had an idea that it would turn up the following week.

That afternoon, Mama and Daddy came to the farm to visit, along with my aunts and uncles, who were the other cousins' parents. I assured Mama and Daddy that I wanted to stay one more week, but I didn't tell Mama about the missing bookmark. I was too embarrassed. I made Granny promise not to tell Mama, because I hoped to find the bookmark during the next Sunday church meeting.

We all went outside under the big pecan trees to have some watermelon together before the relatives who were planning to leave got on their way back home. Granddaddy had chosen a huge, elongated, striped watermelon for the afternoon treat. We sat down at the picnic tables in the shade of the pecan trees; the adults sat at one table, and we children sat at the other one. We watched as Granddaddy prepared to split the watermelon. As he cut into the melon's flesh, I thought about King Solomon and his wish for an understanding heart rather than riches and material things. I appreciated my family in a special way on that afternoon as we ate the juicy, sweet melon.

I knew that Mrs. Kate had wanted us children to grasp this lesson of the heart from the Bible so that we would remember it as we grew older. She got her wish as far as I was concerned. To this day, I think about King Solomon every time I eat watermelon. We cousins even acted out the motions of those verses every summer after that one for years when we picked and ate Granddaddy's watermelons.

The following Sunday it was just my older cousin and I who made it back to church with Granny and Granddaddy. The younger cousins decided one week was long enough away from home. We greeted Mrs. Kate, telling her that this Sunday would be our last one with her until the next summer because we would be going home later that afternoon. She hugged us and said that she was certainly glad we had come to Sunday school.

I sat down next to my cousin at one of the tables, as we got ready to sing, "I've got the joy, joy, joy, joy, down in my heart." It was at that moment that I saw the little blond girl grinning and playing with my bookmark as she sang along. At first, I wanted to reach across the table and grab my bookmark away from her right then and there, and I almost did it, too. At the end of the song, Mrs. Kate told us to get our Bibles ready for the weekly sword drill.

As we stood up with our Bibles to participate in the drill, I whispered to the little blond girl, "That's my bookmark you took last Sunday, but maybe you need it more than I do. Maybe God wants me to give it to you to help you with your Bible lessons. If you really want it and need it, you can have it. I think my Mama will understand if I explain it to her, since she embroidered it."

The little blond girl burst into tears and ran out of the room right as we began singing. When she came back later, she handed the bookmark back to me, and said she was sorry she took it. I looked at Mrs. Kate, and she nodded at me as she read on through our lesson in the Bible. I was learning how to get through to the heart of things.

Before there were fast food restaurants?

"Grandmother would always make a little "snack lunch" for us grandchildren so we could get all the way home without having to ask Mama and Daddy to stop along the way for a snack. She would put in the box (usually an empty animal crackers circus box with the elephants, tigers, and bears painted on there) all of my favorite "eats," like peanut butter crackers or whatever she had on hand that day. Most of all, her love was packed in there for me and I knew it! I couldn't wait to visit again!"

When music was printed on vinyl albums you played on record players?

"Actually, I owned many of the old 78s as well as the 45 rpms! I have vivid memories of dancing around my childhood bedroom in Atlanta to the vibes of 'Davy, Davy Crockett, King of the Wild Frontier' and 'Little Red Riding Hood.' I distinctly remember hiding under the bed just before the wolf growled at Grandma! My cousin and I sometimes danced and sang along in her family's garage with her recording of 'Does your Chewing Gum lose its flavor on the bedpost overnight . . . ?' Those were the days."

When watching a movie meant going to a drive-in theater?

"I remember Mama dressing me in my pajamas and settling me into the back seat of our 1951 Plymouth many a time as she and Daddy and I headed off to our neighborhood drive-in for movie entertainment. Hiding in the back seat under my blanket was especially convenient when I got too scared of scenes from movies like the *Hounds of the Baskervilles!* I would always fall asleep part-way through the movie."

— Lynda Holmes,
Getting To The Heart Of The Watermelon

Ants Gotta Bite, Sun Gotta Burn

BY JULIA HORST SCHUSTER

"Well, they're Southern people, and if they know you are working at home they think nothing of walking right in for coffee. But they wouldn't dream of interrupting you at golf."

— Harper Lee

Queen Esther Ashcraft Gaston was my grandmother's name, and she lived up to its loftiness, certainly not in wealth or social stature, but in the richness she passed down to her wisdomless clan. I fancied her a royal, but she was far from stuck on herself. She was genteel and kind, with a unique way of humbling herself to mingle with us "relative" commoners who needed someone to teach us what was what.

My family always visited her in the summertime, usually during the month of July, when the humidity in Deland, Florida was at its peak and could suck streams of perspiration out of you, drenching your shirt and

60

underdrawers in nothing flat. I remember those visits as some of the happiest days of my young life. All except one summer, that is.

Oh, I must have been about five or six years old. Our pea-green, 1959 Chevrolet Impala Estate station wagon crunched along the shell road toward Granny's house. We'd been driving since midnight. I couldn't wait to get out of the car and away from my brothers — John, who relished tormenting me, his baby sister, to the point of making me scream or tickling me to the point of wetting my pants — and Arthur, who had just reached puberty and had not yet learned the advantages of deodorant.

Once a week did not cut it, and ninety-five degree heat only made the fumes rise faster to my nose. The boys hogged the back seat; I was sandwiched in the middle and never allowed to "claim" the window seat. How did our parents ever survive those trips without Nintendo, DVDs or at the very least, CDs or cassettes? Better yet, how did I ever survive them?

Before our tires came to a complete stop in front of Granny's house, I vaulted over John and forced open the car door, eager to escape the stale air. I jumped out with sandaled feet, and without noticing the ant mound. It took a few seconds for my travel-numb limbs to react to the bites, but when the pain hit, my siren wailed.

A regiment of tiny red soldiers charged up my legs and into my shorts. They covered my lower extremities in a matter of seconds; even got into my panties. My white flesh turned angry red from the six-legged poison machines. I howled. I kicked, goose-stepping, and squealed, searching around frantically for something to rub up against.

With me dashing about like a Comanche meeting the warpath head-on, Mother had a dickens of a time catching me after she clambered from the car. "Julia, be still!" she yelled. She slapped at my legs with her headscarf. Daddy cursed. Even John and Arthur chipped in to beat off the little bug-gers. I'd never been so happy for a whip-ping. But fire ants fight to the death. They were not giving up.

By the time Granny heard the ruckus and made her way from out back near the fern-packing shed — she grew and sold the kind of ferns used in floral arrangements — to the front porch, I had hundreds of bites from my waist to my feet. Granny snatched me up and dashed to the side of the house, where she dropped me into the rain barrel, pushing my head below the surface with great force. Green algae choked me and got sucked up my nose. But when I came up, gasping, I was thankful and certain that my queen had saved me from a horrible death.

"Just sit right there and let the water soothe you," she said. "I'll fetch the salve, and I'll be right back."

She disappeared around back of the house, unfazed and unruffled. I wondered how she had managed to remain so calm. Royal blood, I figured. She hadn't screamed, "Lord, have mercy, my baby, my baby," like Mother had. She had just acted, swiftly and with total control of her senses. I had known and loved this woman my whole life, but only then did I realize she was a woman to be admired.

I did okay for a few seconds, just bobbing there in the barrel, the water cool on my burning legs. Then I realized that I was alone on the side of a house so eerie and mysterious it took me weeks to overcome the nightmares that followed me home. It didn't exactly resemble a castle. A rundown old Florida homestead was more like it, sitting on cinder blocks and listing slightly to the left. Live oaks dripping with Spanish moss domed the property. Their shadowy crown added a horror flick atmosphere that fueled the imagination of this grandchild ripe for suspense. Their shade was essential for Granny's Plumosus fern business, but to me the gloom concealed monsters who lurked under the blades, waiting to jump out at the next passerby or the next child left alone in a rain barrel.

I screamed.

Where had the rest of my family gone? Had they all been attacked by the biting varmints? Were they out front in a battle with the tiny foe? Or what if . . . what if . . . what if the fern monsters had gotten them and eaten them all up?

"Aheeeeee!"

"Julia? Julia!" Finally my mother's voice came to me from someplace above. I looked up and found her. She stood inside the screened porch, her face pressed against the mesh. "Oh, baby girl, are you okay? I'd come down there but those critters are everywhere. This place is crawling with them, just like it always was when I was a child."

"I want out," I wailed.

My mother was scared out of her wits. I could tell by the way she scanned the ground around me. I could tell by the way her hands rubbed her arms as if she were cold. What other reason could keep her away from me in my time of need? I had never witnessed her in such a state. It caused me to pause in my pain and wonder how itsy-bitsy red bugs could wield the power to cause such a horrible thing — a mother paralyzed with fear.

But fear is contagious. I caught it and quaked. "I can't get out. I want out. I want out NOW! It hurts, Mother, it hurts soooooo bad." Tears rolled as my agony recharged. Green slime and imaginary water beasts threatened to gag me again.

"It's okay, doodle bug, just hold on. Granny will be right back with the salve, quick as a minute. She's immune to those dad-blamed creatures. They gave up on her long ago. But she'll fix you up like she always did me."

Thankfully, Mother was right. Granny reappeared and lifted me from the muck. And for a woman of close to eighty, she was one strong broad. But now, slime dripping from my toes was the least of my worries. The air hit my bites like a thousand needles. I started yelling and I didn't quit until a dose of paregoric kicked in.

The next few days remain a blur to me. I guess doping me out of my mind was easier than listening to me lament like a captive damsel in distress. When I finally recovered, I had major catching up to do. My brothers had already been to Silver Springs to ride the glass bottom boat, see the mermaids, and marvel at the human pyramids of championship water skiers who dazzled the crowds there seven days a week. Plus, they'd been down the St. John's River fishing with Uncle John A. I had missed out on everything. This vacation was from hell. I was cranky and bite pimpled, and it was time for high-style Julia pampering. I deserved better than this.

When Daddy carried me to the car, (because I refused to place my feet anywhere near the ground) I sported a pity-party attitude that I was certain would gain me extra trinkets at the local souvenir store. Boy, was I wrong. Granny didn't react kindly to emotional blackmail. I was lucky to get to go to the beach, or so I thought.

Daddy drove and Granny rode shotgun. "Daytona, here we come!" Granny rattled off directions, pointing left, and then right while I sat in amazement in my usual spot in the middle of the back seat. This was a curious thing, I thought, a first in my five-year old history. No one had ever told my daddy where to go. But there he sat in the driver's seat, quietly following Queen Esther's commandments, and never raising his bushy left eyebrow or grumbling under his mustache.

Normally, I thought of Granny as a vanilla woman, who wore only regal shades of gray, beige and white. She had Clorox-white hair, braided and coiled into a crown on top of her head, as cottony soft as my pillowcase. I recall her as if she were perpetually seated in a black and white photo, even when she was right there before me in the flesh, with sepia shades being the boldest her personality could muster up. But here, in her domain, Granny took on an air of authority that she could have never pulled off in Memphis on her visits to see us. She spoke and everyone listened. With words delivered with a smile and in a quieter-than-normal tone, her meaning came across with clarity and kid glove force.

At the beach she said, "Julia Elisa, come here and let me slather on this here Coppertone." I wrinkled up my nose, but obeyed. "Your momma and John A. will be comin' to git me real soon. I can't stay out here with y'all an' bake all day. I got work to git done back at home. Those ferns gotta be cut, packed an' shipped today. But you mind my words, now, young'un' — in a little while you're to put on this here shirt your daddy brought, and sit here underneath this umbrella so'ens you don't get scorched.

Don't forget, now, or those bites will come back to life and have you ruby red and wailing all over again."

"Yes, ma'am," I replied, taking no mind.

By bedtime the blisters rose. My shoulders puffed up with a septic ocean boiling just below the skin. Hot red, I couldn't sit, I couldn't stand, and I certainly could not lie down. There was no position of comfort, no salve that could ease the pain. Granny cut five stalks from the aloe vera plant, smeared me up good and prayed to the Lord Almighty that I'd get some relief. Then it was once again time to bring on the dope. Mixed with peanut butter to kill the taste, Mother spooned paregoric down me, and before long oblivion took me to a place of tormented dreams, fern monsters and fire ants bigger than the flying monkeys in the Wizard of Oz.

The next morning — as I awakened from sitting straight up all night on my cot in the corner of the dining room — I overheard my brothers discussing how Daddy had just stood there and taken it when Granny reamed him up one wall and down the other for not watching out to make sure I didn't get charbroiled at the beach. First taking directions, and now a good reaming out? This woman, Queen Esther Granny, must have some kind of power to accomplish all of that in these few short days, I thought.

A few more miserable days of healing passed. They seemed to go on forever. I was not a happy camper, but I knew better than to moan too much. I was bored out of my mind but reluctant to leave the house. It seemed that the out-of-doors that had once been my playground now held painful dangers my young years had never experienced before. I started to understand why my mother seemed so jumpy. I was more than just jumpy. I was ready to bolt.

Arthur came into the kitchen one afternoon in search of some needle-nosed pliers to fix his fishing line. I was helping Granny make fried chicken for dinner. It had taken all I could muster to stand on the back porch and watch her swing that poor bird by the neck till it was dead. I was a city girl. I had never seen anything so tragic. Now, I stood across the room while she chopped the creature to bits. My stomach churned just a little, but I managed to choke it down.

I guess she figured a little cooking would keep me occupied since I had run out of things to play with and had refused to set foot off the porch for fear of another ant attack. After all, those little varmints knew I was there and that I tasted good. They were sure to come back for course number two of me.

Granny's hands were caked with flour, so she pointed Arthur and me to search through some of her less-used kitchen junk drawers for the pliers. I was glad for the distraction. I rummaged through a couple and then came upon one drawer with a stubborn attitude. It refused to pull out. I tugged hard, leaning backward. I tugged once, tugged again.

When the drawer finally gave way, it gave way with gusto. It flew open, tossing me onto my rump in the floor and something black and hairy into my lap. The beast scampered across my belly, ran up my arm, and around my tender shoulders before scurrying off in a mad dash to escape human wrath. Screaming at a pitch that would break Hobnail glass, I leaped into my brother's arms. My fillings quivered.

"Whoa, watch out there," Arthur stuttered, but Granny didn't even pause from dredging chicken parts.

"What's all this commotion about?" she asked calmly.

"It's a rat, or something, Granny," Arthur said, struggling to hold on to me and not let my feet touch the ground. "He's gone now, Julia. It's okay, I won't put you down."

Granny took her time milking and flouring the last breasts and thighs. She placed the pieces on the baking sheet and covered them with a dishtowel before even coming over to see if I had survived. Dusting her hands off on her yellow checkered apron, she leaned over the drawer, which now lay in the floor, as if investigating a crime scene. "Hum, what have we got here?" she said. "Looks like we got us some good eats for dinner."

Arthur moved a few steps closer, with me hanging around his neck like a talisman of bad luck. That remark had even piqued my interest. Had I heard her right? What on God's green earth could be in a drawer that we'd want for dinner? I wriggled out of my brother's arms, being careful where I stepped, and leaned tentatively over the drawer.

There, eight tiny rat-lings lay nestled in with the canning tongs and Mason jar lids. Their eyes weren't even open yet. They squirmed close to each other, searching their dishrag nest for the mother they knew had been there just moments ago.

My hand caught the first droplets of vomit. No way was I eating baby rats. I ran out the back door toward the outhouse, and under the arbor of wisteria, but I only made it as far as the packinghouse stoop. When I returned, still green and queasy, I slumped into a vinyl kitchen chair. Granny was just lifting the first few chicken legs from the hot oil.

"We're not really eating those little critters for dinner, are we, Granny?"

She didn't answer. She just raised her eyes to me and smiled one of those smiles that are impossible to decipher. "Did any ants attack you on your way to the john?" she asked.

I thought for a minute. "No, ma'am."

"Any other catastrophe besiege you? Wasps, hornets, yellow flies?"

"No, Ma'am."

"A fern monster grab your leg while you upchucked?"

I shook my head.

"So I guess you're gonna help me wash the fern fronds tomorrow and get them packed, iced and ready to ship off to florists all across these fine United States then?"

The snakes my mother had mentioned that slither amongst the ferns and often visit the packinghouse came to mind. I had to pause before answering. Could I really do it? Could I handle being out there with danger lurking at my feet, just waiting to bite me, burn me, or jump into my lap? I wasn't sure. "I'll have to ask Mother," I said.

"Your momma is a wonderful woman, but I did her wrong raising her up. I coddled her to the point of making her wimpy. It's my fault, not hers. I didn't want my baby to suffer. I didn't want her to have to deal with pain and strife. But it don't have to be like that, you know. You're a strong little dickens. Just look how you handled yourself with those pesky old ants. And I've never seen a child brave a sunburn like you've got as well as you did. This here is a prime opportunity to face those big bad monsters you've created for yourself. Them ants gotta bite and that sun gotta burn, but you, young'un', gotta snub your nose at it all. You can either be a shrinking violet or stand tall like a hardy mum. It's your pick."

Granny turned back to tend her chicken.

I sat there for a long while. I traced the flower pattern on the vinyl tablecloth with my finger, not having the courage yet to answer or to join Granny at the stove. Finally I moved to stand beside her. I tugged on her apron. She stopped and looked down.

"How do you keep those ants from biting you, Granny?" I asked.

She tussled my hair. "Meanness, for one thing, pure meanness. They know better than to mess with Queen Esther Ashcraft Gaston. I can be as mean as a snake, if need be, you know. But more than that, young'un', I tread lightly. Yep, I tread lightly and I watch out where I place my feet."

Queen Esther dished up a fine dinner that night, double-coated fried chicken, scrubbed clean potatoes, mashed with homemade butter and fresh milk, lady peas, angel biscuits and tomato slices the size of pancakes. I didn't try the casserole she prepared, though, even after she encouraged me that it was a fine way to snub my nose at my fear. It resembled her cornbread-dressing recipe, usually my favorite. But the eight grayish lumps just visible below its crusty surface reminded me too much of baby rats in a drawer.

"What are those?" I asked, pointing to the mounds.

Granny smiled another one of her unreadable smiles.

Daddy scooped a huge helping onto his plate and announced, "Chicken livers, them are chicken livers and gizzards, too. Good ones, I might add. Give 'em a try."

I swallowed hard and hoped no one ever pulled one over on me like had just been pulled over on him. I wanted so badly to prove to Granny that I was brave, but her fried chicken had been so good, I wanted it to remain in my tummy where it was. Arthur, usually the garbage disposal of the family, didn't indulge in the mystery casserole either.

I guess I wasn't the only fearful subject in Granny's kingdom of scaredy cats.

When Grandma and Grandpa Went Shopping In The 1950s

- Coke-a-Cola came in glass bottles and cost ten or fifteen cents.
- A gallon of gas cost fifty cents.
- A hamburger cost less than twenty cents.
- The average family of four lived on an annual income of about $5,000.
- A dozen eggs cost sixty cents.
- First-class postage was three cents.
- TV shows were in black and white.
- Favorite TV shows included westerns like *Wyatt Earp* and *Gunsmoke,* and variety shows such as *The Milton Berle Show.*
- Favorite singers included Pat Boone, Bobby Darin, Perry Como and Patti Page.

Have A Coke and A Smile

"As a teenager I worked in the drugstore of my small, south Georgia town. Old men would gather there every morning and order what they called 'a glass of dope,' with no ice and no 'fizz.' Then they'd sit on benches outside the drugstore and drink it. This was their tonic.

"The 'dope,' of course, was Coke-a-Cola syrup. This was back when the soda jerk mixed a soft drink for you, squirting Coke syrup into a glass then adding carbonated water and ice. Even though everyone knew Coke had no 'dope' in it, the old men were convinced of its eye-opening powers."

— Sandra Chastain,
The Green Bean Casserole

A PRESBYTERIAN COOKBOOK

BY BERT GOOLSBY

"Within the South itself, no other form of cultural expression, not even music, is as distinctively characteristic of the region as the spreading of a feast of native food and drink before a gathering of kin and friends."
— John Egerton, from "Southern Food, at Home, on the Road, in History"

"I don't want neither one of y'all to get me anything for Christmas," Mamaw declared immediately after we finished our dinner in celebration of Thanksgiving 1944 and before anyone could leave the table. "Charlie — you and Davy. Y'all hear me?"

Mr. Charlie and I looked at each other. I could tell her statement troubled him as much as it did me.

"Does that mean I don't get nothing either?" I asked, concerned that my Christmas might once more be a bleak one. The year before Santa Claus brought me only a

New Testament, a pair of homemade socks, and an aviator cap — none of which I'd asked for.

Ever since my parents died three years before in a railroad crossing collision, I had lived with my grandmother and her second husband Charlie Kranshaw, folks with plenty of love but not much money. Mr. Charlie worked as a produce clerk at the Jitney Jungle in town while Mamaw eked out a small income from some cows and chickens they owned.

I had yet to get used to being what I considered "poor" and not getting the gifts I wanted when Christmas came around. My dad had been a salesman of industrial containers and had made a good living for his wife and only son; but being a man with little or no foresight, he'd left no insurance, either on himself or on my mother. Worse yet, a jury later ruled fault for the accident lay with him and not the railroad. He'd been drinking.

Mr. Charlie drew a deep breath and shook his head. "And what iffen I done already got you somethin' other, Treace?"

Mamaw pushed back from the table, stood, and picked up the platter that held what little remained of the hen she had baked. "Then you can just march yourself on back down to the store and return it, that's what you can do," she said, ignoring my question in favor of Mr. Charlie's.

"But what iffen they won't take it back, then what?" he asked, his head tilted sideways.

"You just make sure they do, that's what."

"But Treace —"

"But Treace, my foot. You take that thing back, whatever it is, and I don't mean maybe. You hear me?"

Mr. Charlie frowned. "All right then. But come Christmas and I ain't got you nothin', don't you forgit you done told me not to git you nothin'."

Mamaw whirled around and stomped off to the kitchen with the platter and one other serving dish in her hands.

I never quite knew what to do in these situations. When Mamaw's birthday approached, she would usually pull the same stunt. We never knew from year to year whether Mamaw really meant she didn't want anything or she wanted something special but didn't want to say what it was for fear of being disappointed if she didn't get it.

"Mr. Charlie," I whispered, once the door between the dining room and the kitchen swung shut, "what'd you buy her?"

He leaned toward me, a hand to his mouth. "I got her a cookbook. They was sellin' them down there at First Presbyterian for only fifty cent a piece."

My mouth flew open. "A Presbyterian cookbook!" I exclaimed in a whisper, glancing at the swinging door and expecting Mamaw to return at any moment for the other dishes. "Golly Pete, Mr. Charlie, a Presbyterian cookbook ain't something you'd give Mamaw at no time, much less for a Christmas present. I ain't but eleven years old and I know that."

"How you know it ain't?"

Before I could answer him, the door banged open and Mamaw returned to the dining room. "What you two still sitting in here for? Eat so much you can't move?"

"No, huh-uh. Me and Davy, we was just sittin' here talkin', you know, 'bout Christmas and all and what he wants Santa Claus to bring him this year."

Mamaw scraped two plates and stacked them on top of the one Mr. Charlie had used. His didn't need scraping. It never did. "I hope you realize, Davy, wanting and getting, they're two different things, especially this day and time."

The best I could recall, I'd learned that lesson the first Christmas after my folks got killed. I'd wanted a Shetland pony, and I didn't get it. Instead, I got a wagon. As Mamaw had explained it at the time, "You don't have to feed a wagon or clean up after it."

"Can I tell you what I want anyway, Mamaw? Although I know I won't get it," I said.

She stood just behind Mr. Charlie at the head of the table, the stacked plates in her hands. "Well, yeah. What?"

I swallowed and began to talk fast while I still had her attention. "Uh, I want a Mark Tidd book. I like reading them. And I want a new basketball. That's because a truck run over my old one yesterday when me and Earl were out playing with it. I meant to tell you about it, but I plumb forgot to. And, uh, I'd like a radio for my room so I can listen to my programs without bothering y'all. You know, like when 'Gangbusters' comes on, on Wednesday nights?"

"A Mark Tidd book and a ball and a radio so you can listen to 'Gangbusters,' " she repeated. "Have you read that New Testament I gave . . . I mean, Santa brought you last Christmas?"

"Nome."

"And you let your old basketball get out

82

into the road for a truck to run over, did you?"

"Well, I didn't exactly let it. It —"

"And you brought home a report card last week that had a B, three C's, and two D's and you're wanting to listen to the radio on a school night?"

I could tell Mr. Charlie felt for me. He looked at me, gritted his teeth, and squinted as if to say "Ouch." Thank goodness Mamaw didn't see him do it. If she had, she probably would've bopped him with the plates, not caring that they were her good china.

"I guess what you're saying, Mamaw, is I'm not gonna get any of those things and so it ain't no need for me to even ask for them, right?"

"Right. Now y'all get on outta here so I can clean up. I swear. I've never seen anybody who could mess up a table worse than the two of you can. Can't neither one of you eat a soda cracker without getting it all over you?"

Mamaw pushed her rear against the kitchen door to open it. "Oh, durn it all. I nearly 'bout forgot. I've gotta go to the hospital and see Cola Wells when I get done here. She's laid up with appendicitis."

Cola Wells belonged to Mamaw's missionary society. I never quite knew whom they "missionaried" to. Mostly, I think they just sat around, sipped coffee, ate pound cake, and gossiped about people.

The way I heard it, Mrs. Wells and Mamaw once almost had a falling out when Mamaw married Mr. Charlie just a few months after Damon Enfinger, Mamaw's first husband and my real grandpa, died of a heart attack a little less than a year before my parents got killed. Mrs. Wells thought that Mamaw wasn't showing proper respect for her dead husband in marrying so soon after his death and that Mamaw hadn't known Mr. Charlie long enough to marry him anyway. Mamaw met Mr. Charlie at an all-night sing or, as she often told the story, "Between the second and third stanzas of 'Love Lifted Me' when he come sat down by me there in the pew. I took it as a sign."

Mr. Charlie and I left the dining room and strolled out onto the front piazza where we picked up our conversation about the cookbook. "Now tell me now how you know the cookbook ain't a good Christmas present for your grandma, Davy?"

Before answering him, I made sure the front door was shut all the way. Even then, I talked in a low tone — a real, real low one. "Well, it might be good to get her a cookbook for Christmas, but, like I tried to tell you in yonder, I wouldn't give her no Presbyterian one. Mamaw feels like — and I thought you knew this, Mr. Charlie — if it's Presbyterian, she doesn't want anything to do with it. Why, for you to give her a Presbyterian cookbook, it'd be like giving her a slap in the face."

"Huh! I ain't thought about that," he said, making a face. "That's one thing I ain't never understood — why come she don't like Presbyterians. Them's Christians too, I always thought. They just don't shout and carry on. Not the ones I seen, don't."

"Oh, I think it's because of Granddaddy Damon. Wasn't he a Presbyterian?"

"I don't know what he was. I ain't never asked."

"Mamaw, she didn't like nothing about him, mama always said. Whatever he was for, she was dead set against. If he liked jelly, she liked jam. They argued all the time, mama said."

"I ain't surprised none. She's a strong woman, your grandma is. Iffen she don't git her way or somethin' other she wants, Lordy mercy, look out."

"Mama said Mamaw used to say, 'The only things Damon Enfinger ever gave me were a beautiful daughter and a hard time.'

But Mama, she kinda thought it was the other way around, Mama did. It was her that gave my grandpa a hard time."

Mr. Charlie sat quietly for a moment or two. "Wonder, then, how I could go 'bout findin' out what she does want so I can go git it for her?"

An idea hit me. "Why don't we call somebody over at the hospital and see if we can't get them to have Mrs. Wells ask Mamaw when she gets there in kinda a round-about way what she'd like to have for Christmas and then, if Mamaw tells her, she could tell them what she says and they could tell us. Know anybody there?"

Mr. Charlie slapped his knee. "Dad burn it, Davy, that's a good idea. Yes, sir. A real good'un."

He walked to the edge of the piazza and peeked around the corner. "Tell you what. Let's me and you watch and see iffen Treace goes to the outhouse and, iffen she goes, I'll call over to the hospital. I know somebody there, sure 'nuff. She's a nurse what works the second shift and I bet she'd ask Mrs. Wells to do it for us, iffen I asked her to. Her name's Miss Gloria Deery. I see her near 'bout ever' afternoon when she comes to the store 'fore she goes on her shift there at the hospital. She buys them seedless grapes we sell. Says she eats them for snacks since all the candy we git nowadays got worms in it, seems like."

We moved from the front porch to the side yard where we had a clear view of the privy. As we waited for Mamaw to finish up inside and perhaps answer a call of nature before she left for the hospital, Mr. Charlie and I threw a football back and forth. After about twenty minutes or so and as we hoped she'd do, Mamaw came out through the back door and hurried to the privy. Once she shut the door, Mr. Charlie took off for the house.

A few minutes later Mamaw emerged from the outhouse just as Mr. Charlie came out onto the back porch, a big smile spread across his ruddy face.

"What you grinning about?" she said as they passed each other on the steps.

"Nothin'," he said. "I'm just grinnin', I reckon."

Mamaw reached the porch and turned around. "You've been up to something, haven't you?"

"No, I ain't neither," Mr. Charlie said from out in the yard.

"Well, I know you have."

Although Mamaw could spot with blinders on a fib a mile off on a foggy night, she went inside the house without pursuing the matter further. Both Mr. Charlie and I breathed a sigh of relief when we saw the back door slam shut.

The next afternoon Miss Gloria came into the Jitney Jungle to buy her grapes and to report to Mr. Charlie what Mrs. Wells had told her. According to Mrs. Wells, Mamaw wanted a phonograph record of "Mairzy Doats" to play on her Victrola; a nightgown she'd seen in J.C. Penney's that had yellow and blue butterflies on it; a silver-looking knob from Montgomery Ward's to put on the steering wheel of her Dodge truck; and a best-selling book from the Book and Art Shop that she'd heard so much about, *A Tree Grows in Brooklyn.*

Christmas Day arrived and the three of us gathered around the Christmas tree in the parlor. As I might have expected, Santa Claus brought me stuff I hadn't asked for: a book entitled *Bible Readings for the Home,* a pullover sweater one size too big, a toy Tommy gun made of wood, and a toy British helmet made of cardboard. While "he" was there, Santa filled one of Mamaw's old worn-out stockings with two oranges, a tangerine, a grapefruit, a red Delicious apple, and a bag of parched peanuts from Romer's "If You Can Buy a Better Bag Buy

It" Peanuts.

I said what I was expected to say. "It's just what I wanted, Mamaw." What I said was a bald-face lie, of course. She knew it and I knew it. Mr. Charlie, though, looked wall-eyed at me. I think he thought I meant what I said.

After I hugged Mamaw for the Santa Claus things, she surprised me by reaching behind the sofa and picking up two presents, one of which was round like a basketball. I tore into the wrapping paper of the round gift first. Sure enough, it was a basketball, fully inflated and ready for me to roll into the highway the first chance I got for another truck to run over. The other gift turned out to be a used copy of my all-time favorite Mark Tidd book, *Mark Tidd in the Backwoods*.

As I flipped through the pages of my book, Mamaw put her arms around me and said, "Davy, honey, I'm sorry we couldn't get you that radio. Maybe next year or for your birthday. Okay?"

I kissed her on the cheek. "Thank you, Mamaw," I said. "I'd much rather read about Mark Tidd than listen to the radio any ol' day." I did mean that.

I started to run outside with my new basketball when I heard Mr. Charlie ask

Mamaw if she was going to open her presents. I decided to stay for the show.

"What presents!?" Mamaw snapped, wagging a mean finger right in Mr. Charlie's face. "You better not have gotten me anything, Charlie Kranshaw! You just better not've!"

Mr. Charlie pranced into the dining room, opened a drawer, and returned to the parlor, carrying four presents. When Mamaw saw them, tears welled in her eyes and inched down her cheeks. She wiped the tears away with her fingertips, opened the first box, and squealed. " 'Mairzy Doats'! It's a record of 'Mairzy Doats.' Charlie, how did you know to get me this?"

"Mrs. Wells —"

"That woman! She can't keep her mouth shut." She handed the record to me. "Here, Davy, go wind up the Victrola and play it for me. And don't you scratch it, neither."

I hated the stupid song. It was one of those that, once I heard it, I could never get it out of my mind.

After opening the packages that contained the Montgomery Ward's steering knob and the J.C. Penney's nightgown and while "Mairzy Doats" played in the background, she kissed Mr. Charlie squarely on his lips and said to him, "Charlie, this is the happiest Christmas I've ever had."

But then, she always said that.

I pointed to the fourth present at her feet. "You forgot that one, Mamaw."

She blew her nose and wiped her eyes again before picking up the box and shaking it. "I just bet this is *A Tree Grows in Brooklyn,* whatcha wanna bet? Oooooo-eee. I can't wait to open it." She scowled at Mr. Charlie. "You devil, you."

"Treace. It's uh . . . it's uh . . ."

Before Mr. Charlie could finish his thought, Mamaw pulled the bow and ribbon to one side and tore apart the wrapping paper. When she opened the box, her face turned the color of raw beef. "What!? What's this!?" she exclaimed. "A Presbyterian cookbook! Charlie Kranshaw! How could you!?" she screamed and slung the book clear across the room, knocking off the mantelpiece a photograph taken on a Christmas Day of a sad looking little boy pulling a wagon — me. The picture fell into the Victrola, causing a grating sound that brought the spin of "Mairzy Doats" to a premature and final end.

"Now look at what you made me do!" Mamaw cried.

I found Mr. Charlie sitting on the front

steps, nursing a glass of sweet tea and smoking a roll-your-own cigarette. He looked hangdog. I sat down beside him.

"What did Mamaw give you for Christmas, Mr. Charlie. I never did see."

He took a swallow of his tea and wiped his mouth with the back of his hand. "A brand new pair of skivvies. My sister, she sent me the same thing. That's all I ever git. I betcha I got a hundred pairs."

I tried to appear sympathetic.

"Davy?"

"Yes, sir?"

"Much oblige for the Burma Shave."

I nodded. Then it occurred to me. He probably had a case of the stuff.

We sat for a while, neither of us saying anything. I broke the silence first. "Could I ask you something, Mr. Charlie?"

"Shoot."

"I thought you were gonna take that cookbook back."

"Tried to, but they wouldn't let me. Said the back cover looked kinda bent a little."

"Well, why come you give it to Mamaw?"

"What else was I gonna do with it?" he said rather glumly. "I done spent fifty cent on it. 'Sides, it's got a real good recipe in it for a pumpkin chiffon pie." He looked at me as serious as can be. "You don't reckon

Treace'd fix me one sometime, do you?"

"Don't count it," I said. "Not unless you know how to turn a Presbyterian cookbook into a Baptist one."

He took a drag of his cigarette. "Hmmm. Make it Baptist. I'll have to think 'bout that some."

Mr. Charlie succeeded the following week in converting the Presbyterian publication into a Baptist one. He had a print shop make him a cover that he pasted over the front of the cookbook. It read, "Recipes for Baptists."

Mamaw accepted the re-titled cookbook without batting an eye. After he got off from work the next evening at the Jitney Jungle, Mr. Charlie found a pumpkin chiffon pie waiting for him on the kitchen table with a note that read, "To my husband Charlie. I know this may be a little late, but Merry Christmas anyhow. I love you, Treace."

When he asked her how she knew to fix him the pie using the recipe out of her new cookbook, she winked my way and said, "Charlie, haven't you learned by now? I'm a durn mind reader."

A 1960s Trip To The Clothing Store And The Car Dealership

- Boy's slacks cost two dollars
- A woman's coat with real fur trim cost less than $100
- Women's stretch pants were seven dollars
- Men could buy a suit for seventy dollars and a tie for fifty cents
- Men's Oxford shoes cost thirteen dollars
- Women wore "nylons," not panty hose, and a pair of nylons cost about a dollar
- A Cadillac De Ville cost $5,400
- A Chevrolet Corvette cost $4,500
- A Ford Fairlane cost $2,100
- A Volkswagon Beetle cost $1,700

"What Did You Just Say, Grandma?"

"Get outta my clean kitchen with those dirty feet, you yard apes!"

Yard apes were unruly children. In other words, go play in the yard.

"Yum! Pour some of that pot liquor over my cornbread."

Pot liquor was the rich juice left in the stew pot after boiling black-eyed peas, turnip greens and other good Southern vegetables.

"That man's got so much gray hair he must be older than dirt!"

Older than dirt meant really old.

"Com'ere, hon, and give me some sugar."

Sugar was a kiss on the cheek.

"I'll nuss that child 'til it settles down and quits cryin'."

Nuss meant to hold, cuddle, or rock a baby or small child.

"That woman is tough as nails and twice as sharp!"

Meaning the person was tough and smart.

"Don't go lecturing me. You're just preachin'

to the choir."

If somebody already agreed with you — the way a church choir naturally agrees with their minister — you didn't need to convince them.

A Doll With Red Hair

BY CLARA WIMBERLY

"A Southerner is distinguished by a sense
of neighborliness, a garrulous quality, a
wish to get together a lot."
— Charles Kuralt in "Southerners: Portrait
of a People"

It was the summer of 1948 when the Vines
family rented my grandparents' old house.
Grandpa Rogers had died in the spring and
Grandma decided she didn't want to stay in
the big old house any longer.

"It's too much for me to clean," Grandma
said one Sunday after church.

"Why, Maude," Mama said. "You were
always the best housekeeper in the county.
And the best cook."

"That was a long time ago, Bess,"
Grandma said. "I'm too old now." She
shook her head. "I can't get up and down
the stairs the way I used to. Besides, it's too
quiet there without Grandpa. I don't have
the heart to clean and cook any more."

"No reason why you should," Mama said. "You've done your share of cooking and cleaning. You need to take some time for yourself. And you know you're always welcome to have your meals here with us."

I looked down at the table, pretending to concentrate on the damp circle my tea glass had made on the white tablecloth. I felt Daddy's hand on my shoulder and looked up to see him smiling at me. Then he winked.

No one could cheer me up the way my Daddy could. He was always funny. And he always understood me better than anyone.

I smiled at him, even though I didn't feel it in my heart. It was sad about Grandma and I hated it for her.

"What do you want to do, Grandma?" he asked. Daddy sometimes called her Grandma even though she was his mother. "You want to sell the house —"

"Heavens to Betsy no," she said. "I couldn't bear to see the place sold to strangers. When I'm gone you and your brothers can do as you please with it, but while I'm still alive . . . no. It will not be sold."

"You should get a little apartment in town, Maude," Mama said. "You'd have neighbors; you'd be close to the grocery store and shopping."

"Oh," Grandma said with a frown. "I could never live in an apartment. No yard. No garden. For goodness' sakes, Bess."

"You can move in with us, Ma," Dad said. "We have plenty of room. You won't have much peace and quiet, but you sure won't be lonely," he said with a laugh.

My mother got up from the table and started carrying dishes into the kitchen.

I looked at Daddy and he made a funny face. It wasn't that my mother didn't like Grandma Rogers. She was just funny about people sometimes. Even people in our own family.

"Your Mama can be a mite standoffish," Daddy once said.

I'd brought a friend home from school and my Mother was so cool and unfriendly that I felt embarrassed. It hurt my feelings and it certainly hurt my friend Carrie's feelings.

"It doesn't mean she doesn't like Carrie," Dad had told me. "She's just funny around people she doesn't know."

But she knew Grandma Rogers. So I couldn't understand why she wouldn't be happy about her moving in with us. I loved the idea.

"That's what I'd hoped you'd say, Clay," Grandma said. She reached over and patted my Dad's arm and he got up from his chair and came and hugged her.

"But I hope your offer didn't put a crimp in Bess's bonnet," she said.

"I'm sure Bess is happy to have you here," Dad said.

But when he looked at me over Grandma's head he made a funny grimacing face. I couldn't help laughing.

"I won't get in her way. And of course I wouldn't think of trying to tell her how to run her own household," Grandma said.

"It'll be okay, Mama," Daddy told her. "When do you want to move?"

"Oh law, now that's another story ain't it?" she said. "I've got so much stuff at the house. We'll have to get rid of it. Of course you and Bess can have anything you want. And I'm sure your brothers will want some of the old furniture. I'd like to have the place rented by the end of the month."

"You want to rent it?" Dad said. He seemed surprised.

"Well, of course I'm going to rent it. You don't think I'm going to let it just sit there and go to ruin, do you?"

"Well, knowing how particular you've always been about that house, I'm a little surprised. Renters can do a lot of damage."

"If they do they can just fix it!" she said,

her lips growing thin.

"Easier said than done," Daddy said.

"Clay Rogers," Grandma said. "Are you going to help me or are you just going to give me reasons why I can't do this?"

"I'm going to help you, Mama," he said with a sigh. "Whatever you want is what we're going to do."

Mama had come through the dining room and now she came back, carrying a large bundle of crumpled linens in her arms.

"Bess, what are you doing? Why don't you sit down a minute?" Daddy asked.

"I'm cleaning out the back bedroom for Grandma," she said, not missing a stride. "I'm sure Maude will want her own linens and quilts in there."

Within a couple of weeks Grandma Rogers had moved into our house. I loved going in her room before bedtime. She'd usually be sitting in her rocker, knitting or piecing together a quilt. I'd lie on her soft bed while we talked. With my hands behind my head, I'd gaze up at the ceiling and at the rose patterns on the wallpaper.

A few days after she moved in, Daddy came in to say he'd found renters for her house.

"Who?" Grandma asked.

"The Vines family."

"Where from?"

"I think they came from White Oak Mountain," Daddy said. "Used to know a Vines man lived over there. Your renter says he's kin to him."

"Are they nice?" Mama asked.

"They seem nice," Daddy said. "Friendly. Glad to have a place big enough for their six kids."

"Six?" Mama asked. "Good Lord."

"Six and one on the way," Daddy added. "They don't have much. I take it Mr. Vines has had a hard time making a living on White Oak. Hopes to do better here. I told him he could farm the land, give you a share of the profit for part of the rent. I hope that's okay, Grandma," he said.

Grandma sat nodding her head.

"That's fine, son. Nothin' wrong with being poor. Long as you don't mind working."

"He'll have to work with six kids," Mama said with a grunt.

"Seven," I said.

"Seven then, Millie," Mama said. "Not that you need to know about such things at your age. And you certainly don't need to discuss it with adults."

I rolled my eyes. Mama never wanted me to know anything. Of course, in 1948, pregnancy was not discussed openly and certainly not with an eight-year-old girl.

"We'll help them all we can," Grandma said. "I'm just glad the old place won't be standing empty."

"You might not feel that way by the time they get through with it," Mama said.

"Now Bess," Daddy said quietly. "You don't have any reason to think the Vines will do any damage to the house."

"I saw them as they went by. Their rattle trap wagon looked like it barely held together and the old nag pulling it is going to eat up more than Mr. Vines can make. There wasn't much of anything in the wagon," Mama said. "Except kids."

"Sounds a lot like me and Grandpa back in our young days," Grandma said, her voice wistful. "And we came out all right. You can't always judge a book by its cover, Bess."

"Let's give them a chance, Shug," Daddy said.

Mama shrugged her slender shoulders and pushed her hair back from her face. She knew she was outnumbered. But I could see she wasn't pleased.

Early one morning a few weeks later, someone knocked at the door. I could hear Daddy talking to a woman and her voice sounded urgent. Tearful, even.

"Millie," Daddy said over his shoulder.

"Tell your mama I'm going over to the Vines place. Mr. Vines has had an accident."

"Can I go, Daddy?" I asked.

"Sure, sweetpea," he said. "But you'll have to stay out of the way. Now run tell your mama real quick while I get the car out of the garage."

Mrs. Vines was waiting outside on the porch. The first thing I noticed about her, besides the fact that she was expecting a baby, was her bright, reddish-gold hair. Freckles covered her face and arms and her eyes were an odd, bluish-green color. She looked awfully young to have six children and be expecting another.

"Hi," I said shyly. "Daddy's getting the car."

Mrs. Vines was just as shy with me.

"I told him I could walk, but he insisted," she said, her voice soft and quiet.

"Oh Daddy would never let a lady in your condition walk," I said without thinking.

Mrs. Vines smiled, covering her mouth as she did. I noticed that several of her teeth were missing and others were stained. I looked away, pretending I didn't notice.

When we got to the Vines house, Mr. Vines was sitting in the driveway holding his arm. The wagon wheel was off, lying in the grass beside him and the children were cluttered about him. Daddy went to kneel beside him. The Vines kids stared at me and I stared back at them.

There were three boys and three girls; the oldest boy looked to be about twelve and there was probably two years' difference between the rest on down the line.

"The boys here are Matthew, Mark and Luke and the girls there are Ruth and Rebecca and Baby — well, she don't have a name yet. We just call her Baby."

The tiny little girl looked to be about three years old. She was very frail and fragile-looking and so small that she looked like a doll. Her skin was pale, with no freckles like the other kids had. I guess they all saw me staring at her.

"She's sick," Matthew said. "She was born with something wrong with her heart."

"Oh," I said. "Is she okay?"

"She's much better," Mrs. Vines said. "Aren't you, Baby?"

The little girl shook her head and put her thumb in her mouth.

"She don't talk much," Mrs. Vines said.

Baby had red hair like her mother and the rest were tow headed, though some had reddish highlights. They were skinny too, but not the same way that Baby was. Their clothes were threadbare and none of them wore shoes.

"What happened?" Daddy asked.

"The durned wheel come off on me," Mr. Vines said. "Pinned me to the ground. The kids managed to get it off, but I think my arm is broke." He was obviously in pain, but trying hard not to show it.

Mrs. Vines stood back, not saying much. I found that strange. If it had been my dad, my mother would have been on her knees beside him, fussing and trying to help. Mrs. Vines seemed completely at a loss, as if she had no idea what to do to help.

"Can you walk?" Daddy asked.

"I . . . I think so," Mr. Vines replied. "If you can help me to my feet." He looked very pale and when he stood up he wavered a bit, as if he might faint. The pain on his face as he cradled his arm made pains shoot down my chest.

"If we can get you in the car, I'll drive you into town to the doctor."

"Oh, no," Mr. Vines said. "No need for that. If you'll help me set it and put a splint on it, I'll be fine. Can't afford no doctor."

"Lord, man," Daddy said. "I'm not about to do that. Don't worry about the doctor. I'll take care of that."

"I can't let you do that." Mr. Vines said, setting his mouth stubbornly. "Don't accept charity."

"Well, unless you want to wrestle me down, you don't have any choice about it," Daddy said, grinning.

I giggled, knowing how silly my Daddy could be. But neither Mr. Vines nor Mrs. Vines laughed. I supposed they didn't understand Daddy's sense of humor.

"Get in the car, Millie," Daddy said. "I'll drop you off at home on the way to the doctor."

"Let her stay," Mrs. Vines said. She reached out and touched my hair shyly. "I just made breakfast and the kids would love to have a new playmate."

"I don't know," Daddy said. "Your mother —"

I knew what he was about to say. My mother would have a fit at the thought of me having breakfast with these poor mountain people.

"Please, Daddy," I said.

"You sure?" he asked, looking at me oddly.

"Yes," I said. "I'll walk home later."

"I'll stop and tell your mother where you are then," he said. But his look told me that I'd be the one to face the consequences when I got home.

After they left, Mrs. Vines gathered the children and we went into the house that I was so familiar with. This had always been a place of homecoming to me. My grandparents had made the old farmhouse into a warm and beautiful home. It was where we had always gathered for holidays and special occasions, and I was sad that all that was gone.

When I walked into the front hallway I was shocked.

There was nothing much in the house. No rugs on the floor, no pictures on the walls. Not really much furniture at all. In the living room were two beds, and I imagined that's what most of the rooms were used for. Bedrooms for the large family.

But going into the kitchen I soon forgot about that. There was the most delicious smell of chocolate in the air. I imagined we would be having hot chocolate when Mrs. Vines seated us at the oil-cloth-covered table and began serving breakfast.

She placed a buttered biscuit on each plate, and then from a huge iron skillet she began to ladle a black syrupy mixture onto the biscuits. It smelled wonderful. Then she poured each of us a tall, cool, glass of sweet milk from a blue, earthenware pitcher.

"Chocolate?" I asked, staring at the syrup.

"Chocolate gravy," Mrs. Vines said with a certain amount of pride. "Mr. Vines says I make the best chocolate gravy around."

"Hum," I said, tasting it gingerly. "Never had chocolate gravy before. Reckon I never even heard of it."

"Never heard of chocolate gravy?" the kids yelled. They laughed and giggled as they ate, smearing chocolate all over their mouths.

It tasted as good as it smelled. And soon I was asking for seconds. My mother would have been horrified to know I also asked for thirds. Mrs. Vines beamed as she ladled more onto my plate. I loved chocolate and this was like manna from heaven.

When I got back home, Mama and Grandma asked so many questions it made my head spin. I answered as best I could about Mr. Vines' arm and told them how nice Mrs. Vines was and how funny the children were. I told them about the little red-haired girl with no name.

"They just call her Baby," I said. "And she's probably two or three years old."

"Poor little thing. They probably didn't think she'd live," Grandma said. "Used to, people didn't name children when they were born with serious ailments."

"But . . . she did live," I said. "So she'll be okay, won't she?"

"We hope so, dear," Mama said, giving

Grandma a look.

"How does the old place look?" Grandma asked. I knew she changed subjects intentionally.

"Empty," I said. "And kind of sad."

"Oh, now — don't let it made you sad, darlin'," Grandma said. "Life goes on and we have no choice but to follow. I should have left some of the old things in the house for the renters."

"Goodness, Maude," Mama said. "You wouldn't want to do that."

"Why wouldn't I? They need it and I've got it. Why not?"

"Your things were always so nice, that's why."

"Yes," Grandma replied. "In later life we did manage to acquire some nice furniture. We had a nice home. But it wasn't always that way. And I'd hate to think that people saw us in the same light as some people see the Vines family."

"Oh piffle, Grandma," Mama said. "That's unlikely."

"And why is it so unlikely?" Grandma asked, bristling.

I hated it when Mama and Grandma bickered.

"Mrs. Vines made the best breakfast I've ever had," I said.

They both turned and looked at me, staring as if I'd lost my mind.

"What?" Mama asked.

"The best breakfast," I repeated. "Chocolate gravy and buttered biscuits. Grandma, you know how to make chocolate gravy?"

"Chocolate gravy?!" The look on my mother's face was one of horror. "On biscuits?"

I nodded my head.

"Why, I've never heard of such a thing," she said.

"Now, Bess Rogers, don't you go acting all uppity like you never heard of chocolate gravy," Grandma said. "You know many a poor Southern family served their family chocolate gravy — sometimes every morning. It's hot and filling and Lord knows with all that sugar it has plenty of energy for a growing child."

Mama sniffed as if her feelings had been hurt.

"We certainly never ate chocolate gravy," she said.

"I'm sure you didn't, dear," Grandma said dryly.

"It's good," I exclaimed.

Grandma laughed. "It *is* good," she said. "I used to love it myself. But it's been a long time since I've even thought about it."

"I don't know what your Daddy was thinking," Mama said. "Letting you have breakfast with those people. Why you're liable to be sick, eating chocolate for breakfast."

"It would be worth it," I said, remembering the delicious chocolate concoction.

"Millie Ann Rogers," Mama said as if she meant business. "Don't get sassy with me. You are not to eat anything ever again at the Vines' house. Knowing your daddy, he'll have you over there with him, but you don't have to eat there."

"But Mama . . ." I complained.

"Don't Mama me," she said. "You just mind what I say unless you want to go outside and cut me a switch."

"No, ma'am," I said. "I mean yes, ma'am."

I sighed as I left the room. There was just no talking to Mama when she made up her mind about something. She never seemed to like anyone I liked and she never wanted me to do anything fun!

Summer passed quickly and as Mama predicted I was at the Vines house often, always with Daddy. He helped Mr. Vines as much as he could, but by then summer was almost over. Their crops were meager and I often heard Daddy talk about what a hard time the family was having.

In the fall, Luke Vines was in my class. He was a quiet, polite boy but because of the poor way he dressed the other kids often made fun of him. None of the Vines children seemed to fit in at school.

One day when Luke was absent, our teacher, Mrs. Fitzgerald, took the opportunity to talk about him with our class.

"There is no shame in being poor," she said. "Jesus was a poor carpenter. Would you make fun of him if he were in this class?"

"Noooo," the class said in unison.

"A person can be poor, but as long as he's clean and works hard, there's nothing wrong with that — isn't that right children?"

"Yes, Mrs. Fitzgerald," we sang out.

"Now, when Luke comes back I expect things to be different. You children will treat him with respect. He doesn't deserve to be treated badly for something he has no control over. Do you understand?"

"Yes, Mrs. Fitzgerald," we said.

After school I'd go to Grandma's room. We'd have a snack and sit and talk before I did my homework. That day I told her what Mrs. Fitzgerald had said about Luke.

"Mrs. Fitzgerald is a good woman," Grandma said. "And a fine teacher. I hope Luke will have an easier time when he gets back."

I nodded. I felt so grown-up discussing such things with Grandma. In a time when children were supposed to be seen and not heard, my grandmother was very open and honest with me.

Autumn passed and the weather grew cold. I began to be excited about Christmas vacation. Christmas was always a happy time at our house and even though Grandpa would not be there that year, I was happy at least that Grandma was living with us. She enjoyed Christmas as much as I did — maybe that was why it had always been so special to my dad, because she had made their Christmases so much fun.

My dad made everything about Christmas fun, too. From going out to find a tree to finding just the right gifts. On Christmas morning my stocking, usually one of his old hunting socks, would be heavy with crisp apples, juicy oranges, nuts, hard candy and chocolate drops. And even though I'd always find the boxes of apples and oranges after Santa left I pretended that it was just a coincidence because I knew it pleased my dad.

As soon as Christmas vacation began that year Daddy started our search for just the perfect tree. The week before Christmas, Mama and Grandma began making cakes, pies and candy. We used hickory nuts in the fudge and for several nights we'd sit near the stove in the living room, picking out the delicate pieces of nutmeat to be stirred into Mama's special fudge.

The weather had turned frigidly cold, but I didn't mind. Our house was warm and cozy; we had plenty of food and it was the best time of the year. I didn't know how anyone could ask for more than that. Except perhaps a white Christmas.

I remember vividly Daddy coming in on that Christmas Eve night. I was excited because we were going to church for the Christmas play and afterward all the children would receive bags of candy and fruit, and perhaps a small toy. The singing of Christmas carols made me feel warm and happy and I thought the holly wreaths and white candles in the windows were the most beautiful sight in the world.

As I was getting ready I heard Daddy talking to Grandma and Mama. Their words were low, but the tone sounded serious and it aroused my curiosity. I walked quietly to my door and listened.

"It's been a tough year for them," Daddy said. "Besides the fact that there wasn't much money from crops, Mrs. Vines is having problems and has been ordered to stay in bed until the baby comes. The little girl — the one they call Baby — is very sick. The doctor says she might not live through the New Year."

I felt an odd heaviness in my chest, and I felt like crying. I couldn't believe it. I'd never known a child who died. All I could think of was Baby's bright blue eyes and her shining red hair. She always seemed so sweet and happy.

"Oh, Clay," Grandma said. "My heart aches for them."

"What about Christmas?" Mama asked.

"Nothing," Daddy said. It was unusual to hear such sadness in my daddy's voice. "I should have checked on them sooner. There's not enough money for food, much less toys for the children. And the house is cold. I told Mr. Romines to take them a truck load of firewood today."

"Well, we must do something to help them," Grandma said. "That's all there is to it."

"I have plenty of baked goods," Mama said. "There's enough to share."

"I can give them one of the hams from the smokehouse," Daddy said.

"We have plenty of eggs and I think we can spare some of the potatoes from the root cellar," Mama said.

I smiled when I heard Mama. When it mattered she was just as generous as Daddy and Grandma.

Daddy looked at his watch. "Maybe I can get a few toys at the hardware store if I hurry, but everything else is closed by now. I'll have to miss the church play," he said, looking apologetically at Mama.

"It's all right," she said. "You go ahead. See what you can do about toys for those children. We'll catch a ride with the neighbors."

Daddy sighed.

"What's wrong?" Mama asked. "Something else is bothering you — I can see it on your face."

"It's the little girl — Baby," he said. "She said she only wants a doll with red hair for Christmas — one that looks like her."

"Oh, Clay," Mama murmured.

I thought Mama was going to cry and that wasn't like her. I rarely saw her cry about anything.

Daddy rubbed his chin. "I doubt the hardware store will have any dolls. Do you think Millie has a doll she could give to the child?"

"You know," Grandma said. "I think she might even have a doll with red hair — the one Santa brought her a few years ago. I could probably make a new dress for it from quilt scrapes.

I felt my heart lurch. Not Mandy, I thought to myself. She was my most favorite doll in the entire world. How could they expect me to give her away?

I slipped back into my room and quietly closed the door. I went immediately to the row of dolls sitting on the cedar chest and picked up the red haired doll. I was still standing there when Daddy came into the room.

"You heard?" he asked.

I nodded, not looking at him. I didn't want him to see the tears in my eyes.

"Can't I give Baby one of the other dolls?" I asked. "Mandy is my very favorite."

"Why Millie, I'm surprised at you," Daddy said. "This could be the last Christmas that little girl has. She's not asking for much — just a doll with red hair. You have plenty of dolls."

"I know," I said, frowning. Still I didn't let go of the doll.

I saw Daddy clench his teeth. I rarely saw that look on his face — one of anger and disappointment.

"You will give her the doll," he said angrily. "We're going out to the Vines place early tomorrow morning and take them

Christmas and you will take the doll and give it to Baby."

Holding the doll tightly to my chest I hurried past him and threw myself on the bed, crying. Daddy stood for a moment looking down at me — I could sense his anger. But what hurt worse was that I had disappointed him.

I couldn't understand myself why I behaved as I did. Why was it so hard for me to give away a doll to a little girl who might be dying? Mama came in later and said we wouldn't be going to the Christmas play because she and Grandma had decided to make doll clothes and prepare more food for the Vines family. I cried most of the night and the guilt I felt was something I'd never experienced in my young life.

I woke up on Christmas morning feeling not excitement, but dread. I felt as if my Daddy would never look at me the same way again. I was sure I had disappointed him beyond forgiveness.

Sometime during the night Mama and Grandma had come in and taken the doll. That morning she was dressed in a beautiful blue gingham dress with a blue satin sash at the waist. She had been cleaned and her red hair brushed and arranged with tiny blue silk flowers. She was more beautiful than she was the Christmas morning that I received her.

By the time I was dressed Daddy was ready and waiting for me in the old truck. In the back was a large red wagon filled with colorfully wrapped Christmas packages, a large ham, several sacks of groceries and containers of cakes and pies and candy.

I walked slowly to the truck with Mandy held in the crook of my arm, being careful not to wrinkle her new clothes. It was very cold that morning and there were flurries of snow falling on the windshield of the truck. Even that didn't lift my spirits. Daddy said nothing on the short drive to the Vines house.

When we got to the mailbox, he pulled over and stopped.

"We'll have to walk from here," he said. "It sleeted during the night and the driveway is probably pretty bad. Can't take a chance on getting stuck."

I got out of the truck, still carrying Mandy. Daddy got the wagon out of the back and handed me a couple of things to carry. Then we set off toward the house.

The road was frozen almost solid, and as Daddy pulled the red wagon it rattled along noisily. Snow fell against my face and I put Mandy under my coat so she wouldn't be wet when we arrived. The pine trees that lined the driveway were frozen and heavy with sleet. I could hear the hiss of snow falling and the quiet murmur of wind in the pines.

Here I was dragging along, feeling sorry for myself, not even realizing that I had gotten my wish. Christmas day was a white one. But as we walked in the quiet, just the two of us, through the tunnel of snow-covered evergreens, I felt my heart begin to fill with such gladness. I wanted to laugh and dance. It was the most beautiful Christmas morning I could ever remember.

I glanced at Daddy and he smiled at me, his look sweet and loving. Apologetic, even. My eyes filled with tears and suddenly my heart felt as if it would burst from my chest.

As we approached the house we could see smoke coming from the chimney.

"I'm glad to see Mr. Romines got the wood here," Daddy said. I could hear the relief in his voice.

I nodded and smiled at him.

"You okay, squirt?" he asked.

"Yep," I said, trying not to cry. His goodness and his sweetness were almost my undoing.

Mr. Vines opened the door and his look when he saw the wagon and our gifts was one of quiet joy. But there was pain in his eyes too. He'd rather have provided all this for his children himself. I knew that, even as young as I was.

"You shouldn't have done all this, Mr. Rogers," he said.

"It's Christmas, man," Daddy said. "Glad to do it. There have been times when we barely had enough to get by. This year we have plenty and I'm glad to be able to help."

I had never been so proud of my daddy. He was right. He was doing the right thing the way he always did. I'd known it all along. But still I'd selfishly wanted to keep the doll for myself. I was glad my parents hadn't allowed me to do that. I never would have understood what a joyful gift they were giving me that Christmas morning.

Mrs. Vines was in one of the beds I'd seen in the living room. In the other was the little girl called Baby.

Mr. Vines summoned the other children and they came noisily to gather around the beds. Mrs. Vines' eyes were bright and shiny as she watched Daddy hand out packages from the wagon. When it was empty he pulled the handle around toward Matthew, the oldest boy.

"This is yours, son," Daddy said.

"Wow," Matthew whispered. "Always

wanted a wagon," he said.

Daddy stepped back and looked at me. I smiled at him and stepped to the bed where Baby lay quietly, taking everything in.

Her breathing was loud in the half-empty room.

I pulled the doll from under my coat and handed it to Baby. She reached out for it eagerly and hugged it to her chest as a huge grin spread across her face. Then she held the doll out for her mother to see.

"Yes, I see," Mrs. Vines said. "What a pretty doll. She looks just like you, Baby."

Baby smiled.

"Her name is Mandy," I said, pointing to the doll.

"Mandy," Baby said. I think it was the first time I ever heard her speak.

"That's good, Baby," I said laughing with her.

"Mandy," she said again, pointing to the doll. "Mandy," she said, pointing to her own chest.

All of us laughed. She was just so cute.

"No, your name is Baby," I said. "The doll is Mandy."

Mrs. Vines reached over and took her daughter's tiny hand.

"We can call her Mandy if she wants us to," she said. "I guess its time she had a real name anyway — don't you think so, Daddy?"

"I guess so," Mr. Vines said, his voice a little hoarse with emotion. He stepped to his little girl's bedside. "You want to be called Mandy?" he asked.

"Mandy," she said, nodding.

Mr. Vines looked at his wife and smiled and so just like that, Baby had a name.

"We need to get home, Millie," Daddy said. "Before the weather gets any worse."

The Vines children gathered around us, their eyes bright as they held their new toys. Mr. Vines placed more wood on the fire in the fireplace and the little red-haired girl snuggled in the bed with her doll tightly against her.

As we said goodbye, I looked back and thought the old house seemed warm and alive for the first time since the family had moved in. I had never felt such peace and happiness in my life. It was that feeling of knowing that everything was right. That I had done something right and made some-one happy.

That Christmas morning my Dad taught me what it really means when you say it is 'more blessed to give than to receive,' reluctant though I was at first to accept that lesson.

By the time we got back to the truck, I was freezing. I snuggled next to Daddy for the short ride home.

We hurried into our warm, cozy house, and I'd never been more thankful for my home and family. Under the tree was a new doll for me, one with shining black hair and a beautiful bonnet with a fluffy black feather on it. There was also a red-metal cash register. When you pushed the keys it rang and the money drawer opened to reveal several shiny new quarters.

"Let's eat breakfast," Mama said after we'd opened all our gifts.

I was hungry; the house was filled with the delicious aroma of Christmas dinner, which would be ready later.

"Sit down," Grandma said to me when we went into the dining room. I thought there was an odd look on her face.

I sat at my place while Grandma placed a buttered biscuit on my plate. Then Mama came in from the kitchen carrying an iron skillet. When she ladled chocolate gravy on my plate I must have looked shocked because they all laughed.

"Well, try it," Mama said. "See if it's as good as Mrs. Vines' chocolate gravy."

"I wasn't sure I remembered how to make it," Grandma added.

I took a bite and closed my eyes.

"It's even better," I said.

They all laughed again and Daddy came around to hug me.

"You did a good thing this morning, Millie. We're all proud of you. I'm sorry if I hurt your feelings, but I knew that when you gave away something you loved, you would understand what Christmas is all about."

He was absolutely right. But I felt a little guilty accepting the compliment after the pouty fit I'd had about the doll. Even though I couldn't express it I was proud of myself too.

That was the best Christmas I remember from my childhood. It was the year I learned the true meaning of that most holy day and I hope I never forget it.

The little girl, Mandy, did make it through the New Year. Mrs. Vines had the baby — a healthy little girl. Mr. Vines' arm healed and he worked part time at a sawmill until the family recovered from their rocky year. One day in early spring, just after school was out, their wagon pulled up in our yard, loaded with furniture and kids. They had come to say goodbye and to settle up with Grandma before going back to the White

Oak Mountains where they could be near their families.

I never knew what happened to Mandy, and that probably was a good thing. I always imagined her alive and well somewhere and as happy as she was that Christmas morning when she snuggled in the bed with her new doll with red hair.

- Dressing up to go shopping, which was always downtown
- Wearing white gloves
- Wearing girdles because there were no pantyhose
- Helping your grandfather slop the hogs
- Watching your grandmother wring the neck of the chicken you later found fried on your plate
- Attending a church in the country and discovering the communion "wine" was actually *wine,* not grape juice!

— Martha Crockett, *Y'all Come*

LISTENING FOR DADDY

BY DEBRA LEIGH SMITH

> "People generally see what they look for
> and hear what they listen for."
> — Harper Lee

Daddy died on a bright, crystalline October morning about the time he should have been having his second cup of coffee. He should have been making his rounds at the big electronics plant north of Atlanta, where he was a supervisor. Someone else sipped his share of coffee that morning.

Someone else checked the plant's security cameras, and joked with the secretaries.

Life went on, as he had always assured us that it would, and if he felt the least bit perturbed at the way the steady flow of energy swirled into the eddy he had claimed in our midst, he never mentioned it. I know, since I listened hard every time he whispered in my ear.

I talked to him that morning after I got the news. We carried on conversations I told myself couldn't be real. We talked again that afternoon, and that night, and the next day at the funeral home, and on the day of his burial. After the funeral, at the suburban Atlanta farm house Daddy and Mama had shared for all of the thirty years of their marriage, Daddy and I watched Uncle Luther settle into Daddy's rocking chair with a plate of potato salad and fried chicken on his wide lap. The house was full of people, but Uncle Luther filled the whole porch all by himself.

Uncle Luther's special suit, the one he had worn at the other funerals the family had had that year — it had been a boom year for dying — was damp across the immense bottom of his polyester pants, and it left sweat marks on the wooden slats every time he stood up. Not that he stood up often.

Good lord, Daddy whispered distinctly. *I'll have to re-glue the supports.*

"No, mother will have to do that, now," I told him.

Daddy could no longer be held responsible for the flotsam and jetsam of life. We would have to muddle along on our own.

"You need to eat somethin'," Uncle Luther admonished me, as the rocking chair creaked on the concrete porch where my sister and I had grown up bouncing on a rocking horse Daddy had made in his shop. "Your Daddy wouldn't want nobody to go hungry."

I just want old Luther to get his fat butt out of my rocker, Daddy whispered.

I turned away, hiding a smile. Maybe I was losing my mind. There I was, a grown woman, a marketing executive for a cell phone company. I wore expensive dress-suits and drove a Beamer. My home was worth a small fortune; it overlooked the Chattahoochee River. My purse contained a cell phone, a Blackberry, and an iPod. I was a success. A modern Southern gal. A wireless wonder. I shouldn't be talking to ghosts.

I walked inside the big, friendly, whitewashed house and went over to my husband. He looked handsome and somber by a window done in some funky blue drapes Mama had bought at Wal-Mart. I'm not cheap, she liked to say. I'd just rather save my money for eBay. Mama played the on-line auctions with the zeal of a mule trader at a livestock barn. She bought and sold an endless stream of Hummel figurines. They filled the living room bookcases. When we sat in that room, it felt like a stadium full of tiny porcelain people were watching us.

Tim hugged me and kissed my forehead. "Your mother asked me to run over to the minister's house and give him a check and a pecan pie."

"How much money?"

"One hundred dollars." He frowned. "Are you sure this is the way things are supposed to be handled? It seems odd to tip the minister and give him pie."

"When I was growing up, Grandpa killed two hens for the minister who preached Grandma's funeral. At least Mama didn't ask you to execute any livestock."

He sighed, once again a Yankee on the outside looking in. "I'll be back."

I watched him nod to Uncle Luther and stride off the porch, down a fieldstone walkway bordered with red-tinged nandinas, to our Beamer. He was so . . . alive.

Suddenly I thought, *Tim is going to die some day, and so am I.*

I had lost my childhood faith in immortality.

I couldn't cry over that obvious fact; the pain went beyond that. I stood numbly in the tiny, Hummel-lined living room, looking at the flowered sofa with its cat-scratch scars. I looked at the Wal-Mart fake-damask drapes and the hook rugs and the chintz material on the easy chairs. I had no idea why nothing looked the same, but I was struck with an overwhelming feeling that a filter had been taken off the world and I was experiencing it like a blind woman just given sight.

Suddenly Daddy's voice was there again, no place special, running through my mind smoothly and distinctly, as if it had been beamed in from his TV remote, which lay atop the satellite guide he had consulted faithfully during every football season.

It's all right, he whispered gruffly. *Look after your mother. Sit in my chair. Keep the faith.*

The words popped into my mind in short bursts like that, firm and comforting, the drawl on cue, the little catch between sentences not to be mistaken for the voice of anyone else. Daddy had one of those deep, hound-dog-earred Southern voices, slicked back with enough Atlanta sophistication to keep the vowels glued tight. When I was little, I teased him and said he sounded like Foghorn Leghorn, the cartoon rooster.

Ah say, do tell? he boomed.

I went to his recliner and touched it reverently. I tried to remember all I'd ever read about grief syndromes. Did other people hear voices? My third cousin, Veda Jane, from Blue Ridge, who did hard drugs at the University of Georgia and has never been the same since, claims John Lennon talks to her. Imagine that.

"Daddy?" I ventured out loud. "Are you really there? Is one of the Beatles with you?"

I'm near by. I'll be here for a little while, if you need me.

I sat down limply in his chair. "Need you? Of course I need you. My future children will never know their grandfather. You and I had just gotten to be friends. I'd finally grown up. I finally understood all the lessons you were trying to teach me. Don't go away now. Come back. Come back."

Silence. That was the only time I crossed the perimeter of dignity and realistic hope, and I regretted it immediately. Daddy would never come back, not to his garden, not to his chickens or his new four-doored pickup truck with the CD player, or even to the sewer pipe he'd left unmended in the back yard three days ago, before the heart attack.

I'll always be here, he finally answered. *Always. In the muscadine grapes every fall and the first jonquils every spring. In the way you smile and in your sister's blue eyes.*

And then his voice faded away, as if someone had changed the frequency, and I was left with a lot of buzzing mental gibberish.

"People are beginning to leave," my sister said from the doorway. Gwen dragged herself to the couch and sat down. "Thank

God." She looked down at the tops of her slender, high-heeled alligator boots. My sister is a scrappy little redhead who works as a publicist for several obscure country-western bands. Bands with names like The Booty Wranglers and Cowboyz. "I keep expecting to see Daddy come in the door," she added. "Remember when we were little and . . ."

"Don't say that. Please don't. Not yet. I don't want to put Daddy in the category of, 'Remember when.' "

Gwen picked a piece of fuzz on her embroidered denim skirt. "I feel like I'm about ten years old. I don't feel twenty-eight. Do you feel thirty?"

"I feel . . . grown. We can't pretend to be anybody's little girls after our daddy dies. We're on our own. Our parents are a psychological firewall that stands between us and death — you know, when they're gone we become the next generation in line. I understand what that really means, now."

Gwen looked perturbed by the thumbnail philosophy, and I gazed at her sadly for a moment. I left the living room and wandered into the little pink bedroom she and I had shared as kids. In the closet I unpacked *Black Beauty, Grimm's Fairy Tales, Charlotte's Web, A Child's Book of Verse.*

Dusty memories floated off the book jackets into the stale closet air. Dad throwing a softball. Dad holding a frightened horse while the vet squirted medication on its thrush-infected foot. Dad coming home from the office, white-shirted and official, his string tie the only clue that he secretly imagined himself to be John Wayne.

Dad grinning over the summer-Saturday ritual of grilled steaks, his balding head still sweaty from his Saturday labors. He smelled of new-cut lawn and tractor grease and Borax industrial strength hand soap. "Little Injuns get little steaks." He said that almost every Saturday of every summer of our youth. And every Saturday, we giggled.

"We love you, Daddy." The thought ran neatly across my mind, like the digital ticker tape at the bottom of a TV screen, an update on the situation.

I love you, too, he replied, *close by once more. The sadness will pass, just like it should. You'll forget, and twenty years from now I'll just be a dusty old picture on the mantel. I want you to forget. Being alive means you always have to be forgetting things that hurt.*

"I don't want to forget," I pleaded. "I see you everywhere. Aren't you just outside, working in your shop?"

I'm here as long as you need me. And when you don't need me, I'll be gone. My mind went quiet. The books stopped sending Memories. I curled my hand into a fist and thumped a shelf.

"Are you okay?" Gwen asked, behind me. She was a good sister and she had to make sure.

"Hell, no."

"Me, neither."

I almost asked if Daddy had spoken to her, too. But I didn't. What each person draws from their memories is personal. The voice of the spirit sings one song at a time.

That night I told Tim to go home without me. Gwen and I crept into bed on either side of Mama. The three of us held hands. I ticked off one of many firsts — tomorrow would be the first Saturday without Daddy. Next month would be the first Thanksgiving. And in December we'd endure the first Christmas.

The next morning I woke up with tears on my face and stumbled back to the closet in our old bedroom, alerted by a dream to something long forgotten. Patty Sue. A thorough perusal of dusty corners and sealed boxes turned up no sign. Gwen recalled nothing of the vintage cloth doll that had been given to me by Daddy. She had belonged to his mother. Patty Sue had been at least fifty years old when I got her.

Mama simply shook her head and went outside to the concrete porch, to rock and grieve in the morning light. The search for Patty Sue became obsessively important to me. I tore into lopsided boxes, explored the attic and searched plastic bags filled with rags stored in Daddy's workshop. Finally, I had to admit defeat. Patty Sue, like my childhood, was gone.

I sat under an oak in the front yard, leaning against its trunk. I was still dressed in my pajamas and robe. Golden oak leaves drifted down with every rustle of wind. "Gone," I said tearfully.

Look in the old trunk in the barn loft, Daddy whispered.

I hurried down a graveled garden path. The barn, gray and friendly, looked warm in the autumn sunshine. I stood for a second in the central hallway, watching the light shift through open slats in the walls. I looked at the empty stalls, forlorn.

We hadn't owned horses since Gwen and I left for college. Maybe I'll buy myself a horse, I thought.

My bare feet felt good on the bottom rung of the creaky loft ladder. The loft was empty of hay, cluttered with old trunks and ancient boxes and dusty farm gear. A light push-plow hung from a rafter, its slender wheel making a shadow-hoop on the wooden floor. The top of a moldy wooden trunk squeaked as I pried it up. A musky odor floated out — the scent of nature at work. Microbes and bacteria reclaim us and everything we love, eventually. But not yet. I brushed away cobwebs. My heart sank. I saw a few yellowed boxes. I'd expected Patty Sue to be sitting there, looking up at me, waiting.

The enormous silliness of my behavior began to worry me, seriously. Grown woman, hearing voices, looking frantically through old boxes covered in dust and death and cobwebs. One by one the boxes opened under my fingers. They were filled with old Mason jars.

When only one box was left, I sat down on the loft floor with it in my lap. I stared at the box bitterly.

Daddy's voice was only in my imagination. He hadn't been with me over the past few days, and never would be, again. My grief had simply cranked out a few harmless delusions.

I thumped the last, unopened box with a fist, expecting the rattle of more jars. Instead, my fist pressed down on a soft form. With a yelp of delight, I threw the box lid aside. Patty Sue came out of hibernation with a merry grin and only a little sadness in her faded, hand-sewn eyes.

I held her and cried.

Daddy was there, not speaking, but warm and nearby, watching. And then I felt him melting away, leaving me with Patty Sue for comfort. He had been alive in the flesh, and he was still alive in spirit. Just like the child inside me. Just like Patty Sue, who had survived. Always waiting to be heard, again, as needed, waiting to be remembered and loved, a vivid memory etched in a daughter's mind.

I would never stop talking to him.

And I knew he would always be there, listening.

Games we played during car trips —
- "I spy with my little eye."
- The states-on-the-license-tags game

How we carried candy, toys and other treasures —
- Before the Container Store, the treasure box of choice was the cigar box!

What people did for vacation before airfare was cheap and Disney came to Orlando —
- Panama City, Florida! The Redneck Riviera. Remember the bandstand?

How people dressed before Grandma discovered polyester —
- Does anybody remember when you wore your Sunday best to go to the movies?
- And AFTER Grandma discovered double-knit, remember how she never smelled quite the same? Or was that just my grandma?

Vicks VapoRub and other amazing cure-alls —
- I know a lady who cut a big square out of the tail of her nightgown so she could iron it good and hot and slap it down on the

Watkins-green-salve-swathed chest of her child. She couldn't find another scrap of flannel in the house.

What cars were like before seatbelts, airbags and talking maps —
- I used to be able to look through a hole in the floorboard of my mom and dad's 1950-something Chevy station wagon at the yellow lines going by.

Drive-in movies —
- Getting lost on the way back from the concession stand or the bathroom was frightening for a little kid!

Window fans but no air conditioning —
- Remember when the old folks had chairs under a shade tree and sat outside until the bugs started to bite?

Shocking, sinful entertainments: Elvis, the Beatles, and Barbara Eden's exposed belly-button —
- My father thought the Smothers Brothers were terribly subversive. But he never changed the channel! Remember how racy the jokes on Laugh-in were?
        — Susan Goggins, *The Wart Witch*

GRANDMA'S CUPBOARDS

BY SUSAN SIPAL

High on the ridge above the farm
I think of my people that have gone on
Like a tree that grows in the mountain
   ground
The storms of life have cut them down
But the new wood springs from the roots
   underground
Gone, gonna rise again
    — Si Kahn, North Carolina songwriter

Along about the time I was a senior in college, and knew all there was to know about *Life,* and was so much smarter than my upbringing, my granddaddy was hospitalized with a bleeding ulcer for several weeks, leaving Grandma to stay at their ancient farmhouse alone.

Now, don't get me wrong, Grandma was as feisty as any ornery farmwife could get. In fact she'd won blue ribbons at the state fair for her mulish ways. At least that's what Granddaddy muttered, in his age-raspy voice, when she nagged him for tracking red Warren County mud into the house once again. Point being, I'm sure Grandma could probably have managed fine on her own, even with diabetes.

But most of Granddaddy's illness fell over winter break and I wanted to be there, with them, with Grandma. I preferred being at Grandma's farm with the turmoil in my life above anywhere else at the time. Even with Granddaddy sick, still, there was a sort of welcome . . . of peace, less stress, less activity, more simple.

I needed time to sort things out in my life. Where was I going after graduation? More school? A job? Plus there was this guy I liked, and I didn't know how he felt about me. It was confusing. And he was going to be out of state over Christmas, so I wouldn't see him anyhow. May as well hide out, I mean help out, at Grandma's and be of some use. Especially as she didn't drive and would have to depend on neighbors to carry her to the hospital every day.

See, Grandma ran over a piglet as a teenager, and ever since refused to get behind the wheel. In a small community like Arcola, however, this was never a big deal. She walked many places she wanted to go, like nearby neighbors, or off to Harvey's — the small country grocery and gas-stop down the road — and church. Usually, however, Granddaddy, one of her children or neighbors (half of them kin as well), were willing and able to carry her whenever she needed to venture further away from what we grandkids called Plumb-Nelly — plumb in the country and nelly out of this world. Like her weekly go-to-town Fridays to the "big" town of Warrenton — to the bank, hairdresser, and Piggly Wiggly.

But I'm venturing off the story, way too easy to do when you get into that Plumb-Nelly mind-frame. Anyhow, as I mentioned, the hospital was thirty-five miles away, in the next county, as Warrenton had been too poor for too long to currently have a hospital. Grandma, of course, needed to go every day to be with Granddaddy. So I acted as chauffeur and did whatever I could to take care of her, especially as Granddaddy's condition weakened, and she became more upset and sickened with worry.

Then, Grandma started doing something she'd never done in her whole life, at least not that Mama or I could remember. She slept late. Late for her being around 7:30. For a working farmer, though, that was sinful. For some reason, I seemed to reverse time sense with Grandma and awoke with the crowing of the rooster. This left me a good hour of free time in which I devised a special project.

Cleaning out Grandma's cupboards.

If you've ever known anyone who lived through the Great Depression, you'll nod your head and mutter, "Yep, yeah, yes-sirree," under your breath at what I'm about to say. Grandma's cupboards were crammed full of every single piece of aluminum foil, bread bag, twist tie, paper bag, plastic wrap, broken mugs, chipped glassware, and other miscellaneous debris hoarded amid her sixty-plus years of marriage. Aside from the pure junk, her cabinets cached a collection of mismatched china, that ugly jade Fire King (which Martha Stewart somehow thought pretty enough to reissue), green and pink Depression glass pieces in various patterns, and every collectible glass piece ever pulled out of an old box of oatmeal or soapsuds.

She'd never thrown nothing away. Never knew when it might come in handy again. Especially when she'd been a dirt farmer all her life and knew what it meant to go without.

But I was going to clean it up. I knew better. Those cupboards hid cockroaches and disease, as well as the trash. Surely Grandma

146

would feel a lot better with clean, organized cabinets, and would never miss all that junk.

One morning I awoke to the sound of little mice feet pattering overhead in the attic, the pinkish light of dawn peeking through the shades, and Grandma snoring on the other side of the bedroom. I slept in the combination bedroom/family room with Grandma as it was the only one we heated at night. With Granddaddy in the hospital it had become my job to toss another log in the stove when it got low, and keep the cast-iron kettle on top filled with water.

Trying my hardest not to wake Grandma, I eased myself up by the nearby stairwell, the sofa-bed protesting with a give-away creak. Grandma snuffled lightly in her blackened iron-post bed, but kept on sleeping. I grabbed my bedroom shoes and crept across the freezing wood plank floor, cracking the door to the dining room.

Which squeaked loudly in the silent house.

I'd have to remember to oil it.

Crossing my arms against the cold, I hurried to the kitchen, less afraid of noise with the bedroom door now shut behind me.

But where to start?

Heat, obviously.

Watching my breath float in front of my face, I searched for matches to light the knee-high gas furnace, which as a child Grandma'd let me use as a stove to cook oatmeal. It would take awhile for the furnace to heat up, even in this small a kitchen, so I pulled back the faded-pink pantry curtain, pushed aside a hanging country ham, and snatched one of Grandma's threadbare cardigans off a nail-hook, buttoning it to my throat.

Knowing movement would generate heat as well, I opened one of the smaller cupboards and gazed with amazement at the chaos within. A deep breath of pent-up air escaped my pursed lips. I could handle this. I could.

But where to start?

The job was immense. There was no way I could clean all this mess out. This was only one cupboard, and Grandma had one, two, three, four . . . eleven of them.

Still, even if I only did one, it would help. And the lure . . . besides helping Grandma clean up, something she wasn't quite as adept at since gaining the age of eighty-two, was the thrill of discovering what treasures might hide beneath that life-long collection.

I'd developed a passion for Depression glass and antique country collectibles. Just the type of thing Grandma had scattered about, using as food bowls for the cat, slop jars for the chickens, paperweights, or pen-and-small-item holders.

Newly determined, I pushed up my sleeves, positioned one of the sturdier ladder-back, wicker-seat chairs, and climbed to the top cabinet.

The first thing I drew out was a crushed mass of aluminum foil, toast crumbs falling out of the folded corners. Grandma washed and reused these. She'd probably saved enough to fill a major recycling bin.

I crumpled a makeshift ball and scored a wastebasket two-pointer.

I felt no compunction about trashing the endless supply of used bread bags, carefully rolled up Glad-wrap, and bits of ribbon and string, but as the meatier contents of the cabinet emerged, I doubted what to do with the odds and ends — stoppers minus bottles, lids without bottoms, and broken-off pieces of china. This stuff might have a missing part somewhere.

Maybe I should clean the cabinets out, but make piles of things that weren't obvious trash, and have Grandma sort through it.

So, the kitchen warming up nicely and having prepared a pot of Luzianne part-chicory coffee to percolate on the stove, I set about covering the small kitchen table in organized piles of possible junk (the pure junk scoring points in the trashcan), parts to be repaired, and keepers to be cleaned. Of course, I'd had to first organize some of the mess already stored on that table — all the Upper Room Daily Devotionals, small bank calendars dating back twenty years or more, and the white transistor radio that still wheezed out the morning weather — all of which anchored down three layers of plastic tablecloth.

I'd just washed out the last section of one large cabinet when Grandma's slow shuffle crossed the dining wood-plank floor, and the kitchen door screeched open.

A pause of astonishment.

"Susan."

"Good morning, Grandma," I said as innocently as I could pretend.

"What are you doing?"

Her hair beneath her net was squished on one side, looking whiter in the morning sun now streaming through the window, making her appear older, frailer. She'd mentioned a visit to Warrenton soon for another dye-rinse.

"I was just cleaning your cabinets out a bit."

"I won't be able to find nothing."

"Aww, come on, Grandma. It's not that

bad." I grasped her thinning arm and tugged her to the one empty ladder-back chair I'd reserved for her. "Here, sit and help me sort through this."

"You best not have thrown my stuff out." Her chin squared, and the usual glint flickered back in her eyes. "I need it."

"Now, Grandma, I haven't thrown anything away that didn't need ditching. All I've done is clean up a bit, and I'll put everything back where you tell me. Without all that trash in the way, you'll be able to find things better."

I held up a glass chicken nesting on a basket, its tail broken off. "Is this something you need to keep?"

"Goodness gracious." Grandma reached for the busted keepsake. "I'd wondered where that old hen got to." She turned it over in her hands, studying it carefully, her fingernail that needed trimming digging out a bit of dirt from underneath the bird's wing. "You know, I won this along with a blue-ribbon for some blue eggs. That was a rough year. We lost a cow and the pig to the swine flu. I got creative with egg dishes. Found Clarence and the kids liked the boiled ones better if they came out of a pretty shell." She chuckled.

"Right." I carefully took the prized hen

from her and placed it on the newly cleared shelf over the sink. I'd loved finding and eating those blue eggs as a child myself.

On to the next. "What about this?" I asked, passing her a plastic bag stuffed with scraps of faded material.

Grandma snorted. "I ought to get Sophie to finish that up for me," she said, referring to her younger sister, aged only eighty years. "I ain't never been much of one for sewing. That's a quilt I started when your Mama got married."

Which happened twenty-six years ago. "So, it can be dumped, then?"

"Now, now. Don't be in such an all-fired-out rush." She opened the bag and drew out several of the squared-off pieces of stitched cloth. "You know what this here came off of?"

I shook my head, though she wasn't even looking in my direction, her gaze firmly focused on the pile of rags in her lap, caressing a slip of rose satin.

"I wore this dress to your Uncle Junior's wedding." She picked up a piece of flowered muslin. "And this was your mother's dress when she was baptized and confirmed."

She passed the bag back to me. "Put that over by the Frigidaire on top of that pile of egg cartons. Sophie'll be by to dinner after church on Sunday. Don't you let me forget to give this to her along with some eggs, ya hear?"

Visions of all my hard work going for naught, I nodded and dropped the bag on the pile of cartons I'd planned to throw out as well. She'd never let me get away with it now.

Seizing upon the one item I was sure we could ditch, I grabbed the blue-glass measuring cup, chipped in many places and minus the handle. "Surely we can throw this away." I held it up to better study it in the light. "Why, there's a crack running through the side and bottom. It won't even hold liquid."

A frail, age-spot marked hand reached past me, claiming the glass.

"The church gave me this years ago," Grandma whispered. "For years of service as Sunday school superintendent. Said it was a measure of their love for me and my service for God." She studied the ragged edge where the handle was missing. "Your Granddaddy was supposed to fix that handle back on here long time ago. I wonder where he put it?"

Sighing, I reclaimed the measuring cup and replaced it in the cabinet. I'd ask Granddaddy where to find the handle later, though highly doubtful he'd be able to remember. But if so, maybe I could fix it myself. After all, at the age of eighty-two, Grandma was still Sunday school superintendent.

She was one strong woman. Mulish, too.

Grandma wandered on, sorting through her treasures, amid stories of days gone by . . . hunting honey with her pa, churning butter with her mama, and later teaching my mother (who could never sit still long enough for the butter to clot). She told me of organizing church dinners and the church family who was always there, supporting each other as best they could, and of days of scraping and scrimping just to get by.

"You never know when you just might need another bread tie, Pumpkin."

I nodded absently, as I placed most of what I'd removed back in the cupboard. But neater than before, and with more space from the missing bags and wrap. Then I whipped on Grandma's frayed, yellow apron, which matched the walls of her kitchen, and cooked a simple breakfast — eggs and ham, minus the biscuits she usually fixed.

Mine were always hard as a rock.

Ushering Grandma out onto the porch an hour later, after finishing up morning chores and watching as she gave herself the insulin shot, I locked the front door with the skeleton key they still used. Then steadying her elbow, I helped her toward the new Celica I'd bought with my pay from working on campus. Naked trees clawed against the stark gray sky, foretelling of freezing weather to come.

Granddaddy's '46 Ferguson tractor looked forlorn, parked at the end of the drive, where he'd left it from his last jaunt down to Harvey's weeks ago. They'd taken his license away at age eighty-eight, but there was no way they were going to stop him from buying his RC Cola whenever the notion took or jawing with his old friends hanging out at the general store.

"Shall we ride the tractor to the hospital?" I asked Grandma, hoping to raise a smile.

"Shush, Susan." Grandma shuffled on.

We arrived at the ICU to find Granddaddy lying back in bed, an unopened pile of cards on the bed tray in front of him. His face white and his gray hair mussed, Granddaddy looked quite ill — but more from temper than from sickness.

"Hey there, Honey Bee," he greeted me. He'd always called me that. His little honey bee.

I leaned over and pecked his paper-thin cheek.

"That young nurse won't let me be," he grumbled, his faded blue eyes minus their usual spark. "Keeps coming in here and covering up my feet." His legs shifted restlessly beneath the white, sterile hospital blanket. "They can't breathe."

"Stop your complaining, you old man," Grandma said as she carefully uncovered his feet, folding the blanket back neatly. "Those nurses got better things to do all day than cater to your silly whims."

She stepped to his side table and poured him a cup of water, then held his head higher so he could drink. "Thinking your feet could breathe. Losing your mind along with all that blood."

He mumbled something under his breath. "Ol' devil woman gonna drive me to drink yet . . ." being all I could catch.

Stuffing the laugh down my throat, I brought out the measuring cup to distract him. "Granddaddy, do you know where the missing handle for this is?"

His eyes narrowed on the glass in my hand. "Hmm." He paused only a moment. "If I recall right, you'll find it in the top tray of my trunk in front of the stairs. Never did get around to buying that special glue."

"Lots of things you never get 'round to, Clarence," Grandma nagged.

And they were off, bickering between themselves, while all the time Grandma took care of Granddaddy's needs and they both chatted pleasantly with me and an endless stream of company. Grandma and Granddaddy either knew or were related to everyone in that tri-county area. Sometimes related in more ways than one.

I slipped out around noon to fetch Grandma a lunch tray, and buy some Crazy Glue.

Several days later, I'd cleaned through all the kitchen cabinets and was digging out the inner recesses of the walk-in pantry. It had been so full of junk, I'd always been afraid of entering as a child, not sure what kind of critters or spooks lurked in those cob-webby corners.

Now, well, it didn't look all bright and shiny, not enough light from the pull chain fixture, but I'd be hard-pressed to find a monster here. Tomorrow I'd start on the sideboard in the dining room, then the hand-made china cabinet, and then the jagged row of magazine and mail piles decorating the steps up the stairwell.

My mind busy with my plans, I dragged

the last item out of the pantry — Grandma's old dough bowl. Goodness, did I have fond memories of this. Grandma'd made fresh country biscuits every single morning of her married life — until Granddaddy'd gone in the hospital.

She'd bought me and my older sister little red-handled rolling pins when we were younger and would give us each a pinch of dough to roll and pat and bake for ourselves, though mine never made it to the oven. Still like the taste of raw dough.

I've tried over the years to make biscuits like Grandma's, even with the whole-wheat that I now prefer, but never could get mine to come out as anything other than solid bricks. Grandma's, though, were soft and moist and at their best topped with her homemade grape jelly. The older jars that had started sugaring off held the sweetest jam.

Cradling the precious dough bowl in my hands, I hurried to the sink. Grandma'd probably never cleaned this out in her life. It was coated and covered in white flour with hard pieces of dough caked in the bottom. I washed and scrubbed, soaked and scrubbed, and washed some more, until it all came clean.

That's when I saw the error of my ways.

Unfortunately the dough had been holding the bottom of the bowl together. Now I was staring through a worn-thin strip to the bottom of the sink.

"Your granddaddy carved that out of a piece of oak for me when we first married," Grandma said behind me.

Directly behind me.

I turned to face her, her hazel eyes watery.

"Grandma, I-I'm so sorry." I jerked up the bowl, searching for a way to repair it. "I didn't mean to —"

"Ain't important, Sweetpea." Grandma took the bowl out of my hands and shuffled to the table, dropping it amid the day's piles. "That hole's been there for years. Don't mean the bowl's no good. I fixed many a biscuit with the bottom worn out. Plan to fix many a more."

"But . . . but, can we, I mean, can I fix it for you?"

"No need." Her long, withered fingers stroked the aged-smoothened wood. "A good bread bowl's like a good Bible. The more ragged it is, the more it's been used . . . and loved."

I watched Grandma sitting there, her threadbare cardigan covering her slight but sturdy body, the lines on her face testimony to her years of hard work, harder life and determined love.

At her elbow on the table was a picture of her and Granddaddy when they'd first married, taken on the banks of a creek on a church picnic, their faces smooth, young, and lighted with care-free smiles. I'd found the photo stuffed in the back of a drawer during my previous day's explorations, and confiscated an appropriate frame for such a beautiful relic.

Now, looking at the youthful faces, I remembered Granddaddy the day before in the hospital, his breath ragged, his body curled almost in a fetal position, his life visibly leaving him, and Grandma once again uncovering his feet so they could breathe.

I understood; I still had a lot to learn.

But Life has a way of teaching us. Life and the ones we love, hold dear to our hearts. Maybe someday I'd have a granddaughter. And I'd be sure to let her explore my cupboards. Maybe by then, I'd have a story to tell worth hearing.

Three nights later, Granddaddy died. Arriving home to Grandma's from the midnight hospital vigil in an unusual North Carolina snowstorm, I was chosen to sleep with Grandma in Granddaddy's place. All my aunts, uncles, and, of course, Mama had joined us as Granddaddy's condition worsened. Mama took my place on the couch.

Yes, I was almost twenty-two, a senior in college, and better than my upbringing, but I still felt scared and empty climbing into that high iron-post bed with Grandma, her muffled sobs giving way to a low snore. Shivering beneath the covers, the stove having gone out while we were all at the hospital, finally I slept.

Then toward morning, Granddaddy visited my dreams.

You know how sometimes you drift between a state of deep sleep and not yet awake? Granddaddy came to me in just such a awareness, drew me off his place in bed and carried me piggy-back to the kitchen, where he sat me on a counter beneath a cupboard and turned to talk with me, his aged face smoother, younger, lighter than I'd seen it in years.

His blue eyes crinkled as he hugged me and whispered in my ear. "I'm going home now, Susan, and I want you to take care of your Grandma until she rejoins me." He stepped away, squeezing my hand, as he fuzzed at the edges. "You be a good girl now, ya hear." Granddaddy flickered, like a candle in the wind, almost disappearing. "I love you, my little Honey Bee." With a last caress from his age spotted hand to my cheek, he was gone.

I awoke in bed, inches away from Grandma, still sleeping, the sun peeking through the blinds, a nearby rooster crowing, and clutched in my palm was that blue glass handle Granddaddy had asked me to fix.

"I promise, Granddaddy," I whispered, a lone tear burning my cheek. "I'll never forget."

And I never did.

Here's to y'all, Grandma and Granddaddy, joined again these last eighteen years. Grandma hurried to join Granddaddy a scant year-and-a-half later.

I wonder, does God allow bickering in Heaven?

Author's note:

Yes, the dream really happened, just that way.

Want to know how I made my list of the "trash" found in Grandma's cupboards? Besides pulling from memory, I sorted through my own cabinets. Hoarding — a delightful family legacy that drives my husband insane!

REMEMBERING THE 1940s

- Rosebud Salve
- Making margarine in a bag
- Rabbit gums
- Sitting on the front porch with the women of the family snapping beans and peas
- Napping while the women quilted
- Listening to an old wind up Victrola
- Putting a banner on the window or door to show that a member of that family was in the service during WWII
- Blackouts during the war
- Ration books
- Seeing hundreds of airplanes fly over in formation during the war
    — Clara Wimberly, *A Doll With Red Hair*

Homeplace

BY ELLEN BIRKETT MORRIS

"I'm still the little Southern girl from the
wrong side of the tracks who really didn't
feel like she belonged."
— Faye Dunaway, actress

I ran out the back door and took a deep
breath, just like Mamma taught me to do
when I'm upset. Sitting under the maple
tree, I thought, *What was happening to
Granny Bess?*

It was like the time I left my watercolor
painting of a house on the porch to dry and
it started to rain. All the sharp lines got
fuzzy. The solid, red square of the house
lost its shape. After a while, the picture
turned into faded streaks of color. Granny
was fading too.

Granny Bess was a storyteller, the kind of
storyteller that made me want to curl up
under a quilt and listen forever. She loved
to talk about the family homeplace where
she grew up.

164

"Come here, Chloe. Let me tell you about the homeplace," she'd say and pull me onto her lap.

Granny Bess told her stories in a whisper, just for me.

When it was warm outside, she told me about summers when she was a girl.

"When I was your age I'd play in the field behind our house. The ground was covered with wildflowers for as far as I could see. I'd sit under the oak tree and have tea with my doll."

"What would you eat, Granny?" I'd ask.

"We ate wild strawberries and drank drops of nectar from honeysuckle blooms. We'd pretend that the tops of dandelions were small biscuits," said Granny.

Back home, I spread a blanket on the lawn and had tea parties of my own.

In winter, she told me about Christmas when she was a girl.

"As soon as the sun was up, I'd rush downstairs and unhook my stocking from the mantle. It was stuffed with goodies, oranges wrapped in tissue paper, shiny pink and white ribbons of peppermint candy and hand-carved blocks that my daddy would make himself," said Granny.

"No games?" I'd ask.

"The blocks were my game," Granny said,

with a smile.

She'd tell funny stories, too. "I'll never forget the time I took my daddy's antique car from Burkesville to Glasgow to play in the girl's basketball tournament. That car was so darn slow, just put-putting down the road. The other girls were passing me up on foot. I was so mad," she said with a laugh. When she was done telling me her stories, she would squeeze my hand and smile.

She stopped telling stories about the time that she started to ask the same questions over and over again.

Some days she would ask the score of my soccer game four times in an afternoon, introduce me to her cat, Ezra, like I had never seen him before, and even stop talking in mid-sentence. Usually she was fine, making her special no-bake cookies, smiling, asking me about school and doting on Ezra.

But then there was the day we drove to the department store. On the way home Granny got lost.

"Let's see, I go right here?" asked Granny in a shaky voice. I held her hand.

"We go left here, Granny. We go right at the next street."

When we got back to her house, I sat on the floor petting Ezra while Granny Bess stared out the window.

A few weeks later, Mom and I stopped by Granny's house and found her dressed in a thin skirt, colorful vest and straw hat wandering around the back yard. Her long gray hair had escaped from its usual tidy bun at the back of her head.

"I'm looking for the roses. They used to be right by the fence," said Granny. "You're thinking of the yard at the homeplace, Mom," said my mother.

"Look, Granny, here are the hollyhocks we planted last summer," I said. Granny gave a sad smile.

Granny and Mom went inside. I had a strange jumpy feeling in my stomach. Even though she was a few feet away, I missed Granny. After a while, Mom came out back and joined me. She put her arms around me and said, "Don't worry, Chloe. When some people get older they forget things. We're going to take care of Granny."

When I went home that night I lay in bed and went over her stories in my head, trying hard to remember her exact words.

The next week, Mom and Dad told me that Granny Bess was moving to a new home. She would live in a high rise with other grandparents. She would have someone to cook for her and care for her clothes.

When she got settled, we went to see Granny's new place. The woman at the reception desk smiled when we came in. A lady with a green vest and nametag showed us around.

There was a large dining room full of tables covered with white tablecloths. A bright glass chandelier hung from the ceiling in the middle of the room.

Next to the dining room was a square game room, its walls covered with paintings. Two old men in baseball caps sat talking and playing a game of checkers. They took a long time to make their moves.

The television room was full of grandmas and grandpas. One couple in wheel chairs held hands. One grandpa slept sitting upright on the couch. A very small granny sat in a large easy chair and crocheted while she watched television.

There was even a heated swimming pool where Granny could do water aerobics. And Granny Bess was allowed to keep Ezra in her room. Granny's room was clean and bright with a big window that looked onto some tall maple trees. Granny looked happy.

"Who are we visiting?" she asked. "This is your home now," Mom said. We set her favorite chair in the corner of the room and smoothed the double wedding ring quilt over the bed. When we hugged goodbye, Granny held on for a long time.

Now Mom and I visit every Saturday. Sometimes we talk, trying hard not to notice when Granny repeats herself. On other days, she sits in her rocker and stares out the window.

One Saturday, I brought a shoebox and sat close to Granny on the couch. I opened the box and handed her a honeysuckle blossom. She held it to her nose breathing in the past. Granny ate the corner off a ribbon of peppermint candy and ran her fingers across a small antique car.

I talked to her about tea and Christmas stockings and car rides. She listened, her head close to mine. When I was done, she squeezed my hand and whispered, "Home-place."

BACK WHEN ANIMALS COULD TALK SOUTHERN

Some colorful sayings about our favorite critters

Don't go barking up the wrong tree or running around like a chicken with its head cut off. Even though a blind mule finds an acorn every once in a while and sometimes the tail wags the dog. I don't care what anybody says, you can lead a horse to water but you can't make it drink. You can go hog wild, and if you get real lucky you'll live high off the hog. And then you'll be happier than a pig in sunshine.

It might be a coon's age before you get what you're hoping for, and you'll feel like money is as scarce as hen's teeth. Just play possum when things get rough. Don't look hang-dog and don't get your feathers ruffled. Yes, if a frog had wings he wouldn't bump his butt when he hops, but when you're feeling lower than a snake's belly never forget that, at heart, you're finer than frog hair. Don't lose your cool and blow up like a mule eating butter beans.

Maybe it's true that you can't hit a lick with a snake, or you're all hat and no cattle, or that, when push comes to shove, you give up and say, "I don't have a dog in this fight." But even though nobody knows you from Adam's house cat, and nobody'll even say pea turkey to you when you're in a mood, keep smiling like a goat eating briars. Get some rest, go to bed with the chickens, and don't get mad as an old wet settin' hen.

You'll be just fine. Because every dog has his day.

The Tie That Binds

BY SUSAN ALVIS

> "I formally proposed. I'm a good Southern gentleman."
> — Vince Gill, country-western singer

On the day when true love tied itself around my grandmother's house, I was on her upper veranda, reading a book. It took only two hours from start to finish, but no one at my grandmother's house over the age of eighteen was left single. At thirteen years old, I was considered too young to hang out with my older siblings and cousins. I was also too old to be told to take an official nap.

The day this all started was a Tuesday, just like any other summer day in a small Southern town. Everyone was taking advantage of one of Gran's huge pitchers of sweet ice tea with lemon and crushed mint leaves. Even the ice clinked in a lazy, off hand manner against the edges of the glasses. The adults were swirling the sweet elixir before every next sip. There was no more talk of war and the knot of aching sadness for those who would not be coming home was loosening some.

I wandered upstairs and out onto the palm-and-fern-lined porch. I settled onto the old wicker chaise with plans to waste a long sultry afternoon reading a book. Scarlett O'Hara had choices to make, starting with which Tarleton twin to choose.

Snippets of conversation from other parts of the house buzzed up on the summer heat with the stealth of insects. Hummingbirds, ever hungry and always in a hurry, danced with the dragon flies that droned up from the marsh to light on sunny surfaces before flying off to other attractive destinations. It was one of those the magical afternoons when I loved to dive into a story. The very air around me misted with possibilities.

Frank Darling walked through the doorway, not ten feet from where I sat. He wandered over to the opposite edge of the porch. Frank had been coming around to Gran's house since the cousins arrived before the Fourth of July.

Mr. Darling, his father, owned the hardware store in town. Without much prompting, Frank could really go into too much detail about the growing market for electric tools. Thankfully, with his back to me, he didn't look around or he might have seen me in the deepening shadows, underneath the lazy fan.

Frank dropped to one knee, beside the empty porch swing and pulled a ring out from the pocket of his gray pleated.

"Marry me, will you, Minnie Jo?" he said. (He was speaking as though she sat in front of him. She was not there.)

Frank Darling was sweet on Minnie! I almost shrieked with the discovery!

Minnie Jo Radcliffe was a cousin from Valdosta. She was from the wealthy side of our family. Her mother was my mother's older sister. The money was not from our side of the Macy clan, but had been married into, pure and simple. What the Radcliffe's had in dollars and cents, our Macy clan had in Southern proclivities and sense. This is not a complaint. It's just that our blessings don't buy much at the store.

Minnie Jo's golden curls and dreamy countenance combined to enchant most young men. I knew for a fact that the far-off look she always had on her face had more to do with an attempt to keep her list of suitor's names straight than in any single romantic vision. She was not considering spending the rest of her life with any one of them in particular. I had this on the best of authority — eavesdropping.

Minnie Jo often missed the important details in conversations. Then she acted on what she thought she heard. My father said that her absent expression had something to do with all the very dear but empty space in her head.

"I'm thankful my girls will never have to worry about being overwhelming beauties," he said once to my grandmother. "A few freckles will keep the fellows in check long enough to let them see to the souls of my girls instead of getting caught up in their outside packages."

This from the man, my mother reminded him, whose first words to his own wife had been, "Hi there, 'Body by Fisher . . .' " I found out later that this referenced the sculpted lines of the newest automobile available on the market the year they courted.

"Minnie Jo's a real sweetheart," he told my brother, Beau, who was feeling the need to turn Minnie into a true kissing cousin, "But Minnie's got more blue sky in that brain of hers than anything else. When it's all said and done, a man needs a woman he can have a conversation with, not just one to look at."

Nothing really distracted Beau from his recent experiences in Europe, even when we all wished something could. He was still thinking about war and hurt. He didn't smile much anymore. A crush on our cousin was the first sign that life might be returning, my momma said. I guess I really don't understand how he could be anything less than full out glad to be back with all of us.

Brother spends hours in the library instead of helping my daddy sell cars. Beau probably has lots of beautiful girls interested in him. Letting go of Minnie as his ideal woman didn't cause much of a ripple.

Truth of the matter was I was not worried about Brother. Grandpa always said Beau could fall in a pile of bovine fecal matter and still come out smelling like a rose.

Frank Darling, though, was more entranced with Minnie's charms than Beau had ever been. This was not a fleeting crush on Frank's part. Even I could see that, plain as the ring in his hand.

He practiced the proposal three times, in mime, reacting with enthusiasm to her anticipated acceptance. At this point in his rehearsal he would grab the large down pillow off the swing. Squeezing it tightly, he would lower his face into the chintz, placing an amorous kiss on a large cabbage rose in the center of the cushion.

I was fascinated with kissing, not that I'd done any myself. It never occurred to me that practice was ever involved or even necessary. I believed I would probably get my first kiss from a movie star. I had not given much thought to the practicality or the details of how this would actually unfold. I just believed it would. Watching Frank practice made me sure that I would never be able to put my head against that particular pillow again without remembering that moment.

That ol' lover boy was pretty sure of himself! His little production made me clasp both hands over my mouth to keep from howling with giggles. His face flushed with excitement, giving him a ruddy, sweaty complexion. Frank Darling had the look of a man trying to blow a tuba with a basketball wedged in the opening of the horn.

A few deep breaths later, I was able to compose myself enough to sit quietly, not sure what to do. I will admit I was too fascinated to flee this scene, far more exciting than anything in my favorite old county library book. I had never, at my most sneaky, ever heard or seen anything more amazing than this. It occurred to me that if I were discovered, I would miss the scene for which he was practicing, so I pulled my knees up near my chest, anticipating what would happen next.

In a very short time, Minnie Jo came up the stairs, home from her summer job as a stock clerk at the pharmacy. Her heels clamored on the wooden steps between the lower porch and her fate. She walked across the porch to Frank, stopping near him to touch his sleeve.

"You look nice, Frank," Minnie said softly. "What're you dressed up for? Got a meeting at the church?"

Minnie had the mixed scent of a cosmetic counter perfume girl. She sprayed samples for the drug store shoppers, so the breeze caught, and mixed, a number of things no one in their right mind would ever combine. I'd call her smell 'Evening in the Stable,' if I had to name it myself.

"No, I wanted to look nice, just for you, Minnie. I got this genuine silk tie over at the Brookshire Man's Shop. I'm thinking I might always wear a tie from now on, now that I'm an up and coming hardware man, and all." He paused and gulped. "Minnie Jo," he said as he led her to the swing, bands of red ratcheting up his neck above his collar, "I have something in particular to ask you."

I was holding my breath, giddy with excitement. Frank Darling was going to pop the question right here on my Granny's porch! I would watch and listen. No one would ever know! Could there be anything else that could be more exciting!

Perhaps it was my age and lack of experience, but I was as caught up in the moment as Frank.

Down onto his knee he went, just as he rehearsed. Then Frank asked Minnie Jo for her hand. He reached for her, kissing her with great, slurping enthusiasm. That's when Minnie Jo came up swinging.

"Mr. Darling, you are no gentleman!" she squealed. She was thrashing him and wiggling from his grasp. "No! I. Will. Not. Consent. To. Marry. You!" she choked. Minnie talked like she was spitting words through a straw. She banged him on the head with the same chintz pillow on which he had so arduously practiced his lip-lock technique just awhile before.

Boy, was Minnie mad.

She stomped across the porch, letting the screen door offer further punctuation for her definite refusal which was hanging in the afternoon like haze. It never occurred to me that Minnie would be upset. This possibility must not have ever occurred to

Frank, either.

I watched in stunned silence. Frank's tears were immediate and plentiful.

Suddenly the drone of conversation downstairs ceased and both porches were as quiet as a tomb. I could hear my Gran's old clock count the seconds. It always sounded more like a dripping faucet than a time piece: click-throp, click-throp, click-throp. Then the chimes rang. It was only after five resonant bongs that Frank even moved a muscle.

What I had seen happen was crystal clear.

I knew with sudden clarity what was beginning to dawn on Frank: Minnie Jo had just slammed the door on his heart forever. There was nothing he could do now but go down to the lower veranda, pick up his hat and walk down my Gran's front steps for the last time. There would be quite an audience gathered for his departure. Poor fellow. No dissertation on power tools could get him out of there without further humiliation.

He must've thought that an exit down the porch steps didn't have much appeal either. Flopping down on the swing, he put his head in his hands. Closing his eyes, he slowly loosened his genuine silk tie. It was shining and slim, with varying stripes in shades of chartreuse and burnt umber.

Focusing on that neckwear made me wonder if all such ties were that ugly or if this one was just special.

Frank smoothed it across his knee. His hands and lower lip trembled, synchronized in misery. Then, with slow, deliberate care, he tied a square knot. In one fluid movement he slipped it over his head, leaving a strange long, flapping tail. Leaning over the railing, Frank tied another knot to one of the carved white spindles.

"Minnie Jo?!" he sobbed, "I can't live without you!"

Before I could move from the shady chaise, Frank Darling rolled over the edge of the upstairs railing and hung himself off of my Granny's upper veranda.

The soprano screams from all my cousins echoed up Church Street and hung in the breeze. They all ran down the front walk to look at the upstairs railing where Frank Darling dangled as he tried to die.

With Frank's legs still flailing, the knot on his genuine silk tie slipped and he dropped like a rock into the peonies. He lay there, still and pale, among the rocks that edged the flowerbed.

I ran down the steps. There was such chaos that my only thought was to go find help. Off I ran, down the street toward town. Always a bit of the town crier, I told the story as well as I could, while asking if anyone had seen the doc. I dragged Beau home from the library, where I found him reading poetry to a girl from Beaufort.

Young Buddy Branch from the pharmacy ran up the hill, to see what all the hollering was about. Soon after that Doc Pritchard's son, Bradley, rolled up out front, coming to call on Geraldine, Minnie's sister.

Everyone convened out front. All of us were standing in the flower bed, looking down at the corpse of dead Frank Darling when Daddy roared up in his old '39 Ford. I told the story for the fifteenth time in as many minutes, relishing my role as the historian of recent unseemly events. I left out not one detail, from the chintzy practice kisses to Frank's last, sobbing cry.

Just as I finished, the crumpled body on the ground started to moan.

As I've said before, I may have only lived thirteen years, but even after that afternoon's crash course in romance I was willing to bet that a dead man shouldn't make noise.

About that time, Jean Francis, my older sister, decided to try out some of the training she was getting from her nursing classes up at the Medical College in Charleston.

Right in front of God, Daddy, and everyone else in our family, she dropped to her knees and began giving Frank Darling light puffs of air, her lips sealed on his like the lid on a Mason jar of fresh canned peaches. Her shining auburn hair made a wavy curtain, a privacy screen, if you will, around Frank's contorted head.

I remember thinking that his tie was even uglier in the sunlight than it had been in the upstairs shade. Seems the wind had gotten knocked out of Frank, and Jean Francis, quietly and softly, reintroduced the oxygen he needed to return to life.

My father and a couple of the other men waited until Frank seemed to come around a little. They hauled Frank to Doc's office, where the kind physician diagnosed young Mr. Darling with two broken ankles as well as a badly bruised throat.

By suppertime, I was exhausted. I believed it was probably the most exciting day of my life so far and I wanted to think back through it, to relish the details. Back up to the upstairs porch I went, thinking I'd retrieve my book, before washing my face for dinner.

There was Minnie Jo, draped across the porch swing, crying inconsolably in the arms of Buddy Branch. Buddy must've learned the same stuff Jean Francis knew, because he was using his mouth to help Minnie breathe, too, in between her gulping sobs.

Maybe eavesdropping is a little like honey sandwiches: A person can eventually just get too much.

That night when the house was finally quiet and dark, Gran and my parents were sitting out in the navy night, star-gazing and talking. I was back on the chaise, not really listening. I was just trying not to doze.

"When your father was alive," my Gran said to her son, "Before the first Great War, there was a real sense of Southern propriety in our family. The Lord does His work in mysterious ways, doesn't He?"

"That was quite a dramatic interlude today, wasn't it, Mama?" my Daddy answered.

To my surprise, the three of them began to laugh.

"And it proved once and for all, that little pitchers have big ears . . . Come on outta those shadows, Doodlebug, and give your Pa a hug before bed."

I crept forward, on bare feet, to stand by the rocker where he sat. I couldn't figure out where to put my arms and legs, wanting so badly to be experienced like my cousins and wishing I was still small enough to pass for a child. I wanted to climb into my father's lap and hear his laughter from deep in his chest, to fall asleep in his arms like I had for so many summer nights past. That was a long time ago, when I was small, before I reached my current height of five feet and seven inches.

He stood and gathered me up in his arms, hugging me close. We stand almost eye-to-eye. I felt the sandy finish on his cheek, breathed in his bergamot soap and tobacco.

"Promise me, that when it is your time to drive a young man a little crazy, you'll stay on the first floor. I don't want any more hangings prompted by the women in this family," Daddy said.

"I promise. I'm gonna wait a good long time for the man of my dreams . . . and Daddy?"

"Yes, Sugar?"

"Do you think it was all on account of that genuine silk tie? It was really ugly."

"Are you asking if the tie is why Frank Darling is alive or the reason he hung himself in the first place?"

"Lawson!" admonished my Granny, "Don't you egg that child on!"

■ ■ ■ ■

By the end of that summer there were four engagements in the family, all stemming from the romantic events following the hanging on that summer Tuesday afternoon.

Minnie Jo and Buddy Branch chose the first of December for their wedding. She was going to move from Valdosta to manage the cosmetics department at the pharmacy four days a week and Buddy's life on their days off.

Geraldine got engaged to Bradley Pritchard. As soon as Minnie Jo decided what colors her wedding party would use, her baby sister would be allowed to make choices of her own. Geraldine planned on a Valentine's Day wedding.

Brother Beau fell in love with the girl, Joy, he met at the library that day. She followed him home after hearing about all the excitement at our house. Seems to me like Joy just never went home. Everyone said that she looked like me. She was tall and red haired. Her peachy face looked like someone painted exactly ten freckles across her nose with a paintbrush. I had more of those than her.

Best of all, Joy's laughter filled my Gran's

house with a sweet happiness, and the dust from her own contentment settled around my brother with just the right weight to fend off the memories of his days on the European front. Laughter heals, it's true. Their wedding took place that Thanksgiving.

Frank Darling and Jean Francis planned a Christmas wedding, as soon as her nursing course was over and he could walk without canes. They planned to live in Charleston where they would operate a hardware store that Frank's father purchased soon after his son's unfortunate plunge from Gran's porch.

Please understand. What happened that day is never referred to as a suicide attempt. Even to this day, every time one of the males in our family gets dressed up, he will undoubtedly sigh as he ties his neckwear and retells the story of Frank's wrenching fall at the feet of sweet Jean Francis.

I, Margaret Perrin Macy, chose to sit on the downstairs porch from then on, where I could easily be seen from the street. I knew that I would soon be old enough for my own love story. It might even happen when I turned fourteen. My daddy said I should be on the lookout for men wearing truly ugly ties.

Or Cary Grant. I would wait my whole life for Cary Grant.

IF GRANDPA GOT MAD AT SOMEBODY, HE'D SAY . . .

- "Either fish or cut bait."
- "That fool went off half-cocked."
- "He's as worthless as a bump on a log."
- "Don't get too big for your britches."
- "That woman's so stingy she'll squeeze a nickel until the buffalo hollers."
- "Don't bite off more than you can chew."
- "That child could make a preacher cuss."
- "You're slower than a herd of turtles."
- "That girl ain't got the sense she was born with."
- "I'm gonna hop on you like a duck on a June bug."

THE GREEN BEAN
CASSEROLE
BY SANDRA CHASTAIN

"Southerners have a genius for
psychological alchemy . . . If something
intolerable simply cannot be changed,
driven away or shot they will not only
tolerate it but take pride in it as well."
— Florence King, author

Tradition tells us that holidays aren't holidays without gatherings of friends and family. In the South, that means food. It once meant calorie-laden, full-of-fat sweets, hand-delivered, often with a group singing carols. Now, based on the commercials on television, it means a gathering of friends who all bring "the green bean casserole."

I lived in the deep South in a town where the entire community was made up of Methodist and Baptists with an odd, non-practicing Catholic thrown in. I say non-practicing because they didn't have a church or a priest so they were forced to drive long distances or eventually give in and attend

190

the local churches with their friends. I know this sounds odd, but remember, I'm old.

My childhood seems like a million years ago. I now live in the city where on my street alone, we have Protestants, Muslims, Catholics, Buddhists and probably other religions I don't even know. Still, we continue the tradition of the holiday gift-exchange-dinner where the family brings food. It's probably the only tradition that doesn't lead to family squabbles — food. Unless you're a hundred pounds overweight and seated next to a ninety-pound anorexic cousin who works in a fitness center.

This past holiday season, I drew Auntie Emily's name, Auntie being the ninety-four-year old matriarch of the family. Shopping for her is like having the entire family shaking their finger at you when you take your place at our Christmas dinner table. Everyone long ago learned to shop with care for Aunt Emily because you were likely at some future date to get the gift back in return, often wrapped in the same paper.

Auntie Emily is tolerated with feigned amusement by her friends for her forgetfulness and with clinched teeth by her family for her whining. Her favorite expression is, "You'd whine too if all you had to do was sit here and look at these four walls every day." Never mind that her niece has wrestled down Auntie's wheelchair that weighs as much as Arnold Swarzenegger, and routinely spends the entire day pushing Auntie around the mall to find a little blouse that has short sleeves and no gaudy imprints and no low neckline. There is no such thing; I know. I'm the niece.

I try to console the others by telling them, "You'd whine too, if you had outlived everybody you knew." They don't care. I only hope that one day I can fill Auntie's shoes since I'm the second-oldest living member of the clan. It's my house where we all congregate at Thanksgiving and Christmas and I'm the official hostess. During the year, each family takes Auntie for a month so that we won't have to pay exorbitant fees for a nursing home. Since November is my Auntie month, I usually end up having her for December, too. One day I intend to whine — a lot. I just needed to get that off of my chest.

I have to give them credit, nobody refuses to take her in; the rest believe there's money to be inherited at some point. I don't tell them any different.

Back to the point I started to make. Who would ever expect snow and ice to incapacitate the roads around Atlanta the week before Christmas? Who'd believe that I'd have the mother of all head colds and be confined to the house? Since Auntie started the cold chain in November, she's still here looking after me. Well, that's what she says. To compound matters, my daughter, recently divorced, moved down the street from me. She now spends more time here than either Auntie or I are comfortable with. Auntie says she whines.

Because of my grandson, who always managed to find his Christmas gifts, my daughter decided to come to my house and, under the guise of wrapping my gifts and Auntie Emily's gifts, she would wrap his. She'd just leave them here and for once he'd be surprised. A little window of joy in the midst of a sad divorce.

Her plan to send him to a friend's house while she wrapped presents was foiled by the unexpected prediction of an ice storm, so both grandchildren, my daughter and the two coughing and sniffling senior members of the family ended up in my house while my daughter was trying to wrap presents in one of the upstairs bedrooms.

Now, my grandson isn't dumb, except when he wants to be, because he figured out right away what she was doing. One knock after another drove his mama crazy and turned him into a conniving kid determined to find a way to spy on his loot. Finally, his mama sent him downstairs to help with the cooking, with the promise that if he'd help me, she'd let him open one present early.

Thanks, daughter.

"MeMaw, what do I have to cook?" he asked, not bothering to hide his dismay.

"Nothing! Why don't you just watch?"

"Nope, if I'm helping, I'm helping."

Well, I have a certain mean streak in me that kicks in every now and then. For the almost fifty years I've cooked I've served the same basics every Christmas, not necessarily a Christmas menu but one that everyone would actually eat: Turkey, dressing, giblet gravy, mashed potatoes, English peas and cranberry sauce. This year, after watching endless commercials on television, I decided to go wild and make my first green bean casserole.

To my grandson's question, I answered triumphantly, "Green bean casserole."

"Yuck!" said my grandson.

"Yuck!" said my granddaughter.

"It's your choice," I said.

"Can't do it, Granny, I'll make fudge."

"Too late," I responded. "Your sister just used the last of the chocolate morsels."

Grandson thought about it for a moment then, in his best hip-hop move, caught his crotch and heisted up the jeans that were threatening to slide down his rear. "All right, bring on the green beans," he said.

Auntie grinned. I grinned. "First, we have to outfit you in cooking armor." I pulled out an apron, one embroidered by Auntie in her youth. Her tiny stitches outlined a lady wearing a long skirt covered with flowers. The trim finished the bib and ended at the ties that circled the neck.

"I'm not wearing this," my grandson announced, shaking his head.

"Suit yourself," I agreed, standing back and eying his white Abercrombie and Fitch hoodie. "But, your hoodie may turn green. Look at your sister."

He glanced over at his sister and the apron she was wearing, smeared with chocolate. "I'll just take off the hoodie."

"Smart choice," I said. "But you still wear the apron."

He shrugged, fastened the tabs behind his neck and tied the sash. "So, what do I do? Let's get this show on the road."

"Don't know. First we have to get the recipe. It's on the back of the French onion soup box." I turned it around. "Get two cans of green beans out of the pantry."

"Where?"

"On the shelf."

"Which shelf?"

Did I tell you he's thirteen? Well he is. "Look at your apron. The shelf is about rosebud high."

"Whee, I was afraid you were going to say something . . . improper, MeMaw." He compared the design on the apron to the shelves and reached in, retrieving two cans of green beans. "What now?"

"First, you open the beans."

He took the can and turned it curiously. "Where's the tab?"

"No tab. Use the can opener."

"And that would be where?"

"In the cabinet. Just a minute, I'll show you." I wiped off the counter, opened the cabinet door and pulled out the opener. By time, Grandson had disappeared. "Where'd he go?"

Granddaughter didn't have to answer. I heard Daughter upstairs screaming. "Get out of here. You are not going to see these presents."

"But I'm helping with the cooking like you said," Grandson protested. "I just need to know where the can opener is."

"Ask your grandmother. And close that door and don't open it until you're done."

Grandson returned to the kitchen. "How long is this gonna take, MeMaw?"

Did I tell you he's thirteen? "However long it takes, Grandson," I answer.

That's when we heard a peppering sound on the deck just beyond the table where we were working. "What's that?" Granddaughter asked.

I was afraid I knew. I slid open the glass door and the sound grew louder. When a piece of ice jumped into the breakfast room, I announced, "It's hail and sleet."

"Ah," Granddaughter moaned. "Why couldn't it be snow? Wouldn't snow be wonderful for Christmas? We could pull the Christmas tree out on the deck and turn on the lights. They're indoor-outdoor lights. I saw the mark on the plug. It would be beautiful."

"It would," I said, a tinge of worry creasing my brow. Atlanta doesn't get much snow and ice but when we do, it's a mess. It's beautiful, all right. The huge oaks put on a glistening cover of ice and the magnolias and nandina berries look like Christmas decorations. The pine trees are spectacular, wearing divinity icing with silver sprinkles, until they start to snap and fall across power lines.

No power was the last thing we needed

on Christmas Day. I am luckier than most, having a huge fireplace and a set of antique, wrought-iron cooking pots that I'd actually learned to use in past power outages.

"Let's get the cooking done," I said, "if you're going to leave something out for Santa." And pray that the ice and sleet stops, I added silently.

"What next?" Grandson said, impatiently.

I demonstrated how to use the electric can opener and Grandson learned there was more than one way to open a can.

"Remember the first time we left something out for Santa's reindeer?" Granddaughter mused.

Remember? I remembered. It was right after the divorce and the children were pretty much living with me while Daughter got things straightened out. I'd found a pattern in a children's magazine to make feeding baskets for Santa's reindeer. To distract the children I suggested that we make feed bags for each reindeer. That was also the year of that song about grandma getting run over by a reindeer. In our house, it was the year that Auntie repaired the star on the Christmas tree — with her head.

I glanced through the dining room to the living room where this year's Christmas tree was a thing of true glory. It was just as spectacular a year ago when Grandson helped decorate, until the Christmas star refused to twinkle. I'd stepped into the kitchen to take a tray of cookies out of the oven when he decided to pull up one of my dining room chairs and remove the star. That was the moment when Baby, Auntie's new cat, decided to chase Rosie, Granddaughter's elderly Peke-a-Pom — that would be a mixed Pekingese and Pomeranian.

There was nothing malicious in the chase except when it turned around and the dog chased the cat and the cat decided to climb the Christmas tree, by way of Grandson's leg. The upshot was the tree crashed, pushing Grandson off the chair and conking Auntie in the head with the star. It immediately started to twinkle.

Granddaughter went on with the story about the reindeer bags and how they were empty the next morning. But the deer dropped one, ripped it with their hooves and spread the birdseed and oatmeal all over the deck.

Grandson shook his head. "I can't believe you fell for that."

Granddaughter came over, hugged me and whispered, "I believed." Then went on, "You know, MeMaw, no matter where I go, or whatever happens, your house will always be home. We're going to make Christmas goodies every year, forever."

"I hope so," I said, thinking how young she was and how things change as life interferes. "I call this the best kind of tradition."

She leaned back and looked up at me. "No, it's called 'making memories.' "

I covered the choking feeling in my throat with a snappy reply. "If we get iced-in, that'll be a memory," I said and brushed the frosting of sugar from her long, dark hair. "Tell you what, you'd better get back to stirring. It looks like your candy is about ready to pour up."

"Yes ma'am." She clicked her heels and gave a snappy salute.

"Grandson, let's get this casserole going. Where's your cream of mushroom soup? Open the cans while I get our baking pan." I was blabbering as I covered my emotional reaction to my granddaughter's comment about making memories.

"Oh, boy, tabs." Grandson pulled the first tab and made a face at what was in the can. "It looks rotten."

"It's not rotten."

He pulled the second. "This one, too."

"It's not rotten, that's the way it is supposed to look. Let's empty the beans and the soup into the baking pan, along with the milk and a little pepper."

Grandson followed my instructions until I got to a "little" pepper. I just took the container and gave it a couple of good shakes.

He leaned over and smelled the mixture. "Yuck!" he said.

"Now, we cook it for thirty minutes. Then we'll cover them with French fried onions and cook them some more."

"You're going to ruin those onions by putting them in that?" He nodded his head at the pan I was sliding into the oven.

"I am, and you're going to love them tomorrow."

"If we're eating them tomorrow, why are you cooking them tonight?"

"Because I'm going to have the turkey and dressing in the oven tomorrow."

"So, are we done here?" Grandson asked.

I nodded and watched him tear out of the kitchen and up the steps. Sleet was coating the porch now and the tree limbs as well. If this went on much longer we'd definitely have trouble.

Upstairs, I heard my daughter yelling. "You go down those steps. I'm locking this door and you'd better not try to get in again." The door slammed and I won't repeat the word Daughter said, not in front of you, dear reader.

"Now look what you made me do. Mom! I'm gonna kill your grandson on Christmas Eve!"

"You'd better go," Granddaughter said. "This might be the time when Mom means it."

Upstairs, Daughter and Grandson stood in the hall studying the bedroom door, the locked-on-the-inside bedroom door. Bloodshed was eminent. I studied the situation. We were on the second floor but there was only one door into the room. The two windows were locked, or they were supposed to be. Since the room was just above the roof to the carport, I had to constantly reprimand Grandson and his friends for climbing out and stargazing. At least that's what they said. I'm certain it had nothing to do with the female classmate that lived next door. Dare I suggest it?

I did.

"What about this? Do you think you can squeeze through the bathroom window onto the roof?"

He nodded, smiling broadly. "Sure."

He couldn't. When I stripped off the apron and his tee shirt, his eyes opened wide. "What are you doing?"

"I'm spreading lotion on you so you'll slide through."

"But I'll freeze."

"Just pretend you're a popsicle that's started to melt."

"Do it!" Mom said. "Then if the window happens to be open, you can come in and open the door."

With a shove from the rear and a little twist, he went through. "Be careful," I started to say as he stepped out onto the roof and began to slide. Only a quick move allowed him to catch the window and his mother to grab him. "Hold on. I'll get a rope."

I dashed down the stairs and grabbed the clothesline coiled up on a nail by the kitchen door and the box of ice cream salt under the cabinet. Back up the stairs I flew. Rudolph couldn't have been more graceful.

"I hate to ask," Daughter said, "but what are you going to do with a rope? I know I threatened to kill him, but a hanging on Christmas Eve might be a bit more than I had in mind."

"We tie it around his waist to keep him from sliding off the roof. Do that first, then we'll pour this ice cream salt on the roof and see if he can get to the bedroom."

"And tie the apron around his head so he can cover his eyes," his mother directed. It took a couple of false starts but he eventually made his way to the bedroom window.

"Cover your eyes. Don't you dare look at those presents," his mother yelled.

"I'm not looking."

"Is the window open?" I asked.

"It seems to be stuck," he yelled, slamming his hand, or maybe it was his head, against the house. Then silence. "It's open. I'm going in."

"Make sure your eyes are covered good," his mother said. "And just head straight for the door."

"How can I see where I'm going if my eyes are covered?"

"Just do it," Daughter said. "The door is straight ahead."

It took too long, but eventually the door opened and Grandson wiped the lotion off his shoulders with his apron, gave his mother a kiss on the cheek and walked innocently down the stairs, dragging the clothesline behind. "I'm going to check on my casserole," he said.

As it turned out, we cleaned the kitchen, put out the reindeer feed bags and went to bed. When the power went out after midnight everybody gathered in the den in front of the fireplace. We recited *The Night Before Christmas* with some interesting adaptations by Grandson. "Twas the night before Christmas, Santa's reindeers came. They slid on the roof and turned up lame. None of the children were stirring; they were . . ."

A limb fell across the deck, setting off the wind chimes.

"That was the reindeer," Granddaughter said the next morning. "Just think what memories we're making. Fudge, my brother almost falling off the roof, an ice storm that left us without power, and pouring our main dish into a cast iron skillet."

We didn't brown the French fried onions, but the green bean casserole was so good that we all voted to have one every year. "And I'll cook it," said Grandson. "I'll bring the green bean casserole. You think that's where they got their idea for the commercial?"

I smiled. We did make memories. In the years to come, when anybody tells the story of the Christmas when the presents got locked behind closed doors, the thing everyone will remember most is the green bean casserole.

Now Y'all Be Polite, You Hear?

- "She's as cute as a bug."
- "She's as pretty as a speckled pup."
- "He's about half a bubble off plumb."
- "His face would stop a clock."
- "He looks like something the cat dragged in."
- "She's lower than dirt."
- "He's colder than a banker's heart."

ARTIFACTS OF A LOST CIVILIZATION

- Vinyl record albums
- Bottle caps with cork liners
- Band-Aid boxes made from tin.
- Vicks VapoRub and other ointments that came in glass jars.
- Wooden sewing spools that could be re-purposed. When stacked up and properly glued, they would support shelves and make an attractive étagère!
- The iPod of 1960: those little 45 rpm record players you could close up and carry like an overnight case. And when you played Alvin and the Chipmunks records on one, it drove your dog to dis-traction.
- Girdles and other horrible torture devices people used. My least favorite was the garter belt. There was something vaguely obscene about all those dangling elastic bands and fasteners.

— Susan Goggins, *The Wart Witch*

THE WART WITCH

BY SUSAN GOGGINS

"I've always said that next to Imperial China, the South is the best place in the world to be an old lady."
— Florence King, author

I usually liked to ride in the back of the truck, face the front, and let the wind hit me in the face, but I ran the risk of being anointed with tobacco juice if Grandpa forgot I was back there. Since I was going visiting I wanted to stay as clean as possible, so I sat up front.

Grandpa was one of those old men who, when driving, looked everywhere but where he was going. Grandma often said it was a wonder he didn't get himself killed that way. He particularly liked to gaze at the livestock in the pastures he passed. Right now, while he was taking in several Black Angus cows that had gathered under a shade tree in a roadside pasture, I examined a seed wart on the side of my right index finger. Gross. The kids at school would tease me about playing with frogs. Either that or they would shun me entirely. I'd seen the cool kids, as ruthless as only children can be, banish their peers from their circle for less.

It was only recently that I had started concerning myself with flaws in my appearance. I was starting junior high in a couple of weeks, and warts did not figure into the hip new image I wanted to project.

Most summers I was content to help Grandma and Grandpa with chores around the farm, but this summer I was spending most of my time doing exercises I saw in magazines and experimenting with makeup and hairstyles. Grandpa thought all this was pretty silly, but Grandma seemed to understand.

I just knew the autumn of 1969 would be a turning point in my life.

"Grandpa, is this really going to work?" I asked.

"Sure will, if you believe," Grandpa said, and spat out the window of the ancient Chevy pickup.

Grandpa had come up with the idea of visiting Mose one afternoon after hearing me complain about the four warts that had appeared on my hand. Grandma, Grandpa, and I had been sitting under a shade tree shucking corn as Bozo the Chihuahua slept under Grandpa's chair.

Years before, Grandma and Grandpa had gone to Sand Mountain, Alabama, to visit one of Grandpa's cousins who was a mule trader. The man had a Chihuahua that followed him everywhere and sat in the crook of his arm while he auctioned mules. Grandpa thought this was grand, because it reminded him of Xavier Cugat holding his little dog while he conducted his orchestra. So he had a succession of Chihuahuas, of which Bozo was the latest. Grandpa would walk around the farm, gazing at his cows, with Bozo tucked in the crook of one arm.

"I used to know an old man who could witch warts," Grandpa said. "If he's still living, I'll find him and take you to him."

"What's witching warts?" I asked as I picked a strand of corn silk from between two rows of white, juicy kernels. For supper, Grandma would boil a generous pot of these ears and I would eat mine with plenty of butter. Grandpa and the other farmers I knew always called this corn something that sounded like "roeshenyers," and I would be grown before I realized that what he was saying was "roasting ears."

I'd figured out that farmers just had their

own unique pronunciation peccadilloes. Like how they always pronounced "guano" as gyoo-anner.

Grandpa paused in mid-shuck. "He's got the power," he said in a lowered voice. "He looks at your warts and does some kind of spell and pretty soon your warts go away."

Grandma snorted and started to say something but stopped short when the little dog let out an otherworldly howl-whine from underneath Grandpa's chair. Grandpa came up out of the white metal lawn chair as if someone had just lit a fire under it and spilled the shucked and silked ears from his lap into the dirt.

Grandma and I began to laugh and finally Grandpa joined in. "Bozo, wake up. You're having a bad dream," I said when I had quit laughing. The old dog, having been roused by the laughter, got himself to his feet and waddled off with what dignity he could muster.

Mose hadn't been very hard to find. After asking around, Grandpa learned that Mose's son was working at a sawmill in the next county. Grandpa went to see him there, and the man told Grandpa where his father lived. The man said he would tell Mose to expect us.

Mose lived at the end of a dirt road that ran beside an old Baptist church and bisected the church cemetery. Grandma and Grandpa attended the Methodist church in which Grandma was raised, but this church in the next county was the ancestral church of Grandpa's family. And this cemetery held the family grave plot. I had often come here with Grandpa to help him care for the family lot where his baby son was buried.

Back before the advent of the perpetual-care cemetery, people tended the graves of their loved ones themselves. To have your people's graves grown over with weeds would have been a disgrace. Grandpa would put rakes and a sling blade in the back of the truck, and we would pull weeds and rake the white marble chips until they formed a smooth, level surface. Then Grandpa would sling blade around the outside of the plot.

Grandma brought flowers at Christmas and on her baby's birthday and a few other times throughout the year. But when Grandpa came, it was to groom the little grave lot, one that already had a tombstone with their names on it.

Even though I had been to the cemetery many times, I had never been any farther down the dirt road. I had seen cars and trucks full of black people go up and down the road, each vehicle raising a cloud of brick-red dust in its wake. But I had never seen beyond the little bend in the road past the cemetery until the day we went to see Mose.

The first homes we saw once we got past the cemetery were small frame houses sitting on brick or stone foundations three or so feet off the ground, as was the style a long time ago. Old dogs stared listlessly from their shady places underneath the houses. Children played in the yards while their mothers hung wash out to dry. Neighbor ladies gossiped and fanned on sagging front porches. The farther down the road we went, the worse the houses looked. Some had outhouses out back, confirming my suspicions that they had no plumbing. And the farther down the road we went the more people stopped what they were doing to stare at us. Grandpa glanced only casually at the roadside scenery. I guessed that was because nobody here had any cows.

I was beginning to think that Grandpa had missed a turn. The end of the road was in sight and the houses were looking very bad indeed, but still he drove on. Right before the road stopped in its dirt tracks in front of a huge oak tree, Grandpa pulled up in front of a house, the most terrible house on the road, the worst-looking house I had ever seen.

The roof was covered in tar paper. The sides of the house were covered with gray roofing shingles. Part of the front porch had collapsed and the two visible windows had no screens. The whole house was no bigger than some people's living rooms.

No sooner had Grandpa shut off the engine than Mose stepped out of the house to greet us. He must have been waiting and watching. Mose was slender and very tall. He must have been really old because he'd been a grown man when Grandpa was just a boy. But the only clue to his age was his white hair and that delicate, slow-motion gait peculiar to the very old.

Every really old person I'd ever seen stood stooped over to some degree, their backs bowed with age, but Mose stood straight and tall. His clothes were well-worn but clean and although it was hot, he wore his checkered cotton shirt buttoned all the way to the neck.

Mose greeted us so warmly and seemed so happy to see us that I figured he didn't get much company, maybe because he lived at the very end of the road. Grandpa and Mose exchanges pleasantries for a few minutes and then Mose turned to me.

"So this is the young lady with the warts," he said, smiling broadly.

"Here they are." I held up my right hand so that he could see.

Mose's smile disappeared and his manner became all business. He took my hand and examined the warts as seriously and as professionally as if he were a dermatologist. Directly he let go of my hand and smiled again. "Y'all come on in," he said.

Grandpa and I followed Mose up the rickety wooden steps and into the little house. The walls were papered with newspaper and pages out of what looked like the Sears Roebuck catalog. The cracks in the floorboards were just wide enough to see all the way through to the ground. The only furniture was a twin-sized iron bedstead and a couple of straight chairs.

A pot-bellied stove stood in a corner with a white enamel saucepan on top. The small pan was half full of blackberries.

Mose asked us to sit and became very serious once again. I dropped down onto one of the chairs opposite Mose, who sat on the bed. He took my right hand in his and put the index finger of his left hand to his tongue. Then, as he began to touch one wart and then the other with his long, wiry finger, he closed his eyes and mumbled some unintelligible incantation.

I stared at Mose, who was swaying now, with his eyes still closed. It felt like there was something ancient and mysterious about this ceremony, but I wasn't afraid. Mose remained in a trance for a couple of minutes, and then opened his eyes and smiled.

I looked closely at my hand for any immediate change.

"Now, they're not going to come off right away," Mose said. He took a dingy handkerchief from his pocket and wiped it across his brow as if the last few minutes had tired him. Then he stood up and I started to stand up too, thinking it was time to go, but he put a hand on my shoulder. He fished in the pocket of his green work pants for a moment and then held out a quarter.

"Here," he said. "I've just bought your warts from you. In a couple of weeks the warts will come up on my hands."

I took the quarter and reached into my own pocket for the money my mother had given me for Mose.

"Oh, no," he said. "You can't pay me. That would break the spell. I had to be the one to pay you."

"Is there anything I have to do?" I asked.

"Yes," he said, looking at me intently with

rheumy black eyes that looked as old as time. "You have to believe. If you don't believe, the warts won't come off."

We went back out into the yard, and Grandpa and I thanked him and said our good-byes. He seemed sorry to see us go. For the return trip, I took my preferred place in the back of the truck, having made sure that Grandpa had a spit cup available. As we rode, I looked through the particles of red dust that we raised and saw that Mose, still smiling, watched us until we were out of sight.

A week and a half later, I sat drumming my still wart-infested fingers on Grandma's kitchen table.

"What am I going to do?" I wailed. "I start school Monday and these ugly warts haven't gone away yet." Grandpa sat opposite me shelling peas while Grandma stirred something on the stove.

"Oh, I forgot to tell you," Grandma said without turning around. "While I was at the drugstore, I got you some of that wart compound I saw advertised on TV. It's on the medicine shelf."

I glanced over at Grandpa, who was silent. "You know, Grandpa, I've given it two weeks, and nothing's happened yet. It couldn't hurt to use that stuff — just sort of like insurance." I braced myself for some sort of disapproval from him, but he still said nothing, appearing to concentrate on the peas.

I went over to the corner cabinet and looked on the top shelf, which was loaded with all sorts of jars and bottles full of country remedies, both store-bought and homemade. The sight of some of these products made me blanch due to past association. Especially the Watkins green salve, which my great-grandmother ate straight out of the jar every night to ward off colds.

Off to the left, I saw what I was looking for, a small glass bottle with a hexagonal plastic cap. I returned to the table with it and read the directions. I glanced up at Grandpa again, hoping for some sign of approval, but he continued to stare at the peas. I took the cap off the bottle and let a drop of the acid solution slide down the glass wand applicator onto wart number one. Even though the label said it was painless, I felt a sting when the chemical touched my flesh. I decided I would try it on just one wart at first and see what happened.

"It's okay, Grandpa," I said, wincing. "This stuff will take off the warts, and Mose will never know I didn't wait to see what happened."

Grandpa began to make that strange, tuneless half-whistling, half-hissing noise he sometimes made when his mind took him somewhere far away.

The next day Mama dropped me off at Grandma and Grandpa's as usual on her way to work. Grandma wasn't there because she had to go to a meeting of the U.M.W. I could see Grandpa in the pasture a couple of hundred yards away rolling a salt block off the back of the truck. The cows had begun to gather around, jostling each other in their attempts to be the first one to get a lick of salt.

I wandered out to where he was, through two gates, past the chicken house, avoiding cow pies as I went. By that time Grandpa had gone over to where a rope suspended some wound-up burlap bags between two trees. He poured used motor oil onto the bags against which the cows would scratch their backs. This was a home remedy he used to keep the horse flies from biting his cows. It seemed to me that Grandpa thought of everything.

"How're the warts?" he asked.

"I guess that stuff took a tiny layer off that

one wart I tried it on. I'll put it on the others today." I nudged a Betsy bug with my toe as it crawled along the ground, some bit of vegetation in its pincers. "Thanks for taking me to Mose's, though. I really enjoyed meeting him. He's pretty special. I mean, he asked us into his house and didn't make any apologies for it even though it was in bad shape. And even though he was really poor, he wouldn't take any money. That quarter he gave me was probably real money to him."

"Yes, I 'spec it was." Grandpa removed his baseball cap and ran his hand through his thinning reddish hair. "Just because a man's poor don't mean he can't be proud."

"Yeah. He even carried himself proud even though he was so old. But how can people keep their spirits up when they have to live like that?"

Grandpa settled his cap back on his head and reached into his overall pocket for his pocket knife and chewing tobacco. "A man's pride don't always come from the things that money can buy," he said, cutting himself a plug of Brown's Mule. "Mose has a gift that nobody else has. Nobody in these parts anyway. It's too bad he didn't get to use it more. Once the older folks that knew him started to die off and the young folks started going to doctors for every little thing, I reckon nobody much came to him for wart witching anymore. Except us, that is."

Grandpa started back toward the barn. "Would you mind getting my inhaler off the kitchen table?" he wheezed. "Then you can help me feed the cows." Grandpa suffered from brown lung from working in the thread mill for thirty years in addition to farming, and he had to stop working frequently in order to catch his breath.

"Sure," I said. "I'll meet you at the barn."

While I walked back to the house I thought about what Grandpa had said. That was why Mose had been so glad to see us. After a long time, someone had come to him and asked him for help, asked him to use his gift again. It was too bad that more people didn't go to see him.

I looked down at the wart I had treated with the caustic wart medicine. It still stung from yesterday's treatment. I realized that I wasn't sure I believed in Mose's wart witching. I'd proven that yesterday. I hadn't given it the full two weeks before I'd put that stuff on the warts, and Mose and Grandpa had both told me it wouldn't work unless I really believed.

I grabbed the inhaler off the table and put

it in my pocket. Then I stopped by the sink for a cool drink of well water. I stared out the window past the profusion of African violets on the sill and felt a twinge of guilt that I hadn't given Mose's magic the full two weeks to work. Good thing Mose would never know. I would hate to hurt his feelings and his pride.

I reached for the wart medicine, figuring I'd put on the second dose. It would only take a second. My hand froze in mid-air. As I looked at the warts, I felt my eyes grow wide and my face redden with shame. He would know. He would know when the warts didn't come up on his own hands. He might think his powers had deserted him and that would make him very sad. Or worse, he would know that I hadn't believed in him.

I flung open the doors to the cabinet under the sink and grabbed the stiff brush that Grandma used to clean the dirt off of freshly plowed-up potatoes. I scrubbed and scrubbed the dried whitish residue of the medicine off the one wart until the whole area was raw and fixing to bleed.

Then I ran out to the barn and up into the hay loft while Grandpa waited on the ground. I pushed bales of hay out of the loft window and onto the ground beside

Grandpa, who cut the twine from the bales with his pocket knife. Then I joined him on the ground and we called the cows. "C'mon! C'mon!" we yelled.

By the time I'd separated the bales into big chunks, and spaced them out, the cows were filing in from two pastures to the barnyard. Grandpa sat down on the top step of the corn crib to rest and use the inhaler. "So, did you put the wart medicine on?" he said when he could breathe again.

"Nah. I decided to have faith." I joined him on the step, hugged him around the shoulders and kissed him on the cheek.

"That's my girl," he said.

When the warts had not gone away by the time school started, I decided the solution to my social dilemma was Band-Aids. I wore them constantly, and one day as I removed them before a bath, I saw that the warts had disappeared.

Grandpa took me back to see Mose a few times more. Whenever the church would have a barbecue fundraiser, I would take him a plate with a chicken quarter cooked all night over an open fire and slathered with a tangy sauce, coleslaw, baked beans, and loaf bread.

He was always delighted to see us, and I

heard he lived to be ninety-five.

Now a few years ago, I read that you could make warts disappear merely by covering them with adhesive bandages. It's supposed to smother them or something like that, and eventually they go away. But I still prefer to think that it was Mose and his magic — and my faith in an old man's special gift — that did the trick.

A 92-Year-Old Remembers

- When you picked sage only during a full moon in May and August and dried it for hog-killing time in October when you made sausage.
- When you hung your clean laundry to dry on the garden fence or a clothes line.
- When you stuffed your own mattresses with fresh new straw when you cut the wheat.
- When children went barefoot from May until the first bale of cotton was sold. That's when you'd get your new shoes and a pound of cheese.

   — thanks to Maureen Hardegree, *The Good Son,* and her husband's grandmother, "Big Mama"

Things Grandma and Grandpa Probably Didn't Have

- Instant grits
- Microwave ovens
- Cell phones
- More than one phone, period
- Air conditioning
- Central heat
- Carpet
- Doorbells
- Automatic garage doors
- Frozen TV dinners

A Patchwork Journey

BY MICHELLE ROPER

"Because I was born in the South, I'm a Southerner. If I had been born in the North, the West or the Central Plains, I would be just a human being."
— Clyde Edgerton, author

One summer when I was a boy, I had to stay with my grandmother while my mom and dad worked. In the evening, while sitting in her porch rocker, Grandmother would piece together a quilt of patches, and as she did, she told me stories about the patches, and where they came from, and to whom they had belonged. Those patches and my grandmother's stories took me on a journey, which I can still remember forty years later whenever I look at that quilt.

"You'd best eat that muffin because you won't feel like eating anything after your treatment," I told my wife as she sipped her ice water. "You haven't touched your orange juice, either."

"I'm not hungry."

I leaned my cheek toward the sun, savoring the warming rays as my wife and I pretended to enjoy our breakfast outside the local cafe.

My coffee had all the flavor of ground cardboard. Lately, everything tasted like cardboard. Just like Liza, I hadn't had any appetite.

Some people claim their hearts are tied to their spouses. Well, in my case, it's my stomach. Same thing happened during her three pregnancies. I developed cravings for pickles, Chinese food, and Krispy Kreme doughnuts right along with her.

Something cold and wet touched my leg. I looked down to find the cafe owner's Chihuahua, Bob, sporting a yellow knit sweater studded with rhinestones. He sat in a begging position with his little paws extended up in the air.

"Sorry, Bob. Dr. Blackshear put you on a diet. No more handouts."

Liza leaned over and threw him a chunk of her muffin. "Let him enjoy himself. He's still recovering from his trauma."

"Trauma? That sweater is an invitation. I swear it's so bright it's a beacon to every hawk in the sky."

I leaned over the table toward my wife and

spoke in a softer tone so Bob wouldn't hear me. "If he was our dog, I wouldn't dress him like he was a poodle. I'd put him in a leather biker jacket with a skull and cross-bones on the back; make him feel like a man."

Apparently, he heard me. Bob moseyed back into the cafe.

Liza glanced at her watch and turned to me. "If we don't get a move on, we're not going to have enough time to get to Wal-Mart and the bookstore before seeing Dr. Allen."

"Alrighty, let's get you to Wal-Mart, I've got some shopping I need to do before we get ready for our trip."

Liza never argued. She merely tilted her head toward the left when she was upset with me. After twenty-five years of marriage, I'd learned to read her body signals, and they were all shouting annoyance. Her head was tilted now.

On the side street sat the Winnebago I'd bought three months ago. In fact, I purchased it the same day the doctors diagnosed Liza with an advanced case of leukemia. They had said she didn't have long to live. I told her she was gonna beat this thing.

I had to help her climb up in her seat. Today she had stumbled, and I grabbed her upper arm to keep her from falling. But then she stopped and cocked her head to one side. "Do you hear it, Disney?"

"What?"

"Listen."

I heard some ladies talking outside the cafe and an old farm tractor rumbled by. Liza used to always tell me take time to smell the honeysuckle blossoms in the early summer. She'd make me get up from the work I'd brought home from the office and come outside to watch Anna and Mickey shovel sand into piles in the sandbox when they were little. She would say, 'It's the small moments that make our memories, Disney. Make a memory.'

"Listen, it's the creek."

I listened more carefully, and sure enough I could hear the burbles. "Well I'll be darned. Can you imagine what the roars of the Colorado River are going to sound like when we're gazing down at it from the rim of the Grand Canyon?"

She turned and looked at me. "Forget the Grand Canyon. Listen to the creek. Listen, Disney."

As she sat down in her seat, my finger-prints showed whiter than the parchment like skin of her arm. I noted that she needed more vitamins. I'd stop by the health food store later. I had to build Liza's resistance and stamina, so she'd have the strength to ride a donkey down the canyon.

We'd talk about seeing the Grand Canyon lots of times, back when we went camping with the young'uns and all we had was a tent and a Coleman cook stove.

As I cranked the Winnebago, the engine purred like a tiger on the prowl. "Well, my lady, to market, to market we go, and we'll buy you a new television for the back so you can watch it while I'm driving the highways and by-ways of the U.S.A."

She didn't answer but leaned back in the seat and closed her eyes.

Liza leaned against me for support as we walked across the parking lot. Inside the entrance to Wal-Mart, she grabbed a buggy, and rested on the plastic covered metal bar.

"That's a good idea, I can put the television in there," I said.

"Get your own buggy. I'm going to the fabric department by myself."

I was taken aback by her crabby tone. Normally, she wasn't this touchy before her doctor's appointment.

It had to be anxiety over the trip. We'd been talking about it for years, and now that we were finally doing it, she must be anxious to get on the road. "All right, I'll let you pick out your fabric. What are you going to make? Curtains for the kitchen window in the camper?"

She pushed her buggy away without answering me, and didn't even speak to the nice grandmotherly greeter.

I nodded. "Howdy, ma'am."

Then I snatched my own buggy and hurried to the electronics department, which was next to the fabric department. I watched as my wife moved up and down the fabric displays. She stopped to unfurl different bolts that caught her fancy. The red kerchief covering her head reminded me of the kind she wore in college. Now, rather than long blonde tresses, Liza only has clumps resembling dried up corn shucks. I cringed as she held up a bolt of pink material. I didn't want any frou-frou fabric with flowers and bows on it, but if it made her happy.

A television would make me happy. In the aisle next to the boom boxes, I found what I wanted. A television with front audio/video input jacks and a DVD built in. I envisioned Liza, Mickey and Anna watching movies as I drove through traffic in different cities around the West.

I wheeled up to the fabric department with our new television set in the buggy.

Liza had a folded blue square in hers. I didn't get to see what was printed on it, but I was relieved. I could live with blue. It would look nice with the oak cabinets in the RV.

"Did you find what you were looking for?"

"Yes," she said as she glanced at the box in my cart.

"I'm ready to go. I have just enough time to get over to the bookstore."

"You have all the time in the world."

After Wal-Mart, we hit the road to Bigelow. At a red light, a man wearing an Atlanta Braves baseball cap leaned over the steering wheel of his Ford pickup truck to get a better look at the Winnebago. Desire sparkled in his eyes. From his facial expression, I knew the plans he was mentally making, what he was thinking. I could almost hear him say, "If I had me a motor home, I'd do such and such, and I'd go here and there."

Because I had made plans for years and years whenever I saw a motor home drive through our town. Finally, I was making my dreams come true. Maybe, that was why I knew I was the envy of motorists everywhere I went — the RV represented unfulfilled dreams and adventures they yearned to have.

Glancing over at Liza's weary face, I'm glad I insisted on driving it to town, today. At least, she could lie down in comfort on the way home after her treatment. I laughed to myself remembering how she protested about riding in this gas-guzzling mammoth as she called it.

Approaching the mall parking lot, I said to her, "Wake up, honey. We're here." Normally, she refused to patronize the larger discount chains as a matter of principle because of all the Mom-and-Pop bookstores going out of business, but this one was so close to Dr. Allen's office that it had become her refuge.

After treatments, we would always stop off and buy reading material. This way she had something to occupy her over the next few days as she rested and allowed the chemotherapy to fight the cancer. We had never stopped before treatments.

As she picked out her books, I searched for an atlas. I found one I liked, *Maps of the National Seashores.* Liza loved the ocean. It was my intention to take her to every natural beach I could find in the U.S.A. after the Grand Canyon. I also purchased a laminated map of the United States.

Being a gentleman, I paid for her books, *The Fool's Guide to Sewing a Patchwork*

Quilt, hence the need for all that blue fabric and the *Treasured Memories Cookbook of New England.* I didn't know why she would buy a Yankee cookbook. Yankees didn't know how to cook their vegetables, let alone bake a decent cake. I also spied a journal with an angel on the outside cover.

The cashier with a nose ring and eyebrow studs slid our books into a plastic bag and handed them to me. I tried not to stare at the young man, but I was secretly praising the Lord that neither Anna nor Mickey had pierced anything other than earlobes.

Out in the Winnebago, Liza placed the books beside her seat. "Why did you buy The Fool's Guide to Sewing a Patchwork Quilt? Gonna make a quilt for us to snuggle under when we get to the Grand Canyon?" I asked.

"No, you're going to learn how to sew a quilt."

For a few seconds, I was speechless. I blinked at her, incredulously. "Me? Learn how to sew?"

She tilted her head to the left and pressed her hand against her forehead.

I wasn't going to argue with her, not on treatment day. However, the fact was I didn't need to know how to sew. I was a surveyor. Furthermore, I didn't want to learn how to make a quilt. My granny made quilts. You bought quilts at church bazaars from little old ladies raising money for foreign missions. Learn how to sew? Me? Preposterous. I had enough to do getting ready for our trip.

Sometimes, Liza didn't crash for a nap until a couple of hours after her treatment, and today seemed to be one of those days. She insisted we stop at Piggly Wiggly and hauled out the *Treasured Memories Cookbook of New England* from the plastic bag.

As we stood in the baking aisle in front of the bags of shredded coconut, my wife flipped the pages to the middle of the cookbook. "I'm going to show you the top secret recipe for my coconut cake."

"I thought you said this was your top-secret recipe." I pointed to the top of the page. "It says here, this is Alice Huntington of Nantucket, Massachusetts's special coconut cake. I can't believe you went and claimed this woman's recipe as your own. You told me your Great-Grandmother Willoughby had given you that recipe."

"Surprise. I lied," Liza said as she placed baking soda into the cart. "You've had more than your share of helpings over the years, so don't start complaining about the source

236

now." She tiptoed over and whispered in my ear, "My secret is to add extra vanilla."

Stunned, I said, "Next you're going to tell me that your chicken-and-broccoli casserole isn't your special creation."

I loved her chicken-and-broccoli casserole.

"I hate to disillusion you, but your favorite casserole is a concoction derived from desperation. I developed it one night to clear out leftovers from the refrigerator."

Stunned by my wife's cooking confessions, I gazed at the flour, sugar, and three bags of shredded coconut in the cart. "Are you going to make a cake when Anna comes home?"

"No, you are."

Inevitably, exhaustion caught up with Liza. She laid down for a nap after we got back from our errands.

When I went to check on her a couple of hours later, she was sitting up in bed and writing in her new journal. Funny, I hadn't noticed the very dark circles underneath her eyes earlier today. In the afternoon light, it looked as if someone had punched her, and she had two black eyes as a result.

"Just wanted to let you know I got the casserole in the oven," I said. "I'll let you write."

"Disney, don't leave." She patted the space on the bed beside her. "We need to talk."

"Sure thing. What're you writing? All the stops you want to make out West, all the beaches you want to walk along? I'm glad to see you're finally getting into the spirit of the trip."

"Let's stop focusing on the trip for a minute. I'm writing out the list of books I want you to buy for Mickey. I haven't had time to get them all together. So, you'll need to . . ."

I pulled the journal from her hands; the ink had smeared on the pages. "Quit talking like that. You're going to beat the cancer. You're going to be fine."

"Disney, I want you to listen to me. I want you to go up to the attic and bring down the 'the keepers'."

My heart hammered in my chest. I stared at her. The 'keepers' were what we called the blue Rubbermaid boxes that contained our children's special clothes. Each child's newborn outfit, Anna's graduation dress, and Mickey's skateboarding competition tee-shirts, had been lovingly stored: a chronicle of their lives in cloth. For years, Liza's intention was to make a special quilt each for Anna and Mickey from the cloth in these outfits and present it to them at their marriages in the faraway future.

I stood, and then walked over to the other side of the room. I pointed my finger at her. "This pessimistic thinking of yours has got to stop. You're going to get better. I bought that RV for you."

"How dare you say you bought that RV for me? Every time I look at it, it's a reminder of my death and a reminder of all the things we said we would do as soon as the business slowed down." She threw the covers off the bed and slowly stood up. She grabbed the bedpost to steady herself. "Isn't that what you always said to me? Soon as it slows down, honey, we're going to go see the U.S. of A. Guess what? Life doesn't slow down, Disney. You have to slow down for it." She sat back down on the bed. "You bought the RV for you, so you wouldn't have to deal with the cancer or me."

Icy cold fingers of despair clutched at my throat as she continued, "I've been trying to talk to you, and I don't have the energy or the time to argue. I need your help to finish one last project." Coughing, she reached for the Wal-Mart bag from the side of the bed. She pulled out the blue material. She gently unfolded the material and spread it out over her lap. Dolphins leaping playfully over foamy waves lay against the blue ocean of the material.

"You will sew the last pieces for the quilts from this material, but only after you've sprinkled my ashes in the ocean among a pod of dolphins."

I had to get out of our bedroom. I had to get away from her. I had to get away from the reality creeping in my mind that my Liza was dying.

Anger welled up in me. How dare she give up? "That's it, Liza. That's it. I'm not gonna put up with this anymore."

"Put up with what? I'm the one dying. I'm the one who's wanted to talk about arrangements. I'm the one who's wanted to hold onto you at night. I'm the one who's cried herself to sleep wanting comfort. But you've denied me that with your fantasy that I'm going to live."

Her words wove around my heart like a barbed wire fence snaring me with despair and fear.

Liza pulled her kerchief off her head revealing her bald scalp. "You are my best friend, and after all these years together, you've turned away from me. I need you now. I need your help to make the quilts."

I grabbed the Winnebago keys off the dresser. "You are not dying. You're giving up. And I am not making any damn quilt. You're going to live long enough to take this trip out West like we talked about all these years, and then you're going to live long enough to make my life a living hell. You hear me?"

I stormed out of the house. I shoved the keys into the switch. I cranked the Winnebago and drove away. As I turned out onto the highway something slid in between my feet and the gas pedal — *The Fool's Guide to Sewing a Patchwork Quilt.*

Entering Moonheart's Natural Living, I inhaled the aroma of vanilla and remembered Liza's secret about her coconut cake. Damn, maybe coming here was a mistake. After the 'living hell' remark, she would serve nothing but coconut cake for breakfast, lunch and dinner for the next six months until I was sick of it.

On the checkout counter, several white candle flames danced like fiery ballerinas upon a stage of wax.

"Disney. What a nice surprise," Maggie Moonheart said. "What can I help you with?"

Though fifty, Maggie's skin glowed with a vitality that I hadn't seen in Liza in months.

"Hey." said Tag, her boyfriend, who sat on

a wooden stool behind the counter.

I watched as Maggie gazed lovingly at him. Having just discovered love, they were beginning a new chapter in their lives. I had known that joy twenty-five years ago and many other joys since.

"I need some of those special high potency multi-vitamins for Liza."

She frowned. "Sorry, but I'm out. I should have more in a couple of weeks."

My stomach churned with a mixture of uneasiness and dread. Would the hands of fate hold the UPS truck back from delivering them until it was too late? I peered around the store looking for something that would make Liza well. I often came here to research natural remedies and buy bottles of herbs to fuel my hope of improving her odds against the leukemia. Today, my hope was gone. The specter of death had followed me here to Moonheart's Natural Living.

I could feel Maggie watching me, so I turned around and pretended to admire a display of beeswax candles as I blinked back tears.

"I have some special soap I'd like to recommend. A lot of customers who go through chemo love it. One girl drives up here from Atlanta to buy it for her mother," she said as she walked to a wooden shelf filled with willow baskets brimming over with fragrant bars. "The folks who use it say it's gentle on their skin. I make it with coconut oil, vitamin E oil and aloe. It's very nourishing for fragile skin."

"If you made it, then it's got to be as soft as an angel's wing. Liza will love it."

Maggie rang up my soap, and my hands trembled as I pulled out a twenty-dollar bill. She grabbed my hand in hers. Her grasp forced me to gaze into her eyes. "How is Liza?"

"Tired, but she's looking forward to the trip." I couldn't admit to Maggie how truly delicate Liza was at this moment. When I reached for the soap, my wallet slipped from my hand and fell to the floor. Bending down to retrieve it, I hit my head on the edge of the wooden counter, stumbled backwards into a small display of homemade teas, and several stainless steel tea diffusers clattered onto the hardwood floor.

Maggie and Tag came over and helped me stack everything back in place. She placed a box of tea in my hand. "Take this ginger-peach tea as a gift from me. Have a cup with Liza and talk to her. It'll make you both feel better."

I held the tea in my hands and inhaled the comforting scent. Tag placed his hand on my shoulder. "You need to come over to the studio with me. Liza's sculpture is ready."

"Sculpture?" This ought to be interesting. When had she ordered a work of art and how much was it going to cost me?

I followed Tag inside his art studio. I liked him. Here he was, a former Atlanta Falcon, but in middle age had rediscovered a talent for sculpture. He even expressed his creativity with a blue streak in his hair. I wonder what Liza would say if I came home with purple highlights in my curls.

He walked into a back room and returned with a blue velvet covered lump. Placing it on the counter, he smiled at me. I hoped it wasn't some New Age-fangly piece of modern art.

"What is it?"

Like a magician upon a stage conjuring his beautiful assistant from thin air, he removed the velvet hood. Numb, I could only stare at the bronze statue of a young woman riding the back of a dolphin. I touched the delicate features of the girl, and I recognized her.

"Normally, I don't do this type of work, but Liza brought me a photo of her when she was younger and asked. I hope you like it," said Tag.

I nodded. Finally, words came to me. "You've captured her spirit. You've captured the essence of my Liza."

I drove to the desolate parking lot of my surveying business and surveyed my life. Had I dedicated too much time to my business and not enough time to the kids and Liza? Was my life going to be like this asphalt lot without her? Empty?

The setting sun turned the clouds a golden-pink color as I sat there. I listened to the ticking of the clock hanging over the stove in the galley of the Winnebago. I kicked myself for all the moments I'd lost, was even now losing. I picked up *The Fool's Guide to Sewing a Patchwork Quilt,* opened it to page one, then quickly flipped the pages to the back of the book.

My marriage to Liza had started on page one, and we were supposed to stay together until the end. Never did I dream that I'd read the last chapter by myself. A tear spattered on the page, but it didn't smear the ink as I read through "Chapter One: The Basics of Gathering the Cloth for Your Quilt."

When I walked into the living room, Liza slowly raised herself from the sofa. She had one of her mother's quilts draped over her legs; she wore a new kerchief made from the dolphin printed material.

"Look what Mickey made for me."

"He did a great job. You look beautiful. Hey, I saw Tag while I was at Moonheart's."

She smiled.

I sat down beside her and handed her the book. "I can't do this quilt or anything else by myself, Liza. I can't make it without my wife or my best friend. I can't imagine life without you."

She patted my hand reassuringly. "I never intended for you to go through this by yourself. Making the quilts will help you, it'll help me, and it'll help the kids. It'll keep us together when I'm gone. When you need a hug from me, all you'll have to do is wrap up in the quilt, and touch the patches. You'll remember all the good times we had as a family and all the love we shared. And when you think you can't go on, just look at the statue and remember that our souls are threaded together even when one of us has gone ahead."

I gently held her in my arms, never wanting to let her go, I wanted to stitch our souls together so that she wouldn't leave me.

In our embrace, I could feel the truth in her bones, so delicate, so fragile. I would be strong for her and not let her hear my heart break. Tilting her face toward mine, I kissed her gently on the lips. "Liza, Tag's statue is beautiful." I ran my finger down her cheek. "You're beautiful. When did you commission Tag to do it?"

"The same day you ordered that damn Winnebago."

I laughed, glad that I still could. "Maggie suggested some new soap, and gave us a box of her special ginger-peach tea. I'll run out and get them and the statue. Where do you want me to put it?"

"Leave the statue in the camper where it belongs. It will go with you to the Grand Canyon. Send Mickey out for the tea and soap. You need to go on up to the attic."

I pulled down the rickety attic ladder. The brackets holding it weren't very stable; it was always a challenge every Christmas when I had to climb up for the box of ornaments. This time it didn't buck or sway with me. I found Anna's box, and brought it down. Then came Mickey's. I climbed up once more, and in a far corner surrounded by cast off Halloween costumes was Kelly's container. It was lighter than the others. Dust coated the lid.

When I had all the boxes gathered in the living room around Liza, she looked up at me. "I need to rest. We'll start in the morning." As I carried her upstairs to our bedroom, she whispered to me, "Hold me tight, Disney. Hold me tight tonight, and don't let go."

I held my wife in my arms late into the night, listening to her rattled breathing. With each inhalation, I savored her life. With each exhalation, I feared it was her last. I promised myself that I wouldn't sleep to make up for the time I lost this afternoon. I would memorize every last detail of her face from the elegant arch of her eyebrows to the small scar underneath her chin.

When a warm kiss touched my lips; I opened my eyes to Liza smiling down at me.

"Did you sleep well?" she asked.

After a breakfast of Krispy Kreme doughnuts and ginger-peach tea, we began our journey of memories with Anna's box. We laughed as we pulled out small dresses remembering what a tomboy our little girl had been. We discovered Easter dresses, tee shirts, and the homecoming gown of our oldest daughter.

I reverently opened Kelly's box. Liza leaned over and lifted out the small pink Carter nightgowns. She uncovered a pink crocheted baby blanket and held it against her cheek. I wrapped my arms around my wife, just like the day she held our little baby in her arms when we learned Kelly had a congenital heart disease. Our little girl died on the operating table at three months. I think that's when I started working more and more to fill up the loss I felt at Kelly's death.

For a few moments, as I closed my eyes, I envisioned a younger version of my wife holding a baby wrapped in a pink crocheted blanket. I watched as she smoothed the fuzzy down of the baby's head. Would Liza rock Kelly in heaven?

Then we came to Mickey's box. Our son had been a robust nine-pound baby, and the boy had the lungs to match his vitality. He'd kept us awake at night for several months with his howls. Liza laughed as she shook out the Oshkosh overalls. We laughed at the memory of our son's first overnight camp at Zoo Atlanta when we held up his "I'm a Wild Thing" tee shirt. He'd taken a flashlight and a net just in case the snakes got loose. Finally, we smiled as we both remembered the day he'd worn his Wheel-in' On the Concrete shirt and won first place in an X-games competition.

As I started cutting six and a half-inch by six and a half-inch squares from several of

Anna's Easter dresses, the phone rang, and I answered it.

"Hey, Dad, how's Mom?"

What did I tell my daughter? I guess I could no longer deny reality. I looked over at Liza, who had fallen asleep. I could see the blue veins underneath her translucent skin as the late morning sun shone through the bay window. Admitting to Anna she might want to come home early so she could see her mother made me feel like I was losing grip on life. And I was. I was losing my life with Liza.

"She's hanging in there. But you need to come home. As soon as possible."

"Oh no. Daddy. Please no."

"I'm sorry. Your Mom and I are making the quilts from the keepers."

My daughter sobbed over the phone.

"Do you want me to come and get you, sweetie?" I asked her.

"No. Stay with Mom. I can have a friend bring me home. I have someone I want you to meet."

"Be careful, Anna."

"Bye, Daddy. Love you."

Mickey came into the living room, and his eyes widened at the explosion of baby clothes, dresses, and tee shirts. His eyes wandered over to his mother.

"You did a good job on that scarf, son. She's real happy with it."

"Thanks. Guess I'd better move the sewing machine in here. That way Mom can tell us how she wants things."

Liza woke up. "What's going on?"

"Mickey thought you might like to critique our handiwork. He's not going to school tomorrow."

She smiled as she tried to sit up.

With reality-glazed eyes, I saw how my denial had prevented me seeing the progression of the leukemia. How could I have not seen the ravages of the cancer on her body? Even now in the past twenty-four hours of my enlightenment, more and more of my Liza was slipping. "Can I get you anything?" I asked.

"Yeah, I'd like a piece of Alice Huntington's coconut cake."

As I mixed the coconut into the batter, the whir of the sewing machine told me that Mickey was sewing the first two strips of the quilt.

The sweet smell of coconut cake permeated the house. I cut more pieces of cloth from the kid's clothes. Memories flooded my mind of when Liza and I had taken trips up to the mountains with no kids. Then suddenly I had an idea.

I wanted to add something to the quilt, something that symbolized our marriage, something that represented our love among the patches of memories. I ran upstairs.

Once I reached my bedroom closet, I touched the soft cotton of my "red lumberjack of the woods" shirt, as she called it. I smiled. It always turned her on in the winter when I wore it to bring in the first load of firewood. I had looked forward to our trip to the Grand Canyon; I had intended to pack lots of flannel shirts including that one and pay the kids to go for long walks.

Downstairs, I cut three patches from my "red lumberjack of the woods" shirt for the quilt. If I couldn't have my Liza snuggled beside me in years to come, then at least I could touch the red flannel square on cold winter nights.

I heard a car in the driveway as I finished icing the cake and began to drop coconut onto the top.

"Dad. Mom," Anna called as she ran in the doorway.

She hugged me.

"Mom's in the living room."

Dropping her purse on the kitchen floor, she ran down the hall. A young man with shaggy brown hair, a small gold hoop in his earlobe, blue flannel shirt, clean jeans and hiking boots walked into the kitchen with Anna's luggage.

He stood there holding her bags and looking confused. At least he didn't have a pierced nose.

"Just put those on the floor. I'll take them upstairs." I held out my hand to shake his.

Normally, I liked to scare the boys that Anna brought home. This boy's handshake felt different. He had a strong, firm grip. I wanted to put him at ease. I think Anna had a 'keeper.' "Hi. I'm Disney Halbeck."

"Nice to meet you, sir. Tim Huntington."

"You from up North?"

"Yes, sir. Boston."

I looked at the coconut cake and back at him. "You wouldn't happen to be related to Alice Huntington from Nantucket?"

His eyes widened. "No sir, not as far as I know."

I smiled. "Son, have you ever made coconut cake?"

"Yes, sir. My mother taught me how to cook."

"Sounds like your mama is a smart woman."

Tim and I served coconut cake to everyone in the den. "Good cake, Dad," said Mickey.

"I'm proud of you, honey. You can do it, you know," said Liza as she looked at me, her dark green eyes bright.

"Do what, Mom?" asked Anna.

Lisa's gaze held mine. "Your father can bake a coconut cake, he can make a quilt, and he can do a lot of things he thought he couldn't."

Later that afternoon, everyone cut patches from the clothes. We sewed strips of patches together, and soon the patches and strips became quilt tops. We laughed at old memories, entertaining Tim with stories from our lives. We would hold up a shirt and ask, "Do you remember?"

We left the last patch empty on the first quilt. I stared at the blue dolphin material not wanting to use it. When we added the pieces of Kelly's clothes to the quilt strips, Anna and Mickey were quiet. They were remembering a sibling that once was and what might have been.

Would I do that when I wore a flannel shirt? Would I remember what was and what might have been in the years to come?

We worked late into the night and ate coconut cake during breaks. Working on the quilts bound our family together, more tightly. Each piece of material became a part of us, a part of our family story, and each quilt would be Liza's legacy of love to her children, to her future grandchildren, and to me.

Hours later Liza coughed, and I held her as Mickey sewed the last strip onto the last quilt. Anna cut the last three patches from the dolphin material. We now had three quilt tops in our living room: one for Anna, one for Mickey, one for Kelly. I took Kelly's quilt and wrapped my beloved wife in it. She coughed, once more, then opened her eyes, and gave me a slight smile. "Love you," she whispered to me for the last time.

Liza Halbeck died in my arms surrounded by her children just before the first rays of the morning sun kissed the sky.

Water slapped against the boat. Dolphins played around the bow. Mickey cried as he gently let the wind carry his mother's ashes into the ocean. Anna watched hers float into the water. In the distance, a mother dolphin and her baby leaped high into the air, splashed down, and dove under the water. I tipped my portion into the water and thought of the bronze statue and the sylph-like girl who used to be my wife. "Love you. Take care of our little Kelly."

Anna, Mickey and I dipped our dolphin printed patchwork squares in the salt water. When we got back to the beach, we laid each square on the sand to soak up the sun. I watched the waves ebb and flow. I noticed the crabs running in and out of their holes.

At the campsite, I hooked up the sewing machine inside the Winnebago, and with the brass statue beside me, I sewed a dolphin patch onto each quilt top. Liza would've wanted me to end it this way.

The next morning, as I sat on the beach and watched a distant pod of dolphins frolicking in the waves, Mickey and Anna sat down beside me with their keeper quilts draped around their shoulders to keep away the chilly air. I opened my copy of *The Fool's Guide to Sewing a Patchwork Quilt* to the end, and to my surprise my map of the United States fell out. Liza.

I held it up. "Hey kids, want to go to the Grand Canyon?"

WHEN THE DRUGSTORE WAS A COMMUNITY GATHERING PLACE

Across from the depot in our small town was my father's pharmacy. There were high tinned-tiled ceilings and old oiled wood floors, a long marbled-topped soda fountain that served the best of Biltmore Dairy's local ice cream.

In the high-backed oak booths boys played hooky, reading comic books and drinking fresh squeezed limeades, ducking out of sight if a parent appeared. My dad believes as many boys learned the fundamentals of reading from those secret sessions with the Green Hornet as they did their reading primers from the grammar school a few miles away.

Tucked in the back of the store behind shelves of categorically organized pharmaceuticals was a nook with a chair in it where a local minister's wife could enjoy a relaxing cigarette away from all prying eyes and still hear all the conversations from the tables at the back. On any given day, the surveyors from a highway project that is now Interstate 40 or a world famous evangelist might sit and enjoy a milkshake. Town politics were always part of the subject matter as were all the day-to-day happenings that are the heartbeats of every small town.

No one who ever needed medicine was refused, even if the payment came in the form of fresh rainbow trout, a bag of apples or tomatoes, or corn on the cob. Sometimes it was understood that a payment might never be a possibility.

The cough syrup compounded in the back rivaled the potency of the finest brandy, was always cherry flavored and worked better than any remedy still ever marketed. There were bottles with skulls and crossbones on them, but to my knowledge no one ever combined the chemicals in a way that would merit such a warning. I do know that the smelly fish emulsion fertilizer one of the chemical salesmen sold my parents made the perennial beds around our house rival anything in *Southern Living* . . . and it smelled to the heavens when it rained that summer.

Best of all are the memories of a wizened little old man, let's call him Mr. Jones, who used to sit on the bench at the entrance of the store, happily giving tourists bad directions if they didn't stop for respite in the town. I can still hear him saying, "You can't even get there from here. Matter of fact you can't give somethin' to someone you ain't got . . . and you can't come back from someplace you ain't never been. And that's all the advice I can give you, visitor."

— Susan Alvis, *The Tie That Binds*

Air Raid, Southern Style

BY MIKE ROBERTS

"Yes, sir. I'm a real Southern boy. I got a red neck, white socks, and Blue Ribbon beer."

— Billy Carter

If Southerners are obsessed with the Civil War and its relics, perhaps it's because we can't escape them. We are marked from birth as unique natives of the only region to have fought to leave the union. We are reared on the lore of a struggle made more glorious by comparison to the hardships of the peace that followed. We read the countless battlefield markers that point the way back a century and a half. All this nurtures within us a stubborn, poignant pride about what was, what is and who we are. It's a wild violet in our culture: a flower to some, a weed to others, with runners that burrow deep in our psyche and surface to bloom without warning.

I first learned about the war and wild

260

violets from my great-grandfather, Marse Pop. He was a tall, thin man with fine white hair and a presence that made him seem distinguished whether he was in his Sunday-go-to-meeting suit or his gardening overalls.

"Marse Pop" was, of course, a nickname. The family borrowed it from the two young sons of the woman who began keeping house for him after his first wife died in childbirth, fifty years ago. The boys couldn't pronounce "Mister Perkerson" but they could say "Marse Pop."

Now, "marse" isn't a form of "mister," but of "master," and was once used by Southern whites and blacks alike. During the war and for years afterward, many Southerners referred to Gen. Robert E. Lee as "Marse Robert" or just "Marse." I imagine that Marse Pop was flattered to have something in common with the general. I hoped the general, looking down from his cloud in heaven, was equally flattered to have something in common with a man like Marse Pop.

Either out of love or out of pity that Daddy died when I was two, Marse Pop always treated me like I hung the moon. When I arrived for my summer vacation in what Mamma called "L.A." (Lower Alabama), Marse Pop always seemed as glad to see me as I was to see him.

He spoiled me all right, but not with the toys and things he called "gewgaws" the way a teetotaler would refer to demon drink. Rather, he showered me with something better — his attention. He made me feel ten feet tall just by talking to me. When I helped him with his gardening, he'd tell me the different plants' names and explain what each plant needed to grow well.

Part of his gardening ritual was pulling out some flowers with purple petals.

"How come you're doing that, Marse Pop?"

"Because these are wild violets, and if I don't pull them up from where I don't want them, they'll flat take over. I don't want them to grow anywhere but inside those tin borders I put over yonder."

"So why not get rid of all of them?"

"I like their color, and they grow real well without me having to do much to them. They have their place in my garden, and other flowers have their place. Everything in its place — that's the way the world's meant to be."

What I liked best, though, were his stories. After he finished in the garden, he'd sit on Grandma and Grandpa's porch swing with me and spin the tales he'd learned from his grandfather, who'd fought in Gen. Long-street's corps against the bully Yankees. With Marse Pop's words in my head, I day-dreamed of being a Confederate soldier charging forward at Chickamauga or hold-ing off Yankee assaults in the trenches at Petersburg.

By the time I was six, I was quite the little Rebel. I had a store-bought Confederate cap and a plastic cavalry saber with scabbard. A Confederate uniform wasn't to be had, however, so Grandma bought a pair of pants and a shirt my size and dyed them gray. Confederate footwear was less of a bother. Once I found out that many Southern soldiers had to go barefoot, I did, too, sum-mer or winter, only donning shoes when forced to by church, school or frost. And because the north had the gall to win the war, I scrawled, "I hate the North" in a Civil War history book Grandma bought me. I didn't care about or understand the politics of the war, I cared about the drama.

The height of my personal Confederacy came one August afternoon when the air lay so hot and humid that just breathing was sweaty work. Grandma came on the front porch fanning her bodice to move air through her dress, and decreed we had to make ice cream even though we'd just made it two days before. Once the fixings were ready, Grandpa, Grandma, Marse Pop, two cousins who lived down the road and I circled on the porch to crank the handle on the ice-cream freezer. My knees bounced with anticipation, but not just because I wanted to eat. I had a surprise for everybody.

When it came my turn to crank, Marse Pop slid the freezer to me. I wrapped my legs around its rough wooden tub, shivered as melt water from the freezer's drain hole sluiced over my feet and called, "Hey, y'all. Listen to this!" I took a deep breath and let out my interpretation of a Rebel Yell.

Marse Pop didn't seem to mind that I more screeched than yelled. He clapped me on the shoulder and said, "That's my boy." If my britches hadn't been loose already, I'd have split them as I swelled with pride. I was on top of the world.

Too soon, I fell off it. Marse Pop died when I was seven, followed by Grandpa. Our family's land in "L.A." was sold, Grandma moved to Atlanta to live with us, and Mamma remarried. Marse Pop's ice-cream freezer rotted and rusted away. Mamma replaced it with a modern freezer with a plastic tub instead of a wooden one and an electric motor instead of a handle.

No group had to gather to take turns crank-
ing it, but what the new freezer made was
more ice soup than ice cream.

Time brought other changes. My new
father's dog chewed up my Confederate
cap, my plastic saber broke and the book
I'd scrawled in gathered dust on my shelf. I
no longer played Rebel soldier, either.
Inspired by my new uncle, an Air Force
pilot, I built and flew model airplanes.
Yankee kids moved into our neighborhood
and teased me about my bare feet and my
Alabama childhood. To save face, I wore
smothering shoes even in summer, as they
did, and confined L.A. to a locked closet in
my memory.

By age nineteen, I was smart and sophisti-
cated the way all teenagers think they are.
And after years of northern propaganda
from TV, movies and school that alleged
how stupid the South was, I was ashamed
of my Southern roots. Then I met Cale
"Buddy" Adams, a tugboat of a man used
to pushing people around to his way of
thinking or out of his way altogether.
Though he knew nothing and cared less
about gardening, he still managed to teach
me something else about blooming.

We met because of a major obsession in
my life, Jo Beth. She was Buddy's youngest

daughter and the most interesting girl at the Big Bargain discount store where I worked the summer before my sophomore year in college. She was cute, smart, patient, well-mannered and cheerful. Being around her was like being wrapped in a warm blanket on a cold night.

Being around her daddy, however, was like getting a root canal without anesthesia. I learned that when I came to his house to take Jo Beth out for our first date. She wasn't ready yet, so he invited me to sit in the living room to wait and talk.

Within five minutes, it was plain he and I were from different species. After so many years in and around Atlanta, I considered myself a city kid. He had grown up on a farm in South Georgia and hated anything to do with a city, especially Atlanta. I was scrawny. He had a torso like a barrel and arms as big around as my thighs. I'd made fun of the kids who played soldier in the junior ROTC unit at my old high school. He'd been a master sergeant in the army, overseeing the maintenance of attack helicopters. He drove a new Chevy pickup with an American flag on the antenna, a Rebel battle flag in the rear window, and bumper stickers that proclaimed him a "Civil War Re-enactor" and "Southern and Proud of it." I drove a fourth-hand Toyota hatchback with a previous owner's Dead Head sticker holding together part of a rusted fender.

But if I'd already underwhelmed him, I earned his stamp of rejection when he asked me what I was doing with my life.

"I'm about to start my second year in college," I replied.

"Really." His fingers clenched the armrests of his rocking chair.

"Yeah, and I'm looking forward to it. My freshman year was so fantastic."

"I'll bet." He rocked faster.

"I mean, college is helping me understand the world better, a lot better than most people do."

"Better than most people, huh?" Veins bulged in his forehead.

"It's sad, but most people are just dumb, I hate to say it. In college, I get to be around so many brilliant people."

He ejected from his rocking chair, thumped to the foot of the hallway stairs and shouted, "Get the lead out, Jo Beth! You're keeping college boy waiting."

In seconds, I heard soft, rapid footfalls. I reached the hallway in time to see Jo Beth hustle down the stairs, a hair brush in one hand, loafers in the other. She gave him a wide berth, grabbed my hand and pulled me toward the front door.

" 'Bye, Daddy," she called over her shoulder, prodded me through the doorway and shut the door behind her without breaking stride. Still barefoot, she led me along the decorative-gravel walkway to my car, gestured me into it and climbed in the passenger side. Once we were out of the driveway and on the road, she puffed out a breath and sagged in the seat. "What happened in there with you and Daddy?" She swiped at her hair with her brush.

"I was just talking to him."

"What about?"

"About what all I liked about being in college."

She dusted off one foot and jammed it into a loafer. "For how long were you telling him that?"

"A couple of minutes, maybe."

"That was about a minute and a half too long." She brushed the other foot and worked it into the remaining loafer. "I guess he figured you were bragging. He hates that. He doesn't much like college or college students, either, but he knows I'm going to college next year so he's trying to get used to the idea."

My head filled with images of all the bad movies I'd seen with stereotypical Southern pot-bellied rednecks toting shotguns and chasing their daughters' boyfriends. "Don't guess I made a friend of him."

"Don't guess you did."

I slowed the car. "Should I just take you home? I mean, he's not going to want to see me coming around anymore."

"Well, he wasn't that mad. I mean, if he was, he'd have just thrown you out the door or something. You just got off on the wrong foot with him, that's all." She cocked her head, cut her eyes at me in a way that made them look even bigger and greener, and smiled. If I hadn't still been so rattled by my encounter with her daddy, I'd have probably blushed. As it was, I still felt quivery inside even as I realized she was lying through her pretty, kissable lips.

"But if he wasn't that mad, why'd you go so far around him and drag me out the door the way you did?"

"Uh — he smelled bad. You know, he doesn't always use deodorant. It's really disgusting sometimes. I came down and he like to have knocked me out with his armpit stink. Didn't you smell it?"

I humored her and she dropped the subject. Our supper at the Tenderloin Steak House was tasty, but the movie we went to was so bad we walked out half through it.

We left the theater and drove two miles to the little airport managed by my uncle, who'd retired from the Air Force.

The sun was long since down but the airport was well-lit by blue marker lights on the nearby taxiway, a full moon overhead and white office lights shining through my uncle's window. Mamma had said he was working on a presentation to convince Rufus Purcell and the other county commissioners not to sell the airport land to a strip-mall developer.

When I shut off the car's engine, Jo Beth looked at me and said, "Are you taking me parking on the first date?"

Visions of her daddy and his shotgun made me turn the engine right back on. "Ah, yes. I mean, no. I'll take you home right now."

"No, silly." She giggled. "You don't have to do that. I was just funning you." I shut the car off again and we walked around the small propeller planes. I told her their makes and models, and explained a little about how planes flew. She said she liked how the front of one looked like a smiley face. As I walked around the smiley-face airplane, she called, "Wait a minute."

When I turned around, she was barefoot on the reflective stripe that marked the center of an airplane's empty tie-down space. "They sure used a lot of paint on this. It stands up a mile from the pavement." She walked the length of the stripe, turned in place on one foot like a ballerina and walked back on tiptoes with her eyes closed. "You ought to kick your shoes off and try this."

"No — no thanks. Say, where did you learn to turn like that? Are you a dancer?"

"I've studied dance since I was little."

"Oh, I wouldn't have thought you. . . ." I caught myself before I said I was surprised that a south Georgia farm girl would study dance. I'd already put my foot in my big mouth with her daddy. I didn't want to repeat that mistake with Jo Beth.

"Wouldn't have thought what?" Her eyes opened and bored into me. My mouth went dry.

"I — I wouldn't have been able to do anything like dance. I'm not very coordinated."

"Neither am I all the time. Hold your hand out and help me keep my balance." I did as she asked, but she took two steps and stumbled against me. "Wow, thanks for catching me." She smiled.

I knew she expected me to kiss her, but I couldn't put her daddy out of my mind. I mumbled, "You're welcome."

She looked at the night sky and the planes around us. "This is a nice place. You like it here?" I nodded. "You sure know a lot about airplanes. So how come you're majoring in regular engineering instead of airplanes?"

"There's a lot of demand for it and the money's good."

"Oh."

Regardless of what she thought of my college major, Jo Beth liked me enough to continue seeing me. Her daddy was another matter, though. For whatever reason, probably fear he'd alienate Jo Beth, he never waged a frontal assault on me. Oh no. He chose guerilla war.

For example, since he'd started calling me "college boy" he kept at it. He'd say, "Your mamma ain't feeding you good enough, college boy. You need to bulk up so the girls will quit laughing at you behind your back." Or, "Say, college boy, we need to spend some quality time together. How about if me and you go on an overnight snipe hunt?"

At times, he would go beyond insulting me to making me second-guess myself. "Hey, college boy, you'll have to forget half of what those egg-headed turkeys tell you in that place before you'll go anywhere in business. You do know that, don't you?"

But it was when he abandoned sarcasm altogether that he hit me hardest. Once, while he was loading his truck to attend a bivouac for re-enactors, I said, "Isn't this all kind of silly — a bunch of old men going off to play soldier. You're not shooting real bullets, so what's the point? And what about that bumper sticker that says you're proud of the South? What's it done to make you proud of it?"

When he slammed the truck's rear gate, I knew my words had hit home. I was glad for about a second. Then I was worried he'd hit me home. But he just stared at me over one shoulder and said, "College boy, I don't see the point of arguing with you about my being a re-enactor. Some guys climb mountains. Me and my friends re-enact. But you want to know what the South has done to make me proud of it? How could I not be proud of it? Ain't being ashamed of the place that bore and bred you like being ashamed of your own mother?" Then he drove away.

Watching his dust settle in the yard, I felt as small and out of place as a liquor salesman at a Southern Baptist tent revival. I left and drove to the airport. There, I walked around the perimeter fence for about an hour, talking to myself, arguing this point and that about what he'd said. I decided that maybe, maybe he was right in his own way. I also decided that our relationship was destined to stay icy. I wish I could have foreseen what would happen to test me on both decisions. Then again, maybe it's just as well I couldn't.

At the end of my sophomore year, I changed my major from engineering to aviation management. Also, with my uncle's help and some of the money Marse Pop willed me, I bought a small airplane. The Piper J-3 Cub had been restored to its original 1946 configuration, and was complete with Cub Yellow paint and the drawing of a bear cub on the rudder.

When I told Buddy about these transactions, he arched his eyebrows and grunted. "Nice plane, the Cub. I flew in one of those once. Jo Beth says you know a lot about planes."

Another change was my engagement to Jo Beth. It turned out to be one of the longest engagements in history, because Jo Beth and I didn't marry until we were both out of college. By then, I'd paid off the bank loan for the Cub, earned my commercial pilot's license and was working full time at the airport as assistant manager. My uncle, worn out from years of on-again, off-again fights with the commissioners, was glad for the help. I was glad for the work. My uncle and I shared everything from cleaning toilets to giving flying lessons. Jo Beth taught dance four evenings a week. During the day, she pumped gas at the airport to make extra money while we struggled to save enough for her to open her own dance school.

Buddy was struggling, too, and it had nothing to do with me. The details came out one Sunday afternoon when Jo Beth and I ate Sunday dinner with her parents.

Through the meal, Buddy was his usual gruff, outspoken self. Afterward, we went out on the back deck to cut and eat the watermelon Jo Beth's mother had refrigerated. Just then the phone rang, and Buddy disappeared into a bedroom to take the call. He was gone so long my mother-in-law left to check on him. He re-appeared first, looking preoccupied. She appeared seconds later, and asked Jo Beth to step inside to help put away the dinner dishes.

I'd been around the family long enough to know this was code for "Something's up and I need to talk to you about it, Jo Beth." I knew that if Jo Beth's mother had wanted me to know what "it" was, she'd have told me. I also knew Jo Beth would tell me later.

Buddy and I ate in silence.

When Jo Beth came out, she took my hand and said, "I need to walk off my dinner. Let's you and me go to the creek and look for crawfish." The creek was at the back of her parents' property, hidden at the bottom of a shallow but steep-sided draw. We'd often gone there to make out when we were dating — yeah, I finally got up the nerve to kiss her — but it was also a good talking spot.

Once there, Jo Beth shucked off her shoes and waded into the gurgling water. "Come on, slow poke. Get your shoes off and walk upstream with me." Still I hesitated. "Look, do you want to know what's bothering Daddy or not?" Moments later, we were side by side holding hands to keep our balance in the swift current and ankle-deep mud.

"That phone call," she began, "was from one of Daddy's re-enactor friends. You heard about how some computer company from Massachusetts might build a new plant near here?"

"The company's name is Right Tech, I think. Why would that make your daddy upset?"

"Well, the place they're thinking of building is the only good piece of land around here for the re-enactors to do what they do."

"So?"

"And the company would bring its own people down to run it. They wouldn't be hiring anybody from here. But the worst of it is the county commissioners want to let the company have the land tax-free for two years. That's what Daddy's friend called to tell him just now."

"Tax free? Not for the rest of us. We'll be paying extra to make up the difference, and we won't get anything in return."

"Daddy's so mad he's going to the next county commission meeting to try to change those meat-heads' minds."

Not only did he not change their minds, he managed to get himself thrown out of the meeting. Outside the commission chambers, a friend whose wife was a caterer told him more unpleasant news. Chairman Purcell had arranged to flatter a group of Right Tech executives and local big shots with a seafood dinner followed by a round of golf. The event would be held the next Saturday at the county's upscale country club, where only the wealthy were admitted.

As I guessed, that Saturday was a slow day at the airport. Right Tech, at our commissioners' insistence, landed its corporate jet at Atlanta's airport instead of ours. We made no money selling jet fuel. Worse, many of the local pilots who rent our airplanes were no doubt hobnobbing with Purcell and Right Tech instead of flying. Things were so quiet that I was even pleased to see Buddy come through the office door.

As usual, he dispensed with the pleasantries most people found necessary. "I need you to fly me over the country club in about twenty minutes."

I checked the wall clock. "That's when the commissioners will be kissing up to the Right Tech people on the golf course. Why go there?"

"I've got a little greeting I want to give them, you know, an air drop, low altitude."

"Drop what?" The Federal Aviation Administration is persnickety about the dropping of things from airplanes.

"Just a little patriotic display." He patted the duffel bag under his arm. I was about to ask to see what was in the bag when he added, "What's your usual rate?"

"For me and the airplane, a hundred an hour."

"I'll pay you three hundred." He put the bag on the counter and gave me three hundred dollars in fifties and twenties. I eyed the cash and tested the bag's weight. The object inside was light and soft, not likely to hurt anybody on the ground. I hoped. After storing the cash in the office safe, I walked Buddy to my Cub. It was the closest airplane to the office and had already been prepped for flight.

Now a Cub is about the most basic an airplane can be and still be an airplane. It has big wings to lift it, a small engine to pull it forward at a modest pace while making lots of noise, a small fuel tank to feed the engine, a tail to keep the airplane steady in flight and a fuselage to hold all the pieces together. Right behind the fuel tank is a cockpit with two seats. The passenger sits up front with the best view out the windshield and of the instrument panel right in front of him. To balance the weight of passenger, fuel and engine, the pilot sits in back where he must strain to see what few instruments the Cub has.

Once Buddy and I were strapped into our seats, I turned on the ignition switch located over my head on the left side of the cockpit, held the brakes and engaged the Armstrong starter by shouting "Contact!" My uncle, standing in front of the machine, swung the propeller. The engine spat once and roared to life. Five minutes later, the Cub wafted off the runway and I steered toward the country club.

Buddy had said he wanted us to be low for the air drop, but how low was low? The FAA says a pilot can't fly lower than a thousand feet over an open-air assembly of persons, or lower than five hundred feet over a sparsely populated area. Into which category would the feds put a golf course with golfers on it? Considering how much trouble my uncle and I had already had with government, I didn't want to risk going lower than a thousand.

Even the slow-going Cub ticked off the five miles to the country club in good time. I leaned to the right and opened the split door, raising the clear-plastic top half against the underside of the wing and lowering the opaque bottom half against the fuselage.

"We're almost there!" I yelled.

"What bear?" he yelled back.

We got that miscommunication straightened out as I spotted the country club. I could tell my passenger wasn't ready to drop anything yet, so I flew the Cub in a circle to give him more time. He fumbled with the duffel bag.

"Slower," I thought he said.

"Slower's not a good idea," I replied.

"No, lower. Lower!" Suddenly, my control stick jerked from my hands and the Cub pitched nose down enough to make me come off my seat despite my seat belt. Buddy had taken control and I had to get it back. Knowing too well how strong he was, I put both hands on the stick and yanked. Unfortunately, he'd let go already to fumble some more with the bag. With no resistance on the stick, I hauled the little Cub almost straight up. Cubs don't like that.

"What are you doing?" Buddy yelled from up front. I didn't answer him because I was too busy getting the nose down to a normal level before the Cub bit us by whipping into a fatal spin.

Our gyrations made us overshoot the country club. They'd also put us quite low, around four hundred feet. I knew I could have, should have, climbed back to a thousand feet. I also knew that would take another three minutes at the Cub's pace. Better to get the air drop over with and leave. I prayed no FAA hard-noses were down there with binoculars to see the Cub's registration numbers.

"This is it! Get ready to drop!"

In the front seat, Buddy thrashed around with the duffel bag and then settled down. I assumed he'd freed whatever it was he planned to drop. I relaxed and concentrated on flying the sluggish Cub.

As we passed over the country club's fence, I noticed that Buddy had pulled out a Confederate battle flag that was so large it took both his hands to control it. I thought, "Hmmm, that should get an interesting re-action from the Yankees," and went back to planning our escape from the area once we made the drop.

Then it happened. As Mr. Adams turned in the seat to drop the flag, the Cub hit turbulence that bounced the duffel bag over our heads. Mr. Adams grabbed at it and pulled it down. But since the bag's strap had snagged the Cub's ignition switch, pull-ing the bag also pulled the switch to "off."

The roar of the engine was replaced by the wind hissing by the open door and the clanking of the useless propeller wind mill-ing slowly in the breeze. I froze. I'd never had an engine fail in an airplane at any altitude, much less one so low that I could almost reach out and grab leaves off the trees. Regaining my senses, I pushed the control stick forward to keep flying speed and tried to find a place to land. We were already so low that switching the engine back on, assuming the turning prop could start it, would do no good. We would never clear the huge trees at the far end of the golf course.

"Hang on!" I screamed. I maneuvered around a clump of small dogwoods and aimed for a level patch of grass. But I was so nervous that I botched the landing, bounced high and touched down on a steep downhill slope that led to a pond. I pushed on the brakes, but the grass must have been wet from a morning watering because the Cub skidded into the pond and flipped upside down.

The water was only a couple of feet deep and we were in no danger of drowning, but we had to go from hanging upside down by our seat belts to standing upright. Buddy released his belt and splashed into what had been the top of the cockpit. He righted himself and clambered out.

Worried about the damage to the Cub and the fate of my pilot's license, I unbuckled while bracing against the cockpit roof, tucked my legs tight and did a sloppy backward roll to land on my knees. From the outside, I could hear voices, then the braying of laughter. I dragged my soaking self from the plane to see a gaggle of commissioners and strangers I assumed were from Right Tech standing on dry ground. The object of their amusement was Buddy. He'd made it out of the Cub, but without his pants. His face red as a baboon's butt, he groped around, no doubt trying to find his pants in the muddy water.

I felt torn for a moment. On the one hand, here was the man who'd embarrassed and belittled me now getting a taste of his own medicine. On the other hand, the people making fun of him were no friends of mine and they hadn't even asked if we were hurt.

Buddy found not his pants but the oversize Confederate flag and wrapped it around his sagging boxer shorts. Someone in the group of amused onlookers, said, "That's about all that stupid flag's fit for. When will these idiot Southerners get some sense?"

"We're hoping you can give us some, sir, when you build your plant here." That was Rufus Purcell's voice.

To hear Yankees making fun of the South and a Southerner agreeing with them was too much. Torn no longer, I knew what I had to do. I stripped off my shirt and gave it to Mr. Adams in exchange for the flag. I tucked it under one arm like a flabby football and sprinted toward the club house and its flag poles. I heard shouts of confusion and alarm from the merrymakers as I passed them, and when I looked back I saw a few were chasing me. I was younger and fitter than they were, but I was also weighed down by waterlogged clothes. I kicked out of my squishy sneakers and ran faster.

I had a cushion of about fifty yards when I reached the flag poles and stopped at the one that flew the country club's pennant. I had just enough time to haul it down and run up the Confederate flag before Purcell and a sheriff's deputy reached me. Deciding not to argue with the law, I backed away and watched as the chairman brought the battle flag down and threw it on the ground. I saw bursts of light from a camera's flash, but I was too angry to notice who was taking pictures. The deputy was unhappy with me but even more so with Purcell, who was screaming at him.

"You've got to arrest those two! They deliberately disrupted an important event, like those streakers at big football games. That old one there, he was all but streaking, standing there in his underwear."

"Honest, deputy," I said. "We were just going to hold the flag out the door and let it wave when something happened to the engine and we had to make an emergency landing."

Buddy, who'd reached me by then, followed my lead. "That's right, deputy. That was a heck of a piloting job the boy did. I thought he did good not to crash and kill us both, the way that engine quit up there. You ought to give him a medal."

Since the deputy had no evidence we were lying and since no one on the ground was hurt, he charged me with misdemeanor destruction of property for the damage to the country club's grass. That done, he drove us back to the airport so Buddy could get his car and I could arrange to get the Cub from the pond.

While I waited for my clothes to dry, a newspaper reporter arrived and fired questions at me about what happened. As we talked, she said Purcell had invited her to the country club to get quotes and take photos of the Right Tech fete. Her sly smile told me her article might not be the one Purcell wanted.

It wasn't. In a prominent box on page one, the article was anything but happy-talk. Instead, it exposed for public review the sweet deal the commissioners offered Right Tech, the Saturday event's cost to the taxpayers and what happened when Buddy and I became accidental party crashers. The story even quoted what the onlookers said as Buddy stood pants-less in the water. The accompanying color photograph showed Purcell standing on the Confederate flag with his spiked golf shoes.

After that, Purcell did his best to avoid

cameras for the rest of his abbreviated term. Within two months, a coalition of enraged voters, Yankees and Southerners alike, killed the deal with Right Tech and booted Purcell and the rest of the commissioners out of office in a recall drive.

The day after the recall, Buddy came by the airport and handed me a check for two thousand dollars.

"What — what's this for? You shouldn't do this."

"I can do what I want with my own money. Think of that as seed for Jo Beth's dance school and for helping you with your expenses here. I wish it could be more. I owe you a lot, and I like to pay my debts. And for Pete's sake, quit calling me 'Buddy.' Call me 'Pa' or something. Now how about coming down to the lawn-care center and helping me tote fertilizer bags?"

I followed him out the door and stopped, remembering something.

"What are you standing there for?"

"Pa, you think that place sells wild violets? I think I'd like to plant a few."

A Baby Boomer Remembers The Early 1970s

- In the car, parents opened the little side window next to the big window even when it was cold, to let out their cigarette or cigar smoke.
- Very few people thought cigarettes were really bad for you.
- If you wanted air-conditioning in your car, you rolled down the window — with a hand crank.
- There were no leaf blowers. If you wanted leaves and pine straw off the roof, sidewalk, and driveway, you got out a broom and a rake.
- The Zulu Krewe tossed real coconuts during Mardi Gras in New Orleans.
- A martini was composed of gin, dry vermouth, and an olive. The only question was whether you wanted it shaken or stirred.
- Appliances came in Harvest Gold, Avocado, and Brown, and people thought those colors were pretty.
- Running around barefoot in the yard led inevitably to stepping on a toad or two.
- Kids played outside all the time.
- Spare tires were full-sized.
- Department store doors didn't open automatically.

- Cars didn't have seatbelts or special seats for kids.
- In the years between the black rotary dial phone and the touch tone cordless, people would buy long, curly extension lines so they could hold on to the receiver and move freely in their kitchens while chatting on the phone. More often than not, you'd get tangled up in the long cord.
- There was no choice involved in the hot lunch menu at school. You ate the butter beans and chicken-fried steak or you went hungry.
- Teachers used a blackboard and chalk, not a whiteboard and dry eraser.

— Maureen Hardegree, *The Good Son*

Miss Lila's Hat

BY BETTY CORDELL

"The biggest myth about Southern women is that we are frail types — fainting on our sofas . . . nobody where I grew up ever acted like that. We were about as fragile as coal trucks."

— Lee Smith, author

The very first time I saw Miss Lila, I knew she would change my life. I was fifteen and had taken a summer job as the receptionist for the *Evansville Daily Courier* while Mrs. Mavis Tompkins was out having her fourth baby. My daddy insisted that I "put myself to good use" that summer. That meant I couldn't spend all my time at the Donnellys' pool; I had to work. I was proud of myself for getting the receptionist job. I figured it would be a lot more fun than babysitting or helping my mother and Hattie shell butter-beans or field peas for canning. But I was bored. Not much happened in Evansville, Georgia. Even less in the summer. After three weeks on the job, staring at the phone and willing it to ring, I was ready for something else. Then, the door opened and Miss Lila walked in.

At two-thirty on Monday afternoon, June 17, 1957, I looked up and saw an enormous, navy, wide-brimmed hat perched at a jaunty angle on the head of a woman who looked like a movie star straight out of one of my *Modern Screen* magazines. She wore a fancy navy suit with a longish, straight skirt and a jacket that fit at the waist then flared out, just like the suits I'd envied on models in *Vogue.* A red silk rose was pinned to the lapel and matched the red roses encircling the crown of her hat as well as her long, red fingernails and her red, shiny lips. Perfect eyebrows arched over green eyes and rosy pink cheeks set in a perfect oval face with perfect high cheekbones. I couldn't guess her age. She appeared timeless.

She smiled at me and I realized that while I'd been gawking at her, I'd missed what she'd said.

"Ma'am?"

"Would you tell Mr. Woolsey that Miss Lila Cole is here to see him?" She spoke in cultured tones unlike any I was used to. I knew she just had to be from New York City or some other exciting, romantic place.

"Y-yes, ma'am," I stammered, my cheeks hot with embarrassment. I got up from my desk and went to Mr. Woolsey's door, then caught myself and turned back. I'd been so fascinated I hadn't even asked her to have a seat. She'd taken one, anyway, so I went ahead and knocked on Mr. Woolsey's door.

"Come in," he called out.

I stepped inside his office and told him a Miss Lila Cole wanted to see him.

"Who?" he asked in a loud voice. I felt a moment of panic. Was Mr. Woolsey, who could sometimes be a bit gruff, going to refuse to see my newly chosen idol?

"Mr. Woolsey," I said, "Miss Lila must have something real important to see you about. I mean, she's all dressed up and everything."

"Very well," he said, "Send her in." I breathed a sigh of relief and showed her into his office.

Try as I may, for the next twenty minutes, all I could hear from behind Mr. Woolsey's door was low murmurings. Even when the phone rang, all I did was pick it up and put it back down again so I wouldn't miss a chance to hear a single word.

When the door finally opened, Mr. Woolsey wore a really big smile. He stood back and motioned for Miss Lila to precede him through the doorway.

"Allow me to escort you to your office," he said, extending his hand to point the way. "I hope it will be to your liking."

I blinked in surprise. I'd never seen Mr. Woolsey act or talk like that before — I mean, like he was a butler or something.

"That's very kind of you, Mr. Woolsey," Miss Lila replied. "I'm sure whatever you provide will be quite satisfactory."

I loved the smooth, honeyed sound of her voice.

Mr. Woolsey led her down the hallway to the first office on the right.

My heart skipped a beat. My heroine was going to work at the newspaper office!

When I went home that day, I searched through my mother's closet. The only hat I found remotely similar to Miss Lila's had a brim about half the width of hers. I tried it on and angled it on the side of my head. It fell off. I pushed my wiry, dishwater blond curls up into the crown and tried it again, but the hat sort of floated on top of my bunched-up hair. How did she do it? Since we were going to be working together, maybe she'd tell me. My summer job had just gotten a whole lot better.

Miss Lila began as the society editor. Up until then, I didn't know Evansville had a society. She started out reporting on the various bridge groups that met in town. I don't know how she found out who met when, but she always managed to drop by. The next day her column told the whole town about the delicious desserts served and how pretty the home of the hostess was and what she was wearing. Funny thing is, those groups started out serving cheese and crackers and wearing plain old house dresses and, after only a few weeks, they were wearing their Sunday best and serving pineapple upside down cake. The ladies in town soon caught on to the fact that Miss Lila had a major sweet tooth and her most enthusiastic compliments were reserved for scrumptious desserts. Before long, hostesses were branching out into English trifles, chocolate soufflés, strawberry tortes, and crème brulee. Miss Lila had a way of inspiring people.

Within her first month, Miss Lila got a second column: Miss Lila's Literary Corner. In this column, she gave critiques of classics and books nobody had ever heard of which meant that our local lending library had to order them because of all the requests. Not long after that, Miss Lila yielded to the requests of several ladies in town and agreed to form a book club to discuss the books she critiqued. Occasionally, some men came along, too. Personally, I think they were more curious about Miss Lila than interested in the books.

Miss Lila had made my summer job so interesting that I was unwilling to give it up when school started back. Miss Mavis and I worked out an arrangement that suited us both: She would work every day until three o'clock, then I would come in after school and stay the rest of the day. This worked out great. Miss Mavis could spend more time with her children and I could still be around Miss Lila and keep up with what was going on in town.

At Miss Lila's urging, I tried to read all the books she critiqued and attend the book club meetings, unless I had a test at school the next day. Funny how so many of the books she critiqued that year were also on my reading list for school. So, my grades didn't suffer from me having a job. In fact, they improved. And every time I reported a grade of "A" to Miss Lila, she'd say, "Bravo, Caroline. I knew you could do it."

After several months, Miss Lila added still another column to her list, Couture Corner, in which she described the latest fashions in New York and Paris and sometimes included her own sketches. My mother and her friends rushed to the two really good seamstresses in town, Mrs. Richards and Mrs. Walker, to get dresses made to look as much like Miss Lila's sketches as possible.

Between my mother and Mrs. McCall, our local telephone operator, I kept on top of what people were saying in town. I was flattered when Mrs. McCall began checking with me to find out what interesting things Miss Lila was going to have in her columns. After I'd satisfied her curiosity, she'd tell me what she'd heard people talking about. Most of the phones in Evansville were on party lines, so none of us could help overhearing a little of this and a little of that whenever we picked up the phone and found the line occupied. My girlfriends and I sometimes entertained ourselves at spend-the-night parties by listening in to a lot more on a party line than we should have.

With the launch of Cuisine for Company, Miss Lila's columns comprised a full page of the *Evansville Daily Courier.* Mr. Woolsey boasted that his readership had never been so high. The consensus in town — I'm not sure who coined the phrase — was that Miss Lila was a Renaissance woman. She seemed to know something about everything — food, clothes, books, music. The only thing she didn't volunteer information about was herself. Once, when I asked her where she was from, she replied, "Well, my dear Caroline, a Miss Lila Cole doesn't originate in only one place. The entire, fascinating world is my pied-à-terre." I wasn't sure what she meant by that, but thought maybe it meant she'd traveled a lot.

Whatever the occasion, Miss Lila was never without a hat. She reminded me of Miss Hedda Hopper, the renowned Hollywood gossip columnist known for her hats. But to me, Miss Lila was even more glamorous than Miss Hopper. Miss Lila looked like she belonged in a fashion magazine or in the movies. I was enchanted by everything about her. I even kept a list of the hats she wore and figured she had at least twenty.

Whether reporting a wedding reception or a pancake supper, Miss Lila would sweep into a gathering, her wheel-sized headwear bouncing. At times, I held my breath, expecting to see the hat go cart-wheeling across the room at any moment. At the Evansville Fourth of July picnic I stared in awe when, in spite of a sudden breeze that sent baseball caps and sun hats flying, Miss Lila's umbrella topping managed to stay anchored in place. I guiltily began to relish the idea of one day seeing what her hair looked like underneath those headdresses.

I pitied the bride who sought to be the

center of attention on her special day! When Miss Lila arrived, and, to be certain, her presence was an honor earnestly sought, everyone's attention was attracted to her.

She was unlike anyone I'd ever known — unlike anyone anybody in the whole town had ever known. The idea of her doing ordinary things like removing her hat and changing into pajamas at night or relaxing in slacks or even putting on a bathing suit seemed impossible to imagine. Every day she appeared in her "costume" just as she had the day before.

I wanted to be just like her. No . . . that's not true. I wanted to be her. And I wasn't the only one. My girlfriends and I talked about her all the time. She was so refined, so cultured, so learned, so perfect in every way — clothes, nails, make-up. We all thought she was wonderful — well, all of us except one; but I didn't believe for a minute an ugly story Martha Jean Cranston told about Miss Lila, even though she said she'd heard it from her mother. Martha Jean's mother was just jealous and nobody believed it, anyway.

Miss Lila was very kind to me. "Now, Caroline Crabtree," she would say, "you're the daughter of the only dentist in Evansville and prominence brings with it responsibility. People look up to you as an example." Then, she would urge me to read more books and learn to say diphthongs, which she called the bane of the Southern speaker, and to set my sights on either a noble career or a noble husband. She didn't seem to think a woman could have both. I thought about that a lot. I'd never had anybody talk to me the way she did.

If Miss Lila had any flaws at all, I might mention that she was a tiny bit inclined to exaggerate. In fact, sometimes her columns seemed a little like one of the novels she critiqued for Miss Lila's Literary Corner. She loved a good story and if the one she was reporting seemed a tad boring, she spiced it up with a few "extras." From time to time, Mr. Woolsey was forced to smooth a few feathers when the "extras" in a story became more than the subjects of that story could tolerate.

My receptionist job included answering the phone, so I knew who got upset about what. After a brief conversation, Mr. Woolsey would tell me to ask Miss Lila if she would mind stopping by his office when she had the time. Of course, she found the time right away and after a few minutes behind the closed door, Mr. Woolsey, smiling and treating her like a member of royalty, would

299

show her out and escort her back down the hall to her office.

However, the last incident involving Miss Lila's exaggerations caused such an unexpected outcome, Evansville became famous. Our little town was featured in newspaper stories and on television everywhere in the state of Georgia — all because of Miss Lila.

Evansville's claim to fame began in April of 1958 with the news that Miss Mary Elizabeth Farrell, who'd just graduated from Wesleyan College in Macon, was going to be married. She was the daughter of Mr. Augustus Farrell, who owned the John Deere dealership, the cotton gin, and a silo. Everybody said he was the richest man in town. A tea was to be held in Miss Farrell's honor and Miss Lila was assigned to write the story. I wanted to go to that tea so bad I could taste it, but my mother said I was too young and I wasn't invited anyway.

From all I'd heard, Mrs. Martha Barton Farrell, Mary Elizabeth's mother, was absolutely determined that everything be perfect for her only daughter, having also raised four out-of-control sons. I could attest to that since Bart Farrell was in my class at school and I had heard plenty about his older brothers. In her eagerness to give her "baby girl" the perfect bridal experience,

Mrs. Farrell periodically came by the newspaper offices, carrying etiquette books or bridal magazines, to pepper Miss Lila with questions.

Mary Elizabeth's father was a different story. He was known to be a practical minded, salt-of-the-earth kind of man who, according to reports overheard by Mrs. McCall, objected constantly to all the fuss and expense that went along with his wife's perfect plans. He'd even been heard to call the whole process hogwash or perhaps something stronger that Mrs. McCall wouldn't repeat — at least not to me.

Mrs. Farrell became, in her own eyes, Miss Lila's best friend, and regularly sought her advice on the various teas, fetes, and showers given for her daughter. And if, through her amazing writing skills, Miss Lila's reports stretched the truth concerning the beauty of the honoree, the cooking skills of the hostess, the stylishness of the party goers, or the abundance and elegance of the gifts, Mrs. Farrell didn't object one bit — at least, not until the last tea.

The last tea for the town's most honored daughter was to be held at the home of Miss Bertie Mangum, a retired school teacher and a favorite of Miss Farrell. Miss Mangum was famous in Evansville for her but-

terscotch cream cake and almond macaroons. At school bake sales, Miss Mangum's
cake and macaroons were always the first to
be sold. Miss Lila was certain to eat her
share of the wonderful desserts and write a
wonderful review. I envied her ability to eat
as much as she wanted to without ever gaining an ounce.

I was at the receptionist's desk when Miss
Lila returned from Miss Mangum's tea
party. I was dying to know all about it, but,
as usual, she told me I'd have to read about
it in her column. That meant I'd either have
to wait until after school the next day to
read it or pry information out of my mother
who never tuned in to the details of an event
the way Miss Lila did.

At home that evening, my mother
skimmed the highlights of the party for me:
The party started a little late because Miss
Lila arrived a little late; she complimented
Mrs. Farrell's dress that my mother overheard Mrs. Walker say she'd made for Mrs.
Farrell from a Vogue designer pattern; Miss
Lila was very enthusiastic about Miss Mangum's butterscotch cream cake and almond
macaroons; and yes, Miss Lila seemed to
thoroughly enjoy herself. Unfortunately, my
mother didn't remember which designer
had designed Mrs. Farrell's dress from the

Vogue pattern book or what kind of fabric it was made of, nor did she remember what Mary Elizabeth was wearing — all essential information in my opinion.

When I arrived at the Courier offices the next day, the place was in an uproar. Miss Mavis explained that Miss Lila had stretched the truth once again in her column and trouble was brewing. She read the offending paragraph out loud to me. After describing the "moistness and creaminess" of Miss Mangum's cake and the "airiness and crunchiness" of her almond macaroons, the "geniality" of the "beautifully attired" guests, the "welcoming comfort" of Miss Mangum's home, and the "frothy elegance" of Miss Farrell's crepe de chine gown, Miss Lila described Mrs. Farrell's dress as an "Oleg Cassini original gown imported directly from Paris."

Apparently, Mr. Farrell had read the column immediately after receiving a number of bills in the mail and had blown his top. Miss Mavis said that Janie Windom, Mr. Farrell's secretary, told Mrs. McCall that Mr. Farrell had yelled "Paris!" and then, said a bad word. Everyone in his office was shocked because Mr. Farrell was a church deacon and hadn't behaved like that since he'd walked the aisle of Evansville

First Baptist to give his heart to Jesus. But he'd stormed out of the building and walked the two blocks to his Victorian house on Main Street in record time. Once there, he caused such a commotion that people on the street overheard it and stopped in wonder.

In addition, Miss Mavis reported that, shortly after Mr. Farrell's "appalling" behavior, a very upset and sobbing Mrs. Farrell had called to talk to Miss Lila and that, afterwards, Miss Lila had stayed in her office with the door closed the rest of the day.

I didn't know what to think. My heroine was in trouble. I knew Mr. Woolsey had not reacted badly to prior problems with Miss Lila's columns, but this was Mr. Farrell, the newspaper's biggest advertiser and the most important man in town. Of course, as far as I knew, neither Mr. Farrell nor Mrs. Farrell had complained directly to Mr. Woolsey, so I didn't know how bad this was.

I found out the next day. Hattie Mayberry, who worked for the Farrells on Tuesdays and Thursdays, let it be known that Mr. Farrell shook a fistful of bills in one hand and Miss Lila's column in the other in the faces of his startled wife and daughter and shouted "No more! Not another dime! She can get married in a croker sack, if necessary. I'll not spend another red cent on all this phony, baloney bull . . ." Mrs. McCall, my informant, suggested he'd used another bad word.

The news flew all over town. I was bombarded with calls from my friends from the moment I got home. The Evansville wedding of the year not happen? How could the father of the bride not buy her a wedding dress? And what about the reception? Everyone had looked forward to it for months. Surely, Mr. Farrell didn't mean it! Everyone in Evansville immediately took sides. Some were offended by the idea that the richest man in town wouldn't do everything possible to make his daughter's special day memorable. The others thought Mrs. Farrell must have spent a huge amount of money to warrant such an extreme reaction from her deacon/husband. This last group considered his behavior justified and immediately forgave him. They were all men.

I was questioned repeatedly: "What does Miss Lila think? What has she said?"

The truth is Miss Lila kept her door closed and didn't say anything to anybody. I did notice that she began leaving the office earlier and several people told me she visited the Farrell house often over the next few weeks. Unfortunately, no one was able to pry one piece of information out of Hattie Newberry. Mrs. McCall claimed that Mrs. Farrell and Miss Lila, who talked on the telephone several times each day, appeared to be talking in code. Nothing they said made sense to her.

In the midst of all this, I received an invitation to a kitchen shower for Mary Elizabeth. Mrs. Grace Parker, the kindest soul in town, invited everyone from sixteen to seventy. I thanked my lucky stars, I had just turned sixteen. Miss Lila made my birthday extra special when she gave me a copy of a book she said had meant a lot to her: *How to Win Friends and Influence People* by Dale Carnegie.

Mrs. Parker's invitation asked everyone to bring an appetizer — Miss Lila called them hors d'oeuvres — to share. I was thrilled to be included. On my break, I ran over to Fletcher's Hardware and bought a pretty, painted trivet for my gift.

The kitchen shower was two weeks later on a Saturday afternoon. My mother and I made cucumber-and-cream-cheese sandwiches out of white bread cut into little triangles with the crusts trimmed off from a recipe in a party cookbook recommended in Miss Lila's column, *Cuisine for Company.*

At least thirty people of all ages were there, including Miss Lila. Mary Elizabeth seemed subdued and acted really grateful toward her hostess and all of us who came. Miss Grace had decorated her house with flowers from her own garden and made Mary Elizabeth a corsage of daisies and bachelor buttons.

Miss Lila looked beautiful, as usual, wearing a natural straw hat with a silk scarf entwined with silk flowers around the brim.

After we'd all had a chance to enjoy the foods from the buffet, she took my hand in hers and said, "Bravo, Caroline. Your cucumber sandwiches are delicious. You'll make a wonderful hostess some day."

I couldn't stop smiling. Miss Lila's approval felt like winning a medal.

Mary Elizabeth's gifts included everything from teapots to picture hooks and she thanked each person convincingly — even when she got a gift just like another. While she was opening the presents, I overheard Mrs. Roberts tell Mrs. Jefferson that Mary Elizabeth was wearing the same dress she had worn to an earlier tea, probably because of her father's edict. Mrs. Roberts said she felt sorry for "the poor dear" and wondered, a little too loud, I thought, what Mary Elizabeth would do for a wedding dress. I looked to see if Mary Elizabeth had over-heard and noticed her, Mrs. Farrell, and Miss Lila exchanging meaningful looks. I couldn't help but wonder what that was about.

When the shower ended, several people remarked that they'd had more fun at this party than at all the others. I thought that was curious and asked Miss Lila about it.

"Caroline," she said, "People tend to feel more comfortable when they're on an equal footing with those around them. And you, my dear, have a gift for making people feel valued and comfortable. I'm certain that one day you will use that gift to benefit not only yourself but also those you love."

I had a gift? Miss Lila said things to me that nobody else did. Not even my parents. She had a way of making me feel important — like I could accomplish things — great things.

The next day, Miss Lila's society column reported the kitchen shower as if it had been a grand ball given by a queen in a palace. Miss Farrell had worn the most "winsome frock imaginable." The description was so completely different, no one would have recognized it as the same dress described in a column after an earlier party. Miss Lila had a natural gift with words. The floral "offerings" were so highly praised, Mrs. Thurston, owner of Evansville Garden Shop, must have turned as green as her plants from envy. And my cucumber sandwiches rated a special mention along with other "delectable" refreshments. She reserved her highest praise for the hostess and the guest of honor, reported to be "so hospitable, charming, and gracious they put all the guests at ease and made each one feel grateful to have been invited to such a superlative affair." She was right. I was grateful. It was the first really adult-type party I'd been invited to and being there with Miss Lila was a treat I'd only imagined.

Six weeks before the wedding date, the bridesmaids were asked to go to Mary Elizabeth's house for a fitting. I knew about this because Sue Ann Phillips, my best friend, told me. Her sister Mary Ellen was a bridesmaid. It was the funniest thing. Mary Ellen said that Mrs. Farrell did all the measuring and everyone knew she didn't sew or she wouldn't have Mrs. Walker make her dresses. And Mary Ellen said the only measurements Mrs. Farrell took were her height, her head, and her hips. She thought that was pretty strange. In fact she was a little worried she might be embarrassed by what Mrs. Farrell would make her wear, but she couldn't back out because Mary Elizabeth had been her friend since kindergarten.

The same week the bridesmaids went for their fittings, practically the whole town received invitations to the June seventh wedding. They were hand delivered by Hattie Mayberry's youngest boy and were written in calligraphy on parchment paper that was rolled up and tied with a white satin bow around a sprig of green silk leaves. I felt like turning a cartwheel when I saw my name written beneath my parents' names.

Meanwhile, everyone remarked how curious it was that Miss Lila visited the Farrells so often. All Mrs. McCall, the telephone operator, could offer to satisfy their curiosity was that Miss Lila had made more than one call to the offices of the Atlanta newspapers. No one knew why. Miss Lila didn't have much to say to anyone around the offices any more and her columns had gotten shorter and shorter.

Two weeks before the wedding, Mary Ellen and the other bridesmaids were told to come for another fitting and bring their high heel pumps. They did and left the shoes at the Farrells. Sue Ann and I wanted to know what the bridesmaids were going to wear, but all Mary Ellen could tell us was that they were fitted in slips to go under the dresses. She and the other bridesmaids had been sworn to secrecy about everything else. We were dying to know more, but, no matter what we promised her, Mary Ellen wouldn't budge an inch.

Two days before the wedding, Mr. Edward Young, Mary Elizabeth's fiancé, came to town with his parents. They had been invited to stay at the parsonage by Reverend Whittinghill and his wife. My girlfriends and I had a chance to see the groom when he went by the Rexall Drug Store. He was dreamy — tall and dark-haired, like a prince from somewhere in Europe. My mother told me he was a law student at Mercer University. We thought Mary Elizabeth must be the luckiest girl in the world.

The day before the wedding — it was a Friday — I was on my way to school at eight o'clock in the morning when I saw people carrying boxes out of the Farrells' house. It was Miss Lila, Mrs. Farrell, Mary Elizabeth, and Hattie Mayberry. They packed the boxes into two cars before I could see what was in them.

After school, I found the newspaper offices buzzing with news. It seems Miss Lila, Mrs. Farrell, Mary Elizabeth, and Hattie Mayberry had spent all day at the church getting it decorated for the wedding. They wouldn't let anybody else help or come in to look — not even Edward Young.

That same day, a woman wearing large square sunglasses and a head scarf was seen driving around town in a red 1958 Chevrolet Impala convertible, and no one knew who she was. Sugar Miles had seen the car featured in her father's *Car and Driver* magazine and was the first to identify it. No one in Evansville had a car like that. Poor Mrs. McCall had been kept busy all afternoon at the switchboard, connecting one person to another, each trying to learn the identity of the mysterious stranger with no luck. I looked for her through the windows of the newspaper office while I was working, but, if she drove by our building, I missed her.

At two o'clock on Saturday afternoon, I was coming out of Woolworth's where I'd gone to buy some Evening in Paris perfume to wear to the wedding, when I saw a big, white van pull into the parking lot of Evansville First Baptist Church. Four men piled out of the van and, while I watched, along with several other people, they erected a large white tent in an amazingly short amount of time.

Soon afterwards, a truck with a sign on the side saying WMAZ-TV, Macon, Georgia, pulled into the parking lot. Men carrying cameras climbed out of the truck along with a petite blond dressed in a raspberry colored suit. She seemed to be in charge and directed them to follow her into the church. I was a bit scandalized by the idea of TV cameras in a church, but I didn't have much time to react because it was getting late. I had to hurry home to dress for the wedding.

When my mother and I — wild horses couldn't drag my father to a wedding — arrived at four fifteen, people were already pushing their way into the church to try to get the best seats. The ushers consisted of Mary Elizabeth's four brothers and two friends of the bridegroom. The six young men looked utterly perplexed when several ladies insisted on aisle seats and competed with each other to get the ones closest to the front, not caring whether it was the bride's side or the groom's side of the church. When they were finally seated, they created additional commotion by making later arrivals climb over them instead of moving to the center of the pews.

When my mother and I had been seated, in the middle on the bride's side half way back, I looked around and was amazed. Chains of white silk roses and gold fabric draped the baptismal pool, garlanded the sacrament table, swathed the organ pipes, and cascaded down the sides of the stained glass windows. Three unlit candles, set in candle stands trimmed with greenery, stood on the platform: one large one in the center and smaller ones on either side. I was used to seeing candles at weddings, but only ones arranged in large candelabras.

The camera men had hidden themselves behind various plants so well, I wouldn't have even seen them if I hadn't been looking for them. The petite blond from the TV truck sat off to the side at the end of the third row on the groom's side of the church. While I was looking around, I noticed another stranger — another blond lady, but older. She was dressed "to the nines," as my father would say and sitting near the front on the bride's side. She appeared to be writing on something in her lap. I was puzzled. I thought I knew all of the Farrells' relatives. I waved at Sue Ann when she arrived with her parents and pointed out the lady, but she turned her hands up and shrugged her shoulders.

At a quarter 'til five, the organist began to play, but not the music I was used to hearing at weddings. She played classical music that I was sure only a few people in the audience would find familiar. I recognized one piece by Mozart from an Atlanta Symphony Orchestra concert I had attended two years before when my freshman class left school after lunch one day and went by bus to the Macon Municipal Auditorium.

At five o'clock on the dot, a red-haired woman I'd never seen before stepped from behind a potted palm to the center of the platform. She was wearing a flowing pink gown and what, in my opinion, was a whole lot of make-up.

As soon as she stepped forward, a tuxedo-clad man with a violin stepped in front of the organ and began to play. A silvery, sweet melody pierced the air as the musician drew his bow back and forth across the instrument. Then, the woman began to sing. My mouth dropped open at the incredible sound. I heard "Oh's" from several people around me as the full, rich tones of an operatic soprano filled the sanctuary. The effect of her voice was so profound I noticed that even Joe Frank Barton, captain of the Evansville High football team and a wannabe country and western singer, sat spellbound in his seat, his attention totally captured by musical words none of us could understand. When the singer and the violinist ended their song, I was so moved I gripped my mother's hand. I looked around. The entire audience seemed dazed.

Then, the Reverend Whittinghill entered from a side door, followed by the groom. At that moment the violinist, accompanied by the organist, began to play a classical piece which has been used at weddings in Evansville ever since. I now know the name of the piece was Pachelbel Canon in D. Back then, all I knew was that it was beautiful. As the music played, the six groomsmen unrolled a white cloth runner over the burgundy rug that ran down the center of the church. When the groomsmen had taken their places on each side of the minister, Mary Elizabeth's tiny niece made her way down the aisle dropping pink rose petals from a little white basket. She wore a dropped waist, organdy dress in yellow and her hair trailed yellow silk flowers and ribbons.

After a pause, the first bridesmaid entered. A gasp went up from the crowd. She was dressed like pictures I'd seen of flappers from the 1920s. She wore a pale lavender, dropped-waist, scarf-skirted dress with shoes covered in a matching fabric. On her head was a headband covered in multi-colored, silk flowers with an attached white plume. She carried one stem of a white silk rose. The other five bridesmaids followed her, each one gowned in a different pastel color. Amid a hushed silence, they took their places in front of the groomsmen. When the music ended, the bridesmaids looked like a beautiful, gauzy rainbow stretched across the front of the church.

I sat, hardly daring to breathe, wondering what Mary Elizabeth would wear, wondering if her father had given in. I guessed he must have or the wedding wouldn't have been as wonderful as it already was. All around me people turned their heads in anticipation toward the rear of the church. I expected to hear "Here Comes the Bride," but, instead, the violinist and organist began to play another classical piece — this time, a piece I learned later was by Bach.

And then, the bride appeared. With a brilliant smile spread across her face, Miss Mary Elizabeth Farrell, on the arm of her obviously uncomfortable, but proud father, stepped onto the white runner and into history as the first "period" bride of the century. *The Atlanta Journal and Constitution* Society Editor — the blonde stranger seated on the bride's side, who I learned later was the mystery woman seen driving through town in her red Impala convertible — described the scene in her column, complete with pictures, the following day:

The bride wore her mother's 1928 wedding gown in heavy candlelight satin, cut on the bias. The draped neckline, long sleeves fitted from the elbows down, dropped waistline, and short train were accentuated by appliquéd silk flowers and beadwork. As the bride and her father made their way down the aisle, Miss Farrell's sheer net veil, attached to a crown of white silk roses, spread out behind her for ten feet, evoking oh's and ah's from the onlookers.

Mary Elizabeth was so beautiful and her fiancé so handsome, they could have been on the cover of a Daphne du Maurier novel. They looked into each other's eyes with so much love; it was the most romantic thing I'd ever seen.

The bride and groom said their vows and exchanged rings and then their parents lit the smaller candles on each side of the platform. The bride and groom took those two candles and lit the big one in the middle. Reverend Whittinghill explained that the lighting of the candles symbolized two families becoming one. The society editor mentioned that, too, in her column. From then on, every time someone got married in Evansville they made lighting candles a part of the ceremony.

After the Reverend prayed for the couple,

he pronounced them husband and wife. Then, to the surprise of everyone, the organist played the "Hallelujah Chorus" while the couple recessed out of the church. Their happiness was contagious. We all felt so relieved that Mary Elizabeth had been given a beautiful wedding after all.

I found Sue Ann and we followed the wedding party through the church doors and into the white tent that had been erected. Inside stood an ice sculpture and a fountain of sparkling grape juice. The Baptists wouldn't have permitted champagne. A four-tiered wedding cake surrounded by white silk roses stood on a sheeted table to one side and on the other side was a table bearing what appeared to be every selection from the party cookbook recommended by Miss Lila in *Cuisine for Company.*

Miss Lila had kept out of sight during the ceremony. I caught a glimpse of her as she held each bridesmaid until her turn to walk down the aisle, but I didn't have a chance to speak to her until the reception. She was dressed in a pale gold silk suit, the same color as the cloth draped in the church. Her hat was covered in the same gold fabric with clusters of gold-and-white silk roses around the crown.

"Miss Lila, it was all so beautiful, so

incredible. I've never seen anything like it!"
I felt like jumping up and down.

"Caroline," she replied, "you are limited
only by the extent of your imagination and
your willingness to work. Remember that
and you will have an exceptional life."

Miss Lila always said the most unusual
things.

After the bride and groom had cut the
cake and shared a piece, the bride cut the
next piece and offered it to Miss Lila. With
tears in her eyes, she said, "Thank you,
thank you, thank you. I'll never be able to
thank you enough."

Miss Lila was a bit teary herself and
replied, "Be happy. That's all the thanks I
need."

The bride tried to hug her, but we could
all see that Miss Lila's hat and the bride's
veil were in danger of getting tangled and
breathed a sigh of relief when they ended
up patting each other on the back.

A shout of laughter drew my attention to
the rear of the tent where several men had
gathered around Mr. Farrell. Being naturally
curious, I eased my way through the crowd
and stood near the group.

"You had to eat your words, didn't you?
This wedding must have set you back thousands."

"Not at all. I haven't paid out another dime — just like I said."

"I don't believe it. That's impossible. You're telling a whopper."

"No. I absolutely, solemnly promise that I left it to my wife and daughter to figure out how to produce this wedding without any more money from me and they did. Of course, they couldn't have done it without Miss Lila. But that's all I'm going to say."

Several voices overlapped, each demanding to know how it was done. They knew now that Mary Elizabeth's wedding dress had been her mother's, so that mystery was solved; but Mr. Farrell's friends wanted to know about the silk flowers, the singer, the musician, the food, and everything else. And so did I. Neither Mr. nor Mrs. Farrell ever fully explained how the wedding had been accomplished without spending more money, but I knew Miss Lila had a lot to do with it.

I saw the cameramen following the singer and violinist around the reception. They filmed the two chatting with Miss Lila, exclaiming over the bride's and the bridesmaids dresses, and standing beside the wedding cake and ice sculpture. Both the TV lady and the Atlanta newspapers' society editor spent a lot of time talking to Miss

Lila. The editor's story on the wedding in the Sunday paper ran a full page with pictures and she praised everything: the originality of the music selections, the performance of the lead soprano for the Atlanta Opera Company and her musician husband, the beauty of the swags of gold fabric and white silk roses in the church, and the symbolic candle lighting ritual.

She reserved her greatest praise for the "period" dress theme of the wedding and the use of color in the bridesmaids' dresses. She seemed particularly touched by the bride's sentimental use of her mother's wedding gown. The society editor concluded her story with the observation that Miss Farrell had set the mark for brides to aspire to for the season, both in Atlanta and the rest of Georgia. Her post note in italics thanked Miss Lila Cole for alerting her to the story and gave her due credit for the astounding success of the event, calling her a "wedding planner extraordinaire, literary critic, fashion maven, culinary artist, and journalist for the *Evansville Daily Courier.*"

Film from the wedding was shown that evening on the eleven o'clock news on Channel 13, the Macon TV station. The petite blond I'd seen directing the cameramen reported on it from the reception. The report showed the bridesmaids walking down the aisle and the bride and groom coming out of the church. It also showed some of the decorations and the singer and violinist. On Monday, the story and pictures were used by Atlanta and Savannah TV stations. By the end of the week, newspapers reported that brides all over Georgia were returning their dresses to bridal shops and digging through the attics in their parents' and grandparents' homes searching for their own "period" wedding dresses.

When I'd arrived for work on Monday, Miss Mavis told me the phone had been ringing off the hook with everyone wanting to talk to Miss Lila. It seemed that a number of Atlanta brides-to-be insisted their weddings would be disasters without Miss Lila's personal intervention. A few weeks later, Miss Lila decided to go where her talents were most needed and moved to Atlanta. It was a sad day for me.

I was at college when my mother sent me an article she'd clipped from the newspaper. The article stated that the Georgia Business Councils of 1958 and 1959 had cited the Farrell-Young wedding as responsible for the twenty percent drop in income of Georgia bridal shops for those years. I wasn't surprised. Mrs. Evalina Deese, owner of

Evansville Bridal Emporium, had been heard to say, "Don't mention that woman's name in my presence" whenever conversations turned to reminiscing about Miss Lila.

I went to a college up north. I never would have even considered applying to such a prestigious school if Miss Lila hadn't suggested it to me when I told her I'd probably go to Wesleyan like Mary Elizabeth. I also did something Miss Lila didn't think was possible. I ended up with both a noble man and a noble career. I met my husband in dental school and we set up a practice together in Thomasville, about forty-five miles from Evansville.

On one of my frequent visits home, my mother, with tears in her eyes, handed me a copy of *The Atlanta Journal.* The first thing I saw was a picture of an ageless Miss Lila in one of her famous rose-covered hats. The headline read: Miss Lila Cole, Arbiter of Taste in Atlanta Society, Dies in Freak Accident.

I gazed at the headline in shock. How was it possible? Not Miss Lila! She wouldn't, couldn't do anything as mundane as dying.

Numb, I read further to see what "freak accident" had killed the person who'd had such an influence on my life. According to the story, Miss Lila had choked on a cream puff at an outdoor tea party after a sudden gust of wind came up that threatened to carry away her "signature" hat. The article went on to extol her skills in writing the perfect review, whether of a wedding or a literary work; her trend-setting fashions; her coveted hats which were credited with increasing Atlanta millinery sales fifty percent in the past ten years; and her renowned ability to produce the most memorable weddings ever.

I continued reading, fondly remembering Mary Elizabeth's beautiful wedding. The newspaper quoted Miss Lila's best friend from childhood, an Atlanta opera singer, as saying that Miss Lila's accomplishments were all the more astounding, considering she grew up as the daughter of a dirt-poor south Georgia pig farmer.

Unbelieving, I stared at the paper in shock and quickly looked to see what else was said. According to her friend, Miss Lila had changed her name from Eula May Dutton to Lila Cole when she'd decided to change her life. She'd succeeded so well, she'd inspired her friend to seek voice training so she, too, could have the life she wanted.

I was flabbergasted. What Martha Jean Cranston and her mother had said about Miss Lila way back then was true. When I was fifteen, I think I probably would have been disappointed to learn that my heroine grew up in such humble surroundings. But now, remembering all that she succeeded in doing and the effect she'd had on my life, I couldn't help but smile and say out loud, "Bravo, Miss Lila!"

DID YOU KNOW?

- In 1940, most farms still didn't have phones or electricity. A lot of people still didn't own a car or truck.
- By the 1950s, 71 percent of farms had a car but only 49 percent had phones.
- Popular hobbies included "paint by number" pictures, wood-burning kits, paper dolls and model car sets. Kids had tree houses, "Lincoln Log" sets, pop guns and toy ovens.
- Popular candies included tiny soft-drink bottles made of wax and filled with sugary juice. Kids could buy candy cigarettes and pretend to smoke them.
- Adults were allowed to smoke wherever they wanted, including movie theaters, airplanes, restaurants and doctors' offices.
- If you wanted ice cubes you had to pop them out of metal trays in the freezer. The trays had metal dividers that rattled.
- School didn't start until September so kids who lived on farms could help harvest the crops.

I'll See You in My Dreams

BY SARAH ADDISON ALLEN

"The past is not dead. It isn't even past."
— William Faulkner

Great Aunt Sophie likes tight, no-fuss perms that sit close to her head, the curls as round as Christmas peppermints. It used to be that she could easily pedal over to the Fashionette for such a coif. But she retired her bicycle about three years ago. Her doctor said it was time. Of course, her doctor started saying it was time fifteen years ago. It just took that long for her to finally agree with him.

I have a standing engagement with Great Aunt Sophie and, when it's time for a perm, I leave early from work and drive her to the Fashionette, past the factory out on Clementine Highway. When she was able, she used to go for a wash and set every week, now she settles for a perm every couple of months. I pick her up at her house, and the first thing she always says to me is, "So, do you like working at Staler's? Did you have a good day?"

And I always answer, "It's all right. A job, I guess," leaving her to guess who actually buys those designer briefs and the boxers with chili peppers on them. She's bound to know the men if I tell her.

I sell men's underwear at Staler's department store. I have the dubious distinction of knowing what almost every man in town wears underneath. Sometimes, walking down Main Street, I imagine I'm getting sheepish looks from the men, especially the older ones. Like I know their secret.

It was a fairly bold move for a factory town store like Staler's to put a woman in charge of men's underwear, but I guess they figured it was a good plan when they found out that more women buy men's underwear for their men than the men do for themselves. There was actually a study done somewhere. Great Aunt Sophie doesn't believe me when I tell her this.

"What kind of person would go up to a stranger and ask her if she buys her man his underwear?" Great Aunt Sophie says. Apparently she has no problem with asking me, though. She called me up last Sunday and said she'd just been to Staler's with her friend Harriet, who still drives. She said she saw this ridiculous pair of men's orange boxer shorts with big green dinosaurs on them that glow in the dark. "Tell me who buys those, Louise," she said to me. "Tell me who actually buys that sort of thing."

I wanted to know what she and Harriet were doing wandering around in the men's underwear department at Staler's when she knows neither I nor Mom work there on Sundays.

Sophie asks me to come in when I take her home from the Fashionette. It's a feverish late September day. It's the kind of hot that sticks to the sides of the mountains, like the colors in this particular Appalachian autumn. As soon as we walk to the kitchen, she opens the back door to let the breeze come in and stands there for a moment, looking out as if at someone. Then she turns around and begins to fuss around the kitchen, her feet whispering against the linoleum.

Her kitchen smells like a combination of apples turning soft and the scent of fine linen napkins that have been locked away too long in cabinet drawers. The smell makes me feel good, like when I was young and Great Aunt Sophie wasn't quite as old. But then it silently reprimands me for not coming to visit as often as I should. Shame on you, Louise, it says.

"So tell me how you are," Great Aunt Sophie says, going to the faded green pie safe in the corner and gingerly bringing out an apple pie. Maybe her stiff, knobby fingers are up to no good again. She doesn't seem to trust them to carry the pie over to the counter. She cuts a piece right there and takes it to the microwave. This is all done before she's even taken off her sweater, or exchanged her going-out eyeglasses for her at-home eyeglasses.

"I'm fine, Aunt Sophie," I say, sitting at the heavy wooden kitchen table covered with a finely-kept, flowered oilcloth, which she's had for as far back as my memory stretches. There's a huge bowl of apples on the table, waiting for her to do what she does to apples in the fall — can, bake, fry, stew, candy, dry, dip in caramel, marinate in sugar to pour over friendship bread. She keeps promising not to touch another apple recipe until the apples decide to peel themselves. But Sophie's not that patient.

She puts the piece of freshly microwaved pie in front of me. Warm curls rise up from it. "Smell that, Louise," she says to me as she hands me a fork. "That's what my heaven's going to smell like. Apple pie. Hot apple pie . . . and leather shoes, new ones.

The dancing kind."

I take a bite because I know she won't move until I start eating. Just as soon as the fork reaches my mouth, she turns and goes to the kitchen drawer to do her eyeglasses exchange. She leans against the counter and rubs her eyes tiredly, at length, before she puts on her at-home eyeglasses.

She sighs and pushes herself away from the counter then she takes off her sweater and ties a blue apron around her waist. "So tell me, how's that best friend of yours, the one you knew in school? Sue? I haven't seen her in a while."

"She's fine, too. I saw her just yesterday. She's pregnant," I say as Great Aunt Sophie turns on the portable radio in her kitchen window. A big band tune comes out softly.

"Pregnant again?" she asks over her shoulder as she starts making coffee in her new automatic drip. The air whooshes into the sealed coffee jar as she opens it. "How many will this make?"

"Just three." I take another bite of her pie. "Her husband wants a boy this time."

"Humph," Great Aunt Sophie says. "Like he can control that."

I smile. Some things I just know I inherited from Great Aunt Sophie and no one else. "That's what I say. She won't listen.

She's in love."

"You're a good girl, Louise. Have I ever told you that? You are. You need to find a nice man and have children. I'm not going to be around forever to tell you this, so you better hurry up." Her automatic drip gurgles and she sways a little to the music as she brings a cup down from the cabinet.

I watch her. Great Aunt Sophie isn't the kind of person you would ever think of as a dancer, but she loves to dance. Not that she ever dances with anyone, but I know that if she's having one of her good days, she'll sometimes dance to her refrigerator and back when she cooks. And when she used to bring her bicycle out of her garage, she would sometimes dance with it all the way to the road.

"I'm sure I'll find a nice man some day, Aunt Sophie."

"Yes, yes. I suppose so. You're only twenty-five. I'd like to see the day, that's all." She pours a cup of coffee and comes to sit beside me at the table.

"Twenty-four," I remind her, thinking that ever since I had that Yes-I'm-old-enough-to-have-coffee conversation with her several years ago, she always seems to make me older than I am whenever coffee is involved, even though she never gives me any. I'm old enough to sell men's underwear. I wonder what she would say if I tell her that.

"I got married when I was twenty. I told you that once, didn't I?" She has the creamy eggshell-thin coffee cup in both of her hands as she takes a sip.

"No ma'am. I don't recall that you did."

"My Harry. He was a good old soul. I had a dream about him." She pauses then laughs. She sets her cup down and leans back in her chair as she puts a hand to her cheek. "When was that?" She shakes her head. "Ha! I can't even remember. Maybe it was as close as last night."

"You had a dream about Harry?" I never knew my great-uncle. He died long before I was born.

"I dreamed I was sixteen again and my hair was long and blond." She pats the sides of her newly permed hair. It's the purest silver you've ever seen, like a new nickel, and it smells something powerful. It makes my nose tingle when the breeze from the open doorway blows the smell my way.

I look at Great Aunt Sophie carefully. "Your hair was long and blond?"

She smiles, a tad mischievously. "Long, maybe. But not blond. But that's what dreams are about sometimes, aren't they? How you want things to be." She nods to the plate in front of me. "Do you like the pie? Harriet's apples weren't great this year."

"The pie is wonderful," I assure her.

"Did I ever tell you how I met my Harry?" she suddenly asks, but distantly, like she's asking someone else in the kitchen, someone behind her in the doorway.

"I don't think so," I say.

"Don't be silly." She's definitely talking to me now. I recognize that tone. "I know I told you a long time ago. When you were little. Remember these things, Louise. They're important."

It's an art, I realize. Guilt is an art. And Great Aunt Sophie is a master artist. When are you getting married? Why don't you stop by and see me? Didn't you ever listen to me when you were little? I would never back-talk Great Aunt Sophie, but the answers are always there: In time, I do, and no. Sophie orbited my world when I was little, large and looming like a full July moon. I used to watch her carefully — the best way to avoid her was to always know where she was — but I never listened to her much. I should have known I was going to be tested later.

"Yes ma'am," I promise her.

"All right, so listen up. There were three girls in our family — Anna, the oldest, me in the middle, and your grandmother Charlotte, the youngest," Great Aunt Sophie begins, counting off each sister on a different crooked finger. "Anna married when she was seventeen to a boy over the state line in Tennessee. She had been married about two years when her first child came along. Mama and Daddy packed me and Charlotte up and sent us on a train to help her out with the baby.

"Mama sent me with secret instructions to have an eye out for every little detail so I could tell her when I got home. Anna married into a family with money, you see. When Charlotte and I got there, the house was as big as any place I had ever seen. But everyone lived there. The whole family. Ma and Pa Coleman, Anna and her husband, another son and his wife, and two daughters, not to mention a couple of housekeepers. It seemed to me that they needed all that space because nobody was ever going to leave. And the family just kept growing. Charlotte and I were put in the same room, the only room they had left, I think.

"It turns out Anna already had a woman to help with the baby, Evangeline, so Charlotte and I weren't really needed. But Anna was happy to have us there and we spent a lot of time together. It was just like when we were girls. Anna was close to twenty then, I was sixteen and Charlotte was going on fifteen. We spent hours just walking around the orchard on the estate. Sometimes we'd go into town and people would remark on what pretty girls we were."

Sophie smiles at the memory. But then she shakes her head. "I always thought your grandmother was the prettiest of us three. I told you she had this beautiful head of golden hair, remember?"

"I remember," I say.

"Somehow, the brown eyes we were all born with seemed to look better on her. Now, Anna was tall and stately and fit right in with money. I was somewhere in the middle, but there we were in this little town in Tennessee and suddenly I was a beauty. There were several dances in town and we were never wanting for a partner. Anna let us borrow her lipstick. Oh, those days, Louise," she sighs. "Someday, when you're old enough, you're going to look back on your life and remember things that, even though you didn't know it then, will make you know who you are now."

"I'm not so young," I have to say.

To that she just laughs. "Anyway, after we had stayed long enough, Mama and Daddy called for us to come back to North Carolina. We were upset something terrible. We'd had the time of our lives. But then I remember Anna coming into the room and telling us that there was another dance that very night in town and we were all going to go. Of course that made everything all right because then we would get to say goodbye to everyone. We had been there almost three months. The whole summer.

"I was wearing my best blue dress that night and my hair was pulled back with a ribbon. There was this boy, you see, that I thought I fancied and I wanted to look nice for him." She laughs lightly, amused at herself. "What was his name? I can't even remember. He always smelled like cloves because he chewed them to help this toothache he had."

"It wasn't Harry?"

"Nooo," she says with elongated emphasis. "That night, someone new, someone I had never met before, asked me to dance. That was Harry. Oh, this is horrible to admit, but I didn't want to dance with him. He was handsome enough, I suppose. His clothes were clean and starched, but old, I could tell. I had become a little high and mighty, spending all that time in that big house, living with one of the most respected families for miles around. But I didn't have a good excuse not to dance with him, and I had to be polite. So we danced. And, Louise, it was like time stood still."

Aunt Sophie holds her hands out and, with effort, makes them freeze for a moment, as if it's very important to her that I understand what she means. "He was such an incredible dancer. Never marry a man who can't dance, Louise. Never do it. He was much taller than me but he moved like grace. Fast dances, slow dances, whatever the band played. His hands felt rough even though he barely touched me. I learned he lived on a farm with his family. He was nineteen and the oldest of eleven. We talked and talked and laughed and laughed. He told me he had come to all the dances I came to, but never had the nerve to ask me until then. That made my heart flip. I was having the best night of my life, and I can say that with confidence, Louise, because I'm old. You can't say that now so don't even try."

"Yes ma'am," I say, but I think about it anyway.

"We danced five dances in a row, then the band leader said goodnight and the band played *I'll See You in My Dreams.* Harry took my hand and put something in it. It was a button, the little bone button I had lost off my sweater the first time I went into town with Anna and Charlotte. He said it was the first time he saw me. He worked afternoons at the local filling station and he said I walked right by him like a queen in a parade and my button fell right off. He was too shy to run after me, so he kept it in his pocket. He said he liked to take it out and think of me. That's when he said he loved me. I didn't know what to say. I started crying right then and there because I loved him, too. That's the way things happened back then."

She pauses to have a sip of coffee and it seems like she's going to stop there. So I ask, "What happened next?"

She shrugs. "I left the next morning. I was so sad I couldn't say a word. And Mama always used to say I was awful to live with for the next few months. But then the next spring, Mama, Daddy, Charlotte and I went to church one Sunday and who should be there but Harry!"

"Here?" I say, smiling at her as I lick my finger and press it against my plate to pick up the last few crumbs from the pie crust.

"Yes, here. I couldn't believe it myself. He was staying at the boarding house that used to be on Carberry Avenue, where the Burger King is now, and old Mr. Johnson had hired him at his filling station. I couldn't go up and talk to him, of course, but Daddy went up and shook hands with him then introduced the rest of us. Charlotte knew who he was but I pinched her arm to stop her from saying anything. She said I left a bruise that lasted weeks."

"He came all the way up here just to be near you?" I shake my head. Of all the people I know, Great Aunt Sophie is the last person I would have suspected of harboring a romantic past.

"Yesiree. He sold all he had, saved up for months, and came to Clementine, North Carolina because he loved me. He called on me a few days later and we started courting. We had to wait nearly three years before we married. He had to save up for a house. Daddy approved of him because he was such a hard worker, and always so polite. Daddy bought a car, his first, and Harry always knew what to do for it. He could fix anything. Old Mr. Johnson eventually let Harry buy him out. Of course, when Harry died, I sold the station to Harlen Duckett. It's a good thing I never learned to drive, Louise. There's too many memories in the smell of a gas station."

She squints then looks down into her coffee cup. "Harry died two days after our twenty-first wedding anniversary. Did I ever tell you that? Life is like living in a house and death is like walking out the door. It's that simple. Harry walked out the door to go to work, and two hours later I got the call. It was a Thursday afternoon. But you want to know something? He loved more in his forty-four years than most people do in a lifetime. He did a lot of things well, Louise, but the thing he did the best was love me. How many people can say that?" She picks up her cup and takes another sip. "Not many, I think."

I push my plate away and rest my chin in the palm of my hand, studying her. "Didn't you ever want any children?"

"I wasn't able," she says quietly and my heart breaks right then and there, so quickly I don't know what has happened at first. I didn't see it coming. No one ever told me. I always assumed it was because Sophie didn't like kids much — their unpredictability, the patience it took to deal with them. She was always exasperated with me when I was younger. I sit up and look at her, startled, sad, ashamed of myself for asking such a question.

She smiles at my silence. "Harry wanted them, but he said he didn't care so long as he had me. The year after he died, your grandmother Charlotte, who had moved to

Maine with that no-good sailor man she married, died. She had one daughter, your mama. She came to live with me, then, and I consider her mine. She was my saving grace, I guess. And she gave me you, of course. So you liked the apple pie, did you?"

"It was wonderful," I say softly.

"Would you like another piece?"

"No, thank you."

"I'll pack up a piece for your mama," she decides with a nod. "You can take it over to her later."

"Okay."

She sighs and leans back in her chair. "Life has been mostly good, all in all."

I smile at her.

She laughs and reaches over to pat my hand. "Remember these things. I'm not going to be around forever." She suddenly looks over at the kitchen door. "Will you look at that! September's not even gone and October is already trying to come in!" I turn to see that the breeze has blown in some dry fallen leaves from her back yard, scattering them across the kitchen floor as if someone had walked in, but then turned and left before we could see him.

Sophie gets up and takes her broom from the broom closet, waving me back down in my attempt to help her.

"So what was your dream about?" I turn in my seat and ask her as she sweeps. "The dream about Harry."

She stops to think. Her breath is a little short already. "I dreamed we were dancing."

She's standing in the kitchen doorway, leaning on her broom, with the sun behind her. I can only see her silhouette, like an echo of her. Like a memory. Like a dream.

"You're a good girl, Louise," she says, walking out the door and disappearing.

Then the only thing left is a door full of sunshine.

Y'ALL COME

BY MARTHA CROCKETT

"When you live in the country everybody is
   your neighbor
On this one thing you can rely
They'll all come to see you and never ever
   leave you
Saying y'all come to see us by and by"
— lyrics from a bluegrass song popularized
         by Jim and Jesse in the 1950s

I was raised in the "*Y'all Come* School of Southern Hospitality."

If you're from the South, you know it well. For those of you who are not, I'll explain. The basic tenet of this school is that anyone who shows up on your doorstep — or who calls or writes to say they're coming — is welcome to a meal at the very least, but also a bed if need be. No questions asked. No payment required. In fact, any offer of payment must be turned away with a show of offense at the offer. This offer is extended not only to friends and family, but also to just about anyone you know and to anyone who might know them.

My father was a Southern minister. Not "Reverend" or "Pastor." He eschewed those titles. "Preacher" was acceptable because he did preach. But as he explained it, he was merely one of the brethren in the congregation, the one that the others paid to minister, so that's what he wanted to be called.

Being raised a preacher's kid — PK, for short — had many ramifications in my life. The one most relevant to this story is the fact that we moved quite often. As much, if not more, than military families. By the time I was eighteen, I'd lived in thirteen different houses. This meant that we had an extensive network of brethren across the South. Colleagues of my father's and friends we'd all made during our brief stays in various places. We were forever hopping in the family Rambler to visit them, or to attend a revival on the other side of town, or for my father to preach a revival for a church in another state, or to visit family who'd stayed put in Florida. There was even a vacation or two thrown into the mix. In other words, my childhood in no way could be considered still. We rarely traveled outside the South — I can only remember a couple of trips above the Mason Dixon line — but travel we did.

You would think that during all these trips, I would've stayed in a lot of motels. But try as I might, I can only remember a handful of rented rooms. And believe me, I remember each and every one because I loved to swim and motel pools were a huge treat. My sister and I could swim at night in a motel pool without worrying about critters nibbling at our toes. They had lights under the water, for goodness sake. If a cottonmouth happened to slip into the water — which did happen (to us kids, any snake in the pool was a cottonmouth) — we could see him coming and swim in the other direction like Johnny Weissmuller chasing a crocodile.

But, as I said, motel rooms were few and far between. The vast majority of family trips were spent in a succession of private homes. I was acquainted with some of the people who put us up, either from one of our brief residences in their fair town or previous revivals there. But like as not, I'd never set eyes on them. Sometimes even my parents hadn't. When someone discovered we were going to, say, Boston (one of the two ventures into bona fide Yankee country), they would inevitably say something in the nature of, "My Great-Aunt Mildred lives two miles from Plymouth Rock." They'd lean closer and confide, "Married a Yankee after the War, bless her heart. She'd love to hear a proper accent again. I'll call her in the morning." So we'd stay with Aunt Mildred. And even through all those impositions, I can't remember a single time when we were greeted with anything but open arms and hearts. And when we left, the last thing my father would say before he backed the Rambler out of their drive was, "Y'all come."

Not the elaborate "Y'all come now, y'here," that *The Beverly Hillbillies* put into popular culture. Just a simple, sincere, "Y'all come."

And come they did. Over the years. my mother must've cooked thousands of chickens. Baked chickens, chicken pot pie, chicken and dumplings. Any way you can cook chicken . . . except fried. Now my mother was a marvelous cook. It was, after all, what she majored in while earning her M-R-S degree. But she refused to fry chicken, and that was my favorite way of eating it. Consequently, I anticipated church dinner-on-the-grounds with great relish, where there was invariably a bounty of chicken fried up by the best cooks in the church. But fried chicken is a story entire unto itself. Suffice it to say, my mother would not drop a single leg into Crisco.

Mother never gave me a satisfactory answer about why the menu invariably featured chicken. When I was old enough to notice the plethora of poultry farms across the South, I concluded chicken must've been cheaper to come by. An important consideration when the Lord is on hand merely to bless the chicken, not to divide the white meat and the dark as he did the loaves and fishes.

The only exceptions I can remember to chicken dishes were the times when the menfolk had gone fishing. Then mountains of crappie and bass replaced the poultry. I understand that many a chicken dish across the South was replaced by venison or quail or duck, but the men in my family were not huntsmen, so game wasn't in the realm of my experience.

The longest stretch of residence we ever spent was in a small town northeast of Atlanta that has since been swallowed up by that massive city. When I was two, my father had been hired by a small group of brethren to build a church from practically nothing. We started meeting in the chapel of an old WWII military hospital. Those were the days when the only way to get to the top of Stone Mountain was shoe leather, decades before they completed the carving on the side. Under my father's ministry, the church grew to almost four hundred people, one of the largest in the area in those days. The congregation was as dynamic as Atlanta, with people moving in and out all the time. So when I was eleven, they began to plan a ten year reunion.

I'm not certain if my father came up with the idea or exactly who, but most members of the church were enthusiastically behind it. They set up committees and spent six months planning the event for the next Fourth of July, figuring most people could take vacation days to drive in if they had to. Since I was still mostly kid, six months seemed a lifetime away. So I shoved it into my peripheral attention and went on with my life.

The trouble didn't start until a few months later. Along about April, I remember Mother telling Dad, "J.C., Myra James called today. They're coming for the reunion. I invited them to stay here."

The Jameses had been friends of my parents' since high school. This was both good and bad news for me. They were an interesting family that we'd seen several times over the years. Not only was the father a rocket scientist, literally, both his and his oldest son's names were Jesse James, which I always got a kick out of hearing. However, the middle son was my age, and a nastier boy you'd never meet in your life. Jerry James was a skinny, buck-toothed, tow-headed boy with a cow lick growing right out of his forehead. He reminded me of Dennis the Menace in every way, and every time we were forced into close proximity I told him that he should've been named Jesse instead of his big brother, because he was the outlaw in the family. I stopped telling him this when I figured out that he actually liked being called an outlaw. The degenerate.

Dad merely nodded to Mother at her announcement and said, "It'll be good to see them."

Nobody asked my permission, of course, even though I would be forced to move in with my sister for the duration of the visit. My sole comfort was that it would be worse for her than for me. Being thirteen made Nona a teenager, and she had all the arrogance that went along with that distinction. Her disdain irritated the stew out of me and I loved to cause her misery every chance I could get. So having the Jameses stay with us during the reunion wouldn't be all bad.

A few weeks into June, I overheard my mother calling my father at the church office. "The Hollingsworths are coming to the reunion, too. They asked if they could stay with us."

I couldn't hear my father's reply, but in the following conversation, I definitely heard Mother say, "the kids can sleep on the floor."

I hated sleeping on the floor. They were called hardwood for a reason.

So when mother hung up the phone, I asked indignantly, "Who are the Hollingsworths?"

She raised her eyebrow, but answered me patiently. "They used to live on the other side of the Dixie Highway. A big yellow house with black shutters. Lots of hydrangeas. You remember."

I didn't remember, which must've been evident on my face because mother continued, "You remember Mark Grady, don't you?"

"How could I forget him? He's the slimy toad who tried to kiss me in first grade." I was not a fan of boys until I hit puberty a couple of years later. "He's coming? And Jerry James, too?" I pictured all kinds of horrible scenarios in their company.

"We haven't heard from Mark's parents

yet. The Hollingsworths are Mark's grand-parents."

So they were old, which meant I couldn't throw a fit about them making me sleep on the floor. "Why are they staying with us?"

"They might not. I'm going to try and see if the Sherwoods can put them up, but right now they're out of town visiting their daughter in Macon. So I can't check with them until next week."

Which meant she'd forget. Mother could remember every recipe she'd ever come across, the steps required for earning half of the Girl Scout badges, and the words to nearly every book in the hymnal, but the details of ordinary life often slipped from her mind. I can't tell you how many times I had to walk home from school after dark because she'd forgotten to pick me up after whatever club meeting I happened to be attending. And if mother didn't place the Hollingsworths with the Sherwoods or somebody, it increased the odds of Mark Grady staying at our house. Jerry James was bad enough. Having both of them would be the end of life as I knew it.

"I'll remind you," I promised her.

She chuckled. "All right."

Mother recognized her forgetful tendencies, but my father was so completely in love with her he thought it was cute, so she had no incentive to improve. If something was very important, she wrote it on the calendar. But that only helped when she actually remembered to look at the calendar. By the time I'd reached the advanced age of eleven, I knew that if I wanted Mother to do something, I had to remind her. Often more than once. To this day, I credit my mother's forgetfulness for both my excellent memory and my tendency to nag.

One week to the day, I reminded Mother she needed to call the Sherwoods.

"I called them yesterday," she said to my surprise.

"And . . . ?"

"They're keeping the Hollingsworths and the Gradys."

"I knew that snarly varmint was com . . . I mean . . . the Sherwoods are really good people." Ebullient with relief at having dodged two bullets — Mark Grady and sleeping on the floor. I started to skip away when my mother's question stopped me short.

"Have you ever slept on cots at any of your friend's sleepovers?"

"Cots?" The only reason she would ask about cots was if we needed them, and needing cots was ominous. "At Amelia's. Why?"

Mother shrugged. "Looks like we'll be needing a few. Remind me to ask Helen at prayer meeting tonight. I'll ask the Mayfields, too."

Nona walked in the back door at that point.

Mother's head turned toward my sister, but mother probably didn't even see her. "Who else goes camping?"

"Huh?" Nona stopped, then recovered quickly. She had two years more than me to be familiar with Mother's ways. "Oh. The Stricklands and the Gutterys went to Red Top Mountain with us last time. Why?"

"Because we need a bazillion cots," I told her in that you're-too-stupid-to-live voice that sisters save for each other.

"Cots?" Nona turned to Mother and said in her best drama-queen voice, "Mother! You haven't invited even more people to stay with us for that stupid reunion, have you? Aren't the Jameses enough?"

Mother's attention came back from the land of cots, and she focused her eyes on Nona. "The reunion isn't stupid, Nona. But, no, we didn't invite them, exactly. They're calling for a place to stay and we can't turn them away."

"Why not?" I asked.

Mother looked at me as if I'd just asked to live in Detroit. "It isn't done."

The classic answer from mothers all over the South. No reason attached to it, but it was backed by many generations and hundreds of years of living inside the Southern box.

"Why can't the Bakers put them up?" Nona asked, thinking along the same lines that I was. "They have three extra bedrooms."

"The Bakers' house is full," Mother explained. "And the Thompsons' and the Abernathys' and the Collins' and everyone else's. When the elders planned the reunion, they never dreamed that so many people would come. But they are coming, and they have to sleep somewhere. The church is paying for the house we live in and it's right next door, so it's only natural that the overspill comes here. We may have to pitch tents in the back yard before it's said and done, but that's what we'll do if we have to. We're happy all these people are returning to celebrate the ten years our church has been serving the Lord. It's a wonderful and important event. Understand?"

Mother strong-eyed Nona into submission. "Nona?"

Nona didn't look happy, but said, "Yes, ma'am."

Mother turned her attention on me. "Martha?"

"Yes, ma'am." What else could I say? Mother was an expert at making my childish concerns seem petty in the grand scheme of things. Besides, with so many people we'd be forced to have potluck dinners, so fried chicken was a sure thing. And since it was summer, homemade ice cream was a definite possibility.

"I'm counting on you girls to help. With so many people, I'll be doing good just to keep up with the cooking. I can't have you girls running off to be with your boyfriends . . ." that was for Nona, ". . . or to run around in the woods." That was for me.

Not escape into the woods? For three whole days?!? Just kill me now!

"But I —"

"Martha . . ."

I may be stubborn, but even I knew when to stop talking. Mother might seem like a mild-mannered preacher's wife, but she'd been known to wield a mean hairbrush to Nona's and my backsides. Besides, I always had back-up plans. I might have to invite company on my treks into the wilderness, but I could stand that for a day or so. While it was true that I valued my alone time in the woods, I wasn't completely anti-social.

"Yes, ma'am. I want to help."

The look she gave me said she suspected I wasn't being entirely truthful, but she didn't say anything. Since I wasn't, I didn't say anything, either.

These were the times when it was best to hide the fact that you weren't quite the good little Christian soldier your parents thought that you were.

The Jameses were the first guests to arrive that Friday afternoon. As far as we knew at that point, we were planning on housing three more families, a total of eighteen guests in all. The four of us added made twenty-one humans and one sub-human (Jerry) sharing a twelve hundred square foot, three bedroom, two bathroom house.

Today I cringe when I think about the logistics of that many people in such a small space. Back then, I didn't have a clue. I was too focused on my personal inconvenience. I had no inkling of the headaches my mother must've suffered.

Mother, luckily, wasn't prone to headaches and never seemed ruffled or put out. She'd grabbed Nona and me before we could slip out of the house that Friday morning, and we spent the day doing slave labor. Which meant we cleaned. We even had to sweep and mop the cement floor of the basement. That's where all of the children would be sleeping — except for the Taylor's baby — plus the two hardiest adults. Mr. and Mrs. Martin weren't the youngest of our adult guests, but they camped and hiked and generally loved roughing it. So they'd volunteered to keep the children in line.

I didn't mind that one bit. Mr. Martin could do magic tricks and Mrs. Martin told the best stories. They had one daughter who was a year older than Nona and therefore of no interest to me. Back then, I categorized adults by whether or not they had children, and then by the relative interest to me of those children. Mr. and Mrs. Martin were infinitely more interesting than Cindy, who talked way too much about boys.

Our full basement was considered semi-finished. It had windows along the back side of the house and a smooth cement floor, but was not finished enough for living space. Nona and I played down there in the cold winter months and during the hottest part of the summer. It wasn't heated or air conditioned, but since it was surrounded by earth on three sides, it stayed comfortable year-round. Mother had secured enough cots and air mattresses to keep everyone off the concrete, so the weekend seemed do-able.

I had just walked inside the front door, having swept the front porch, when a blue station wagon pulled up in the driveway. I recognized the driver and groaned. I'd planned to slip out to the quarry lake hidden in the woods behind the church and hole up until supper.

I eyed the path to the back door. Could I make it?

"Who's here?" Mother called from the kitchen.

I considered lying, but the dangers of hell-fire had been drummed into me since birth. Brimstone had always been a strong deterrent for me. Not that I had any notion of what it was, but it sounded scarier than vampires or kisses from boys.

I was stuck. So I reluctantly answered, "The Jameses."

"Nona?" Mother called. "Run find your father at —"

"I'll go!" A reprieve! Dad was across the street at the church, directing traffic there. I dropped the broom and bolted out the back door before Nona could even look up from her teen magazine.

I took as long as I dared to find my father who, luckily, wasn't in the church office.

When he and I walked into our house, the Jameses had already unloaded their car and were ensconced in the family room with glasses of sweet tea.

Dad, being Dad, exchanged handshakes and hugs all around, and I was passed along the James' line until I got to Jerry. It was the first time I'd seen him in a couple of years. He stared at me with a look I wasn't familiar with — as if he didn't know who I was.

It scared me, and without thinking about where I was, I blurted out, "What's your problem, Doofus?"

"Martha!"

I cringed from Mother's rebuke, adding this public humiliation to Jerry's long list of crimes.

Luckily, my remark had hit its mark. Jerry's scary look was gone, and he covertly stuck out his tongue at me.

Finally something I could deal with. I stuck my nose in the air with a pointed sniff and turned to hug his little sister.

Just as everyone was settling down to their tea again, the Taylors arrived with their four young children in tow. A kind of friendly chaos settled over the house at that point which was not going to let up until everyone left on Monday. I'd been involved in enough

"Y'all Come" situations by then that I recognized the good in them. For a brief span of time, my parents were too focused on other people to pay me much mind. I could pretty much do as I pleased, within reason.

At any rate, it wasn't remarkable.

Yet.

The Martins arrived just as Mother was putting the men to work grilling hamburgers for supper. As I'd hoped, Mother had enough helping hands in the kitchen with the other ladies. They shooed the children outside so they could speculate about the people who were coming for the weekend. They'd talk about such important things as what color hair Myra Hardy would have this year and how much weight Red Thornapple would have gained.

Nona took the two teenagers into her room to listen to records, and I organized the younger children into a game of dodge ball. I tried not to notice that every time Jerry caught the ball, he aimed dead-straight at me. I missed most of his throws, of course. I had dodge ball down pretty good by that advanced age. One time, however, he caught and threw the ball so fast that he got me smack in the side of the head. Even though the ball was soft, it stung.

I swung on him. "That hurt! You don't have to throw it so hard, Doofus!"

I fully expected him to retort snidely with something like, "You're supposed to dodge it, twerp-face. That's why it's called dodge ball."

Instead, he rushed forward with a horrified look and tenderly touched the side of my face, brushing back my hair. "I'm sorry. I didn't mean to hit you. You turned right into it."

Didn't mean to hit me?! What kind of nonsense was that? The whole point of the game was hitting people. That's how you got them out.

I didn't know what was going on here, but I didn't like it.

I shoved his hand away. "Doof—"

"Brother Townsend!"

We all turned to see the church secretary running across the street. Her teased hair was bouncing dangerously, as was every other part of her.

Dad rose from his lawn chair. "Sister Bishop, I thought you'd have gone home by now. What's wrong?"

"I was just heading out," she said breathlessly, "when a VW bus pulled into the parking lot. It's the Rutherfords."

"The Rutherfords?" Dad repeated. "Did

we know they were coming?"

Mrs. Bishop shook her head vehemently. "No, and we have no place to put them. I don't know what on earth we're going to do!"

"Oh dear," Mother said from the top of the back stairs. She'd obviously seen Mrs. Bishop running and had stepped out to see what was going on.

Dad looked up at her. Mother's face tightened almost imperceptibly, then she nodded. "Of course. The Caruthers aren't arriving until tomorrow, anyway."

Beaming with hospitality, Dad turned back to Mrs. Bishop. "Tell them to come on over here. We'll throw a few more hamburgers on the fire and figure something out. You're welcome to stay, too, if you can."

"Are you kidding? I have eighteen guests at my house, waiting for something to eat. I have to go!"

Dad nodded patiently. "I understand. You go right ahead then, but please send the Rutherfords — ahhh, looks as if they followed you here. Good."

Dad moved to greet the family of eight.

I felt nothing but relief. The Rutherfords had a daughter my age among their six children. I hadn't seen Amy in several years, but that didn't matter. It was someone to mitigate the presence of Doofus-Head.

The Rutherfords blended into the crowd — like ages seeking like ages. Just before we sat down to supper, eleven other unexpected guests arrived. Mr. Milam came with his five children in tow. His wife had died two years earlier of cancer, Mr. and Mrs. Harrold brought their two children, and an elderly couple named Rippey had to eat hot dogs because there were no more hamburgers left.

It took Mother until midnight to figure out where to put everyone and get us all settled for the night. Dad and the adult men scrounged the neighborhood for cots and air mattresses. Luckily, they found enough for the thirty-eight people we housed on that Friday night.

The next morning, the flood continued. The Caruthers arrived around ten to find our house over-flowing. By suppertime on Saturday, three more families showed up on our doorstep unannounced, plus the Widow Allredge. That made thirty-six unexpected boarders over and above the eighteen we had been expecting. With the four of us, there were fifty-eight people needing a place to sleep.

Being a kid, of course, I didn't add all this up until later. Still, even I knew it was impossible.

Luckily for my father's wallet and my mother's kitchen (and sanity), we didn't have to feed that many. The church was holding what amounted to a non-stop buffet starting at noon on Saturday and lasting through breakfast on Monday. Doughnuts and biscuits and fruit gradually disappeared, making way for sandwiches and chips and cookies, which changed late in the afternoon to tables and tables of culinary delights brought by the current church families, including a vast variety of the fried chicken I coveted. There was an official starting time for each meal, of course, with a blessing given after announcements and scripture. But there were so many mouths to feed that there was a constant line going down at least one side of the picnic tables set up for the occasion.

I'll never forget that weekend. It was like a huge, never-ending dinner-on-the-grounds. Hundreds of people were there. Most brought lawn chairs and sat in groups talking and eating. Games were organized for the children by some of the more active adults. Back in those days, adults rarely participated in anything more athletic than a bowling or softball league.

Among those hundreds of people, at least

half were children, so I was having a blast. I only caught occasional glimpses of my parents and didn't see my sister Nona at all.

Until late that afternoon, when Amy Rutherford and I wandered into the church basement to cool off in the air conditioning. Mother and Nona stood in the doorway to the large adult classroom, looking in.

Mother brightened as she spied us. "Martha, good. You and Amy run get Jesse James and as many of his friends as you can. I need at least four strong men."

"Which Jesse James?" I asked.

"Oh, right. There are two. I suppose either one will do, but I was thinking about the younger one. Jerry's brother, not his father."

"Yes, ma'am!" I spun to obey orders when she stopped me.

"Martha!"

I halted. "Yes, ma'am?"

"After you find Jesse, go find your father and tell him to beg, borrow or steal at least twenty more cots."

"Dad would steal?!!"

Mother rolled her eyes. "It's just an expression. Go on now."

"On my way. Com'on, Amy!"

After completing our missions, Amy and I wandered back. Mother was in her element, a general marshalling the troops. She had Jesse and his friends removing the chairs and tables from the two largest Sunday School rooms. When Dad arrived with only three more cots, he and Mother had a heated discussion about what to do.

I listened in. When the obvious wasn't occurring to them, I tugged on Dad's rolled-up cotton sleeve. "Dad?"

He glanced down. "Not now, Martha, we're —"

"What about the pads on the pews upstairs?" I asked before he could dismiss me entirely.

Dad and Mother looked at each other in surprise.

"I can't believe we forgot about the pews!" Mother exclaimed.

The church had installed red velvet pads on all the pews the past winter. All the best churches were doing it.

"Out of the mouths of babes . . ." Dad said. It was one of his favorite Bible quotes. I never really understood it, and always bristled at being called a baby.

Mother kissed me soundly. "Thank you for being brilliant!"

"How are we going to do this, Lu?" Dad asked. "They're detachable, but some members might object to us placing brand new pads on a concrete floor."

"Wooden pews would be a much more comfortable base to sleep on than concrete floors, anyway. On the other hand, some might to object to bedding down guests in the sanctuary. And they'll have to be the kids. Those pews aren't wide enough for most adults."

Dad bristled at that. "If any members do object, they won't for long. There is nothing sacred about the sanctuary. Besides, it's called a sanctuary for a reason. Just as the inn sheltered our Lord in his time of need, so will we shelter our brethren who are in need of a place to sleep!"

He punctuated his comments with a finger pointed skyward. Like most preachers, Dad tended to get a bit dramatic when his passions were aroused.

And so the sanctuary became a dormitory for a couple of nights. I slept on the third pew with Amy. The boys slept in the back. Mrs. Martin slept on a cot at the front of the sanctuary to watch over the girls. Mr. Martin slept at the back with the boys.

The only real problem was the lack of showers. In those days, church bathrooms had no baths. And we certainly didn't have a gymnasium with accompanying locker rooms like so many do these days. No, back then, a church was solely a church. Gymnasiums were only at high schools, colleges and the occasional community center.

I tried to offer what I thought was a good solution to the problem. I suggested that the children bathe in the baptistery.

Needless to say, I was not thanked for my brilliance this time. Even my father was appalled at my lack of respect. Since I'd been baptized in the Santa Fe River in Florida with alligators and snakes and fish and frogs and no telling what other critters, I didn't understand the distinction. And to tell the truth, I think that most of my father's reaction was for the benefit of church members within earshot. A lot of what I was allowed and not allowed to do as a child was dictated by the possible disapproval of church members. I resented that fact as a child, but now I understand that every occupation has its own restrictions.

One good thing came out of the bathroom situation. Because all the dormitory residents had to use the shower in our house across the street and use was limited to the capacity of the hot water heater, I didn't have to take a bath until Monday evening. Not that Mother knew, of course. I simply lost myself in the shower shuffle.

Saturday night's supper at the church was

followed by a homemade ice cream party. There must've been fifty churns going. The old-fashioned kind with rock salt and store-bought ice and hand churning. Nothing electric back then.

As I always did at home, I took a turn at churning the vanilla ice cream that my mother always made. After a few minutes of the monotonous activity, I looked up to see Jerry James and Mark Grady whispering together and pointing at me. I stuck my tongue out at them, but didn't scare them away. As I sat fuming, I decided the best defense was a good offense, so when Mr. Rutherford relieved me at the churn, I called to Amy and a couple more of our friends and we chased them into the woods at the back of the church. I pulled my female troop to a halt with a victorious whoop.

That's when I heard Mark call from somewhere in the trees, "Jerry loves Martha! Jerry loves Martha!"

Mortified, I turned to my giggling friends and vehemently denied any romantic involvement with a *boy.*

I couldn't help thinking about Mark's words during down times that night and through the next day. This was the first inkling I had of the heretofore disgusting feelings I'd observed between men and women. Because I couldn't understand those feelings, I dismissed them all as crazy and dismissed any notion that I might one day feel the same. Not that I had any feelings other than abhorrence for that slime ball, Jerry James.

Still, it was as if the first gray light of a romantic dawn had seeped into my awareness.

It worried me.

All that evening as the children settled down on our pews and the next day during the church service and celebration, I caught Jerry looking at me. Then something startling occurred to me. He hadn't denied Mark's accusation.

By Sunday afternoon, I had to escape.

My favorite place in the entire world at that stage of my life was a small quarry lake hidden in about a hundred acres of woods that stretched away from the church. As soon as I could slip away, I disappeared into those woods and followed a familiar path. Just as I reached its granite edge, I realized I wasn't alone. Spinning, I spied the outlaw. He wasn't even trying to hide.

The fear that had been niggling at me for the past twenty-four hours rushed in.

"What do you think you're doing?" I said

with more bravado than I felt.

He shrugged. "I dunno. All that wasn't fun anymore," he waved a hand back toward the church. "I thought maybe . . . I dunno . . . I'd see what you're doing."

"I came here to be *alone.* I don't need any —"

"Jesse said they used to pick blackberries somewhere back in here. Think maybe we could find some?"

I straightened, distracted by one of my favorite things in the whole wide world — blackberries. Nona and I usually picked them in the early summer so Mother could make blackberry cobbler. We hadn't picked any yet this year because we'd been too absorbed with the church reunion.

"They're this way," I called as I started running deeper into the wood. "I hope the birds didn't get them all."

Five minutes later we found the bushes, still laden with very ripe berries. We started picking.

"Oww!" I stuck my bleeding finger in my mouth.

"Oww, oww, oww!" Jerry did the same thing.

Our eyes met and we laughed.

"Now I remember. Nona and I always wear gloves and long sleeves to pick them."

We did manage to carefully pick a few, and ate those. We weren't too serious about it, however, because we were both still full from the enormous bounty at the dinner-on-the-grounds.

I asked Jerry questions about Huntsville, where the Jameses lived, and we talked about how we felt about going into the seventh grade.

We talked as we meandered back to the festivities. We were having a pretty good time, actually.

Then, suddenly, when we were only a few yards away from seeing the church, the outlaw leaned over and kissed me — smack dab on the mouth. It was so quick, I didn't know what he was doing. Then he sprang away and disappeared.

Stunned, I watched him run away. I didn't know what to do. I certainly wasn't going to run after him.

My fingers touched my lips, which stung from the unaccustomed pressure. My first kiss.

A smile crept across my face. It wasn't so bad.

I didn't see Jerry again, except in a crowd. He acted as if nothing had happened, and so did I.

We spent another night on the church

pews, then everyone left the next morning.

The Taylors were the last to leave. As they pulled away, Dad called, "Y'all come!"

I turned to my parents. "You know, if y'all would stop saying, 'Y'all come,' maybe they'd stop coming."

Dad chuckled and wrapped his arm around Mother's waist as they walked into the house.

My parents never stopped saying, "Y'all come!" and people never stopped coming.

■ ■ ■ ■

Dinner
On The Grounds

■ ■ ■ ■

The authors of *On Grandma's Porch*
hope you will enjoy the following tastes of
down-home cooking from family kitchens
across the South.

FORGOTTEN COOKIES

ELLEN BIRKETT MORRIS
Homeplace

Ingredients:

2 egg whites, at room temperature

2/3 cup sugar

pinch of salt

1 teaspoon vanilla

1/8 teaspoon cream of tartar

1 cup M&Ms or semi-sweet chocolate morsels (depending on your preference)

Preheat oven to 375 degrees. Grease a cookie sheet or line it with foil. Beat egg whites with cream of tartar, salt and vanilla in medium bowl until soft peaks form. Gradually add sugar, one tablespoon at a time, beating 4 to 5 minutes or until stiff peaks form, mixture is glossy and sugar is dissolved. Fold in M&Ms or chocolate chips. Drop spoonfuls of the mixture onto the cookie sheet. Place in oven. Turn off oven, and leave cookies inside overnight with the oven door closed.

DADDY'S SATURDAY STEAK

DEBRA LEIGH SMITH
Listening for Daddy

Ingredients:
1/3 cup soy sauce
1-1/2 to 2 pounds flank steak
3 tablespoons Worcestershire sauce
garlic powder to taste
3 tablespoons vegetable oil

Using a fork, tenderize the steak on both sides. Sprinkle garlic powder on both sides. Mix Worcestershire, soy sauce, and oil. Lay steak in dish and drench with mixture. Let it marinate in the fridge for a minimum of eight hours. Turn steak often to make sure the marinade soaks all the way through. Grill over coals. 5 to 10 minutes for medium rare. Slice thin, across the grain. Serves 4 to 6.

GREEN BEAN CASSEROLE

SANDRA CHASTAIN
The Green Bean Casserole

---

5 minutes to prepare — 30 minutes to bake

Mix 3/4 cup milk
1/8 tsp pepper
1 10-3/4 oz. can cream of mushroom soup
2 (14.5 oz.) cans cut green beans. (drain the beans)
1 tablespoon pimento (for color)
2/3 cup of canned french fried onions

Set oven temperature at 350'.

Mix all ingredients except 2/3 cup french fried onions in a 1-1/2 qt. casserole dish.

Cook 30 min. or until bubbly. Stir. Spread onions on top and cook 5 more minutes until onions are golden colored.

GRANDMA'S CORN PUDDING

SUSAN SIPAL
Grandma's Cupboard

I thought about submitting Grandma's biscuit recipe as her biscuits are mentioned in my story, Grandma's Cupboards. Trouble is — there is no recipe, and I've never been able to duplicate anything but bricks. So I settled for her corn pudding, which even I can't mess up . . . well, almost. Sunday dinner wasn't Sunday dinner at Grandma's without her famous corn pudding on the table. Though my uncle will never let me forget the time I was helping Grandma and used salt instead of sugar! But as she kept them both in Mason jars, it was an easy mistake.

1 pint frozen corn, defrosted
2 tablespoon sugar (a bit more if you like sweeter)
2 tablespoon flour
2 eggs
1/2 stick butter

1 cup milk
1/2 teaspoon salt
1/8 teaspoon pepper

Preheat oven to 350. Mix sugar and flour thoroughly, then add eggs and corn. Melt 1/2 the butter in a square 8-1/2 × 8-1/2 inch casserole dish to cover bottom. Add enough milk to the corn mixture until thin. Add salt, pepper and the rest of the melted butter. Pour into the casserole dish and bake at 350 for 45 mins. to 1 hour or until firm in the center.

SOFO 'MATER BISCUIT

DEBRA LEIGH SMITH
Listening for Daddy

Make yourself some biscuit dough. Or buy yourself some biscuit dough at the grocery store. Jazz it up by poking some chopped jalapeño peppers into the dough. Or some onion. Or garlic gloves. Or shredded cheese. Or anything else you figure tastes good mixed with biscuit dough. Except M & Ms. Those won't work. Especially the peanut ones.

Bake the biscuits. If you can't figure out how to do this on your own, get on the computer and Google "Idjit" and see if a picture of you pops up.

Slice your biscuit into a top part and a bottom part. Not all the way through, only No-FoSo's do that! Leave a biscuit hinge on one side. If you do it right, it'll look like a Muppet mouth or a Ms. Pac Man. Stick some sliced tomato inside. On top of the 'mater slice, put some sliced cheddar cheese. Some fried bacon. Some sliced ham. Some fried chicken nuggets. Some fried egg. Not all at once! Back off, it's gonna blow!

LU EVELYN TOWNSEND'S SUNDAY BARBEQUED PORK CHOPS

MARTHA CROCKETT
Y'all Come

One of my mother's most memorable recipes. I've included it in every cookbook to which I've contributed. The pork chops will fall right off the bone (unless, of course, you use boneless)!

Ingredients:
6 or 8 pork chops, 1" thick
1 cup water
1 onion, chopped
2 Tbsp vinegar
1 cup ketchup
1 Tbsp Worcestershire sauce
4 Tbsp brown sugar
4 Tbsp lemon juice

Sear chops on both sides. Combine remaining ingredients and heat; add chops. Cook slowly 1 to 1-1/2 hours. Place chops in baking pan. Heat in 375° oven for 15 minutes. Serve over rice.

ABOUT THE AUTHORS

Sarah Addison Allen has a B.A. in Literature and lives in western North Carolina. Her books include *Garden Spells,* published by Bantam Dell in Fall 2007.

Susan W. Alvis is an English teacher and writer. She and her husband, a Navy Chaplain, live in Annapolis, Maryland, where they are raising six children and being nicely managed by two golden retrievers.

Sandra Chastain, a native Georgian, is the author of 44 novels. Many of her books have been featured selections in the Doubleday Book Club. She has twice been selected a finalist in Favorite Book of the Year by the 8000+ members of Romance Writers of America.

Betty Cordell was born and raised in Dublin, Georgia. She is published in the magazine *Angels On Earth,* the Georgia Writers Anthology, *On My Mind,* Volume IV, and by BelleBooks in *More Sweet Tea* (2005) and *On Grandma's Porch* (2007).

Martha Crockett is an award-winning, best-selling author who has written for Silhouette Books as well as BelleBooks. She has been a finalist in numerous contests — both as a published and unpublished writer — including RWA's Golden Heart and RITA contests, and Georgia Romance Writer's Maggie contest. Her fourth book, *Husband Found,* won *Romantic Times'* Reviewers Choice Award for Best Silhouette Romance in 1999.

Susan Goggins has written romance novels for Harlequin and Zebra. Her romantic fiction has won awards such as West Houston RWA's Emily award, Virginia Romance Writers' Fool for Love contest, and the MICA award from Northwest Houston RWA's Lone Star contest. She also writes horror novels under the pseudonym Raven Hart.

Bert Goolsby is a retired judge in South Carolina. His published fiction includes *The Box With the Green Bow and Ribbon* (Saint

Anthony Messenger, December 1996), *Her Own Law* (Xlibris 1998), *Humanity, Darling* (iUniverse 2000), *Sweet Potato Biscuits and Other Stories* (Cork Hill Press 2003), and *Harpers' Joy* (Grace Abraham Publishing 2005).

Maureen Hardegree wasn't born in the South. She fell in love with the region's rich history and people when she moved to Louisiana at the age of twelve. She's a past president of Georgia Romance Writers and has won GRW's prestigious Maggie award. Her short stories have been published in BelleBooks' Sweet Tea anthology and Mossy Creek series.

Lynda Holmes lives in Flowery Branch, Georgia. She is an instructor at North Georgia College & State University in the Department of Teacher Education.

Ellen Birkett Morris is based in Louisville, Kentucky. Her writing has appeared in *The Girls' Book of Friendship* (Little, Brown & Company), *The Girls' Book of Love* (Little, Brown & Company), *The Writing Group Book* (Chicago Review Press), *Nesting: It's a*

Chick Thing (Workman) and *Hidden Kitchens* (Rodale).

A lifelong son of the South, **Mike Roberts** was born in Birmingham, Alabama, and lives in Powder Springs, Georgia, with his wife Lisa, their two daughters, six cats and one dog. Mike is an award-winning journalist and technical writer. "Air Raid, Southern Style" is his second published short story.

Michelle Roper was born and raised in the North Georgia Mountains. She's been married to her wonderful husband, Jack, for over twenty-five years, and they're the parents of three lovely children. When Michelle isn't writing, she's out walking her three Siberian Huskies, or rather they're walking her.

Julia Horst Schuster is a founder of the Emerald Coast (Florida) Chapter of Romance Writers of America.

Susan Sipal is published in fiction and nonfiction through essays, short stories, and a novel. She is best known for her analysis of JK Rowling's Harry Potter series and has conducted workshops or had papers presented both nationally and internationally. You can visit her at www.SusanSipal.com.

Debra Leigh Smith, a native Georgian, is the nationally bestselling, award-winning author of 35 novels in romance, women's fiction, and general list fiction. Her 1996 novel, *A Place to Call Home,* made the New York Times list.

Clara Wimberly has published more than 20 books in a variety of work, from gothic to historical, mainstream and suspense. Clara writes in a one-room cabin, built for her by her husband and sons, in the woods near her home.